D0879182

Cathead Bay

A Sheriff Hoss Davis Mystery

Also by Robert Underhill

Strawberry Moon (2006)

Cathead Bay

Robert Underhill

Northport, Michigan

Cathead Bay
Copyright ©2008 by Robert Underhill

ISBN 10 - 0-9798526-0-9
ISBN 13 – 978-0-9798526-0-2

Delicti Press
Northport, Michigan
editor@delictipress.com
www.Delictipress.com

Publisher's Cataloging-in-Publication

    Underhill, Robert.
       Cathead Bay/ Robert Underhill.
       p. cm.
       ISBN-13: 978-0-9798526-0-2
       ISBN-10: 0-9798526-0-9

       1. Sheriffs--Michigan--Leelanau County--Fiction.
       2. Leelanau County (Mich.)--Fiction. 3. Detective and mystery stories.   I. Title.

    PS3621.N343F56 2008   813'.6
               QBI07-600310

For Barclay, John, Kristen and Michelle

Acknowledgements

I wish to thank Sheriff Michael Oltersdorf and Sergeant Michael Lamb of the Leelanau County Sheriff's Department for their interest and help.

I also want to thank dott. Patrizia Paccagnella Gamba, a willing guide, who literally went the extra mile.

I have been fortunate to have good friends I can rely upon for honest criticism and valuable suggestions: Susan Ager, James Carpenter, Kathryn and Don Frerichs, Kirby Hall, Vinna and Phillip Mikesell, Rebecca Reynolds, Judith Ruzumna, Duncan Sings-Alone, Kathleen Snedeker and Nancy Terfertiller.

Finally, the whole project would have been neither possible nor enjoyable without Trudy, my constant editor and supporter.

PROLOGUE

What had she gotten herself into? She'd had strong doubts about going out with him in the first place, and now here she was being led down a dark street to his apartment.

He stopped at the doorway of an old, stuccoed building and turned a key in the lock and stepped into the dark entrance and found the light-switch. The dim, bare bulb lighted a small terrazzo-floored vestibule. She noticed the dirty corners that no mop had touched in years.

His impatient hand on her back directed her up a stone stairway. At the top of the stairs, he hit a switch that turned on another low-wattage bulb at the far end of a long corridor. He unlocked and opened the second door along the hallway and stepped aside motioning for her to enter.

"Here it is, my home," he said.

It was a one-room apartment with a bath, the tub of which she could see through the open bathroom door. The place was neater than she would have expected a young man's room to be—as if he were expecting a visit from his mother.

"Do you have a roommate?" she asked to break the tension and to put the moment in a familiar context.

"Don't worry: no one will come: no one will know."

She heard the door being locked and spun around.

"What are you doing?" It was an objection, not a question.

He came to her and began to embrace her.

"No, don't do that. Please. Please let me go. I said NO!"

"What? What? You came up to my room on your own."

"You said we were coming to get your camera."

She twisted, trying to break his grip, but couldn't.

"I thought you meant it . . . getting the camera."

"Don't give me that shit; you knew what I meant."

He pushed her backward until her legs met the bed and she fell backward onto it.

"No. Please don't. I'll scream."

He didn't think she would. She was much too proper and proud to allow herself to be discovered in this way. He reached under her skirt and yanked off her underwear.

"No. Please don't. Please. I've never done this before."

This he believed.

1

"Hey Silvio, come here a minute. We need you to settle an argument."

"Can't right now, Jack. Gotta check on something downstairs. I'll be back up in a few minutes."

"Need any help?"

"No, everything's under control."

Silvio Rossi paused for a moment at the head of the stairs. His eyes passed over the bustling, noisy scene in his expansive, new living room. Forty-plus people were laughing, sipping their mojitos or champagne and celebrating their inclusion on the guest list. A flash of self-appraisal accompanied what Silvio saw. He realized he now stood at the very pinnacle of every element of his life: health, fame, fortune, social position and, yes, satisfaction. Silvio was very satisfied with himself.

He turned and quickly descended the stairs to the lower level. From a cabinet in the spacious game room he took a long, wooden box. Leaving the sliding door open behind him, he carried the box outside. Before him stretched a landscape of sand dunes and beach grass running down to Cathead Bay, which sparkled in the late August sun. Laughter floated down from the deck above. Silvio walked around the corner of his mansion to a side terrace where two large barbecue kettles were giving off wisps of charcoal-smelling smoke. He laid the box on the table where a covered cauldron holding cubed-lamb waited, bathing in his special marinade.

Silvio Rossi currently reigned as America's most celebrated chef. Others in their time had worn that mantle: Julia represented classic authenticity, Wolfgang brought us innovation, Alice preached natural freshness, then Mario followed with a passion for intensity and simplicity, and now came Silvio. "Organic unity", *unita organica*, was Silvio's motto. His cooking methods and combinations of ingredients certainly shattered the mold, but he went further: he saw to it that everything about him was as unpredictable as the next note in a Stravinsky composition.

In the kitchen, he demonstrated true, original brilliance with those things edible just as Stravinsky had with those audible, or Matisse with those visual. His base was Manhattan, his stronghold the Restaurante Lucretius, but his domain extended to all America. Word of his artistry quickly spread around New York, but it was television that introduced him to the nation. Marketers then moved in and took his honest reputation as a chef and extended his name into all imaginable commodities from pots, pans and knives, to even a line of exorbitantly expensive ski clothing (his favorite sport). This kind of progression did not surprise jaded New Yorkers, inured as they were to any kind of crass commercialism, nor did rumors that his taste for invention crossed the threshold from kitchen to many Manhattan bedrooms. What did bring them up short—left his friends and associates staring into one another's puzzled faces—was news they had heard a year ago. They'd learned he was building a magnificent vacation home here on the unknown and remote Leelanau Peninsula of northern Michigan.

A few had already heard the place named, because Silvio's choice of location was neither original nor accidental; another New York celebrity chef, Silvio's main rival and the man he was fixated on surpassing, had preceded him here by three years. But this man hadn't broadcasted the fact; he honestly sought a retreat.

Silvio lifted the lid of the cauldron and saw that the meat was all nicely coated with marinade.

This party would see the sun set on a very satisfying summer. Soon he would head back to New York and center stage there. Was he happy? Yes, he concluded—as happy as he would ever likely be. There were the inevitable problems, of course, ones that arose for anyone who dared to be in the spotlight—and dared to stay there. And yes, some interpersonal problems too. Other people weren't puppets—that was good—but without strings they would have their own ideas and do things that sometimes one couldn't correct as one might a wayward sauce.

Silvio opened the wooden box and withdrew the six, razor-sharp skewers that had been given to him as a gift and placed them within easy reach on the table.

He lifted the lid of one of the giant grills to check the progress of the charcoal. Yes, the timing would be perfect.

2

Gina Rossi, Silvio's wife, was just starting out on an impromptu tour of the architecturally unique Rossi house with three of her women guests. She led the women to one corner of the enormous kitchen, taking care not to get in the way of the kitchen staff, who were concentrating on the many details required to provide the seamless dining experience Silvio demanded. Here, Gina poured softly pink champagne into four glasses already containing a small amount of deep red liquid. She handed a glass to each woman and then led the group up a short curving stair to a small balcony study. Standing there, one could look down over a low wall back into the kitchen. A desk ran the length of the wall. On it rested a computer where Silvio had been working during the past weeks to compile one more of his popular cookbooks. From here he could keep an eye on the action in the kitchen: listen for the call of interval timers or judge the progress of a dish being tried out by his assistants. On shelves covering the other walls of the study were his reference books. Silvio could never really be on vacation, ever aware of the need to keep the wheel of fame turning lest a rising star overtake him and eclipse his own radiance.

Gina smiled down at the feverish activity in the kitchen and raised her glass. "To good food," she said. The friends all touched glasses and drank the toast.

Gina's was an attractive personality, naturally warm, open and unaffected. She interacted intimately and guilelessly with everyone, seemingly unaware of her wealth and vivacious beauty or of the reputed importance or social rank of the other person.

Gina saw Silvio come into the kitchen and say a few words to Paul, the assistant chef, and then walk away rapidly and with purpose back out of the kitchen and toward the stairway to the lower level. She said then to her guests, "If we continue on, we can complete our little tour before Silvio wants us back for the dinner."

Gina led the way through a doorway and then up another short curving stairway into a long hall. They had only gone a few steps along this hallway, when one of the guests, Marla Phelps, a writer for *Gourmet* magazine, stopped suddenly, moaned, then bent over and vomited with force onto the hall floor.

Gina ran to her and put her arm around her shoulders. "My God, Marla, what's wrong?"

She guided her stricken guest into a bathroom only a few yards farther along the hall. Here, she supported Marla over the sink as she continued to retch.

Gina turned to get a towel from the towel bar only to find none.

"Maid forgot . . . Rosa, please take care of Marla. I'll get a towel."

Rosa DeSica, one of the oldest among the guests and the mother of the sous-chef at Lucretius, took over at the sink.

• • •

Paul Treviso held the position of salad chef at Lucretius and was the only member of that restaurant's staff actually working on food preparation for this party. He had reached a minor impasse; the fennel fronds were not fresh. Fennel was a necessary ingredient of the salad he had planned. The vegetable drawer of the giant refrigerator contained fresh dill and this suggested an alternative, but Paul wasn't sure if Silvio was counting on the mild licorice flavor of the fennel to complement the "Lamb Rossi" he planned to serve.

The direct approach would be, of course, to ask Silvio, but he never used that approach with Silvio if it could be helped. He never knew how Silvio would respond: "Excellent idea, Paul", or "That's one of the stupidest things I've ever heard." Paul elected to get Vince DeSica's input. Lucretius's sous-chef, here as a guest, was somewhere out there in the crowd.

"Ann, do me a favor and let that tray of hors d'oeuvres wait a minute and find Vince and tell him to come here. I need to ask him something."

A few minutes later she returned. "I couldn't find him anywhere. I asked Amy, who has been out there for a while passing around champagne. She doesn't know where he is."

"Hmm. OK thanks." Paul said. He reached for the dill.

• • •

House guest Frank Knowles came down from his room on the second floor only after all the other guests had arrived. He stood a moment at the foot of the stairs looking over the pulsing living room scene like a swimmer hesitating at poolside before taking the plunge. Always well groomed and expensively clad, he cultivated a posture of reserved wisdom combined with the insouciance of success. At this moment, beneath the confident façade, he was very tense. He let out a deep breath that approached a sigh; time to make his entrance, and time—if an opportunity arose—to do what he had come here to do. Frank looked among the guests for Silvio, but didn't see him.

The defining moment of success had come for Frank six years earlier in New York as he'd been gathering up his materials after Channel 6's daily talk show, "All Around the Town". He'd been very glum that morning as he automatically went about collecting the production notes and pages of shooting script before shoving them into his briefcase.

His mood originated from a rumor he'd heard that the show was getting the axe and he had no other prospects to take its place. Four months earlier, when he'd gotten the chance to produce the daytime talk show, he'd thought he might finally have found the vehicle to ride-out his remaining years in broadcasting. Instead, it turned out that the celebrity hostess, while vibrant on the Broadway stage, was as dull as a plate of grits in front of the TV camera.

One of the guests on that morning's show approached him. The guy, an Italian chef, recently arriving in New York from the old country, hadn't followed the usual path of taking a job for a few years in an established restaurant. He had struck out on his own, immediately opening a stylish eatery in the West Village. Frank experienced the guy as brash and full of himself. In spite of his bravado, Frank figured the restaurant would probably go under after a few months like most of its kind and the guy would end up working as third chef on the bad shifts at any place that would take him.

The Italian wanted to talk to Frank about producing a cooking show. That's what the world needed, thought Frank, one more cooking show. But, the guy assured Frank he had the money to back it. Frank ended up listening, asking many questions, and finally agreeing (After all, he had no other prospects) to produce "Cucina da Silvio". Now, about to begin its seventh year, it was by far the most popular cooking show on television. It had turned out that the camera loved Silvio as much as Silvio loved the camera. Silvio's easy ability to charm lent itself to close-ups and celebrities fought to be on the show and be included in those close-ups. The celebrity-cooking lesson had been Frank Knowles's addition and thought by many to be the vital element that had made the show a hit. Celebrities came on the show to demonstrate those little favorites they liked to make in their own homes. Silvio suggested additions and techniques and spiced their appearance with his salty and frequently seductive comments. Enlisting top-drawer celebs had been a tough sell at first, but later Frank had to beat them off with a stick, so prestigious had appearing on the show become. Some, who had never entered a kitchen before in their lives, took special instruction from other chefs, so they would have that little "favorite dish I love to prepare for close friends". Last year Cucina da Silvio battled Oprah neck and neck in the ratings. This year it would take the lead.

Last week Frank had heard very disturbing news from Silvio, news that had threatened Frank. Today he intended to take care of the problem.

Frank entered the living room now and caught the serving girl's attention for a glass of champagne. He needed to avoid getting into any conversations that would encumber his freedom to move quickly if he saw an opportunity to catch Silvio alone. As he turned away with his glass, he chanced to see Karen Forbes just coming up the stairs from the lower level. Frank read acute distress in her expression. He knew Karen well; they'd had a couple of weekends together on the Cape. Frank knew her as a woman of evanescent mood. She continued to stand, lost in thought at the head of the stairs. Frank walked over to her.

"What's wrong, Karen?"

Startled at first, she then saw who stood beside her and relaxed momentarily before reminding herself of a need for caution. Frank noticed.

"Nothing," was her delayed response. "Thoughts about the new season, that's all."

Frank didn't believe her. "You were coming up from downstairs." He tried to bend his tone of voice toward lightness.

Karen knew she had to tell him something. "I have a problem I need to resolve with Silvio. I saw him go downstairs to start his barbecuing and I thought it would be a good time to approach him, but I lost courage."

"You didn't talk to him then?"

"No."

"But, it would have been a good time, since you knew he was alone?"

"Yes, but, as I said, I lost my nerve. You know what he can be like. Later, I'll try again later."

So, Silvio was alone, thought Frank.

The serving girl passed by with her tray of champagne. Frank took a glass from the tray and handed it to Karen. Smiling, he raised his glass.

"To solving problems."

• • •

Paul Treviso didn't want to add the dressing to the salad until the right moment but he didn't know what point Silvio had reached with his preparations. He grabbed the arm of the same waitress whom he'd sent on an errand earlier and asked her to run down and ask Silvio where things stood.

Paul sat down on a stool, relaxed and sipped some wine. His thoughts were about how he'd miss the leisurely pace he and his wife had enjoyed these past weeks on this blissful peninsula. Once again he considered the question they'd discussed so much: could they make a go of it with their own restaurant? Could that restaurant be right here in this quiet and beautiful place?

A shrill scream interrupted his rumination. The sound came

from the direction of the large guest-filled living room. Paul rushed to the kitchen door and saw people moving out onto the deck that overlooked the bay and looking about to determine who had screamed. Paul understood, then, that the scream had come from outside and he thought of the waitress he'd just sent there. He ran down the stairs to the lower level. The young woman had just come back into the house through an open doorway.

She saw Paul and choked out, "It's Mr. Rossi!", pointing in the direction of the side terrace and the barbecue kettles.

Paul rushed out of the house and around the corner to the side terrace. He stopped—then walked slowly up to the crumpled and still body of Silvio Rossi. Paul knelt to feel for a pulse even though it was obvious the man was dead. How could it be otherwise with a barbecue skewer thrust through his heart?

3

Deputy Donna Roper of the Leelanau County Sheriff's Department had spent the past half hour directing cars around a gasoline tanker stalled across Northport's main intersection. It had been backing into position to connect its hose to the inlet pipe at the village's only gas station. Twenty or so cars had passed her as she waited for the wrecker from Van's Garage in the neighboring village of Leland to arrive and pull the tanker out of the way. In passing, at least half of the drivers had shouted a greeting to her.

Her task done, she drove around the corner to Barb's Bakery to get a cup of coffee. During the summer months Barb's was crowded with visitors coming to buy her justly famous cinnamon rolls. But the number of vacationers had dropped sharply this last week of August as they'd headed back to the cities to take on another year of work or school.

Four members of the bakery's regulars sat together drinking coffee at the long table that ran along the wall opposite the counter. Immediately they began directing their banter toward the tall, chestnut-haired deputy.

"If you've come to arrest Chip Burrows, you've just missed him—he said he just couldn't wait for you any longer."

"Some people have no patience." Donna returned.

"Has your boss sold his Boston Whaler, because I was talking to a guy who might be interested."

"I'll tell him."

The oldest of the four said, "I've got a grandson I'd like you to meet. He's a good kid; he just needs a damn good-looking girl with some backbone."

"I think I know just the person for him," Donna said.

Having fielded these quips, Donna returned one.

"I was expecting you guys to come down and help me by pushing that truck out of the intersection."

"My coffee would have gotten cold," said one of them.

"I might look strong, but I have no energy until I've had my cinnamon twist," replied another.

The mention of the roll caused Donna to look into the case in front of her and consider one. She usually managed to pass on the delicious but calorie laden goodie. She was about to give in, when a woman's voice announced Donna's call number over the mobile radio attached to her belt. Grabbing her coffee, she said good-bye to the gang and went out onto the sidewalk to answer the call.

Kate Schott, the dispatcher, her voice charged with excitement, said, "Donna, honey, there's been a code five accident reported on Cathead Point Road. The address the guy gave me is Silvio Rossi's house."

"You're sure it's fatal?"

"That's what the man said."

"Scramble the paramedics anyway."

Donna wrote down the number Kate had given her even though she knew where the celebrity's new home was located.

In the past, Cathead Bay, located ten miles north of Northport at the tip of the peninsula, had been a beautiful but seldom visited part of the county for the local farmers. The land near the bay wasn't suitable for farming and their lives had been totally taken up with working their land and the occasional journey to the village of Northport for supplies or church. Once a wild and uninhabited area of sand dunes, the last half-century had seen its shoreline become sought after for the large summer homes of the affluent from cities to the south.

Donna hadn't been up this way for a month. That occasion had been an unsupervised party staged by teenagers that had grown in momentum until angry neighbors called the sheriff. Donna had found herself having to deal with a houseful of sixteen to twenty-year-olds who were so drunk they couldn't even pronounce their own names. One guy with a beer bottle in his hand tried to convince her no one had been drinking. It had taken her hours to sort out and deal with that call.

She drove between the huge boulders that marked the entrance to the driveway of Silvio Rossi's waterfront mansion and drove two hundred yards through dense woods before she encountered cars parked along one side of the road. She could see that a parking area to one side of the mansion's main entrance was solidly filled with cars parked in two neat rows. Three young men wearing black pants and neat white shirts leaned against the rear of an SUV, smoking. Obvious curiosity showed on their faces as the patrol car drove up to the front door of the house and Donna got out.

As she approached the front door of the impressive house, a middle-aged man stepped out and told her the body was at the side of the house and that a man named Paul waited there for the police. Donna turned the corner of the house and looked down. At the bottom of wide flagstone steps she saw a level terrace and a tall man in a chef's white apron and neckerchief looking up at her. She next noticed the two large, smoking barbecue kettles. Only then did she notice what looked like a pile of laundry lying between the kettles.

"My God!" she muttered and ran down the steps. Standing over the crumpled body she exclaimed aloud, "My God. It's Silvio Rossi."

Donna knew about Rossi's house here on the bay, but she'd only seen his picture in magazines, there being no time in a deputy's schedule for televised cooking shows.

Kate had said a fatal accident had occurred—a code five. Now, looking down at the famous corpse, Donna thought with alarm, "This is no fucking accident! This is murder." With almost as much alarm, she thought, "Hoss is out of town!" The sheriff, Hoss Davis, was in Detroit at a Sheriff's Association meeting.

She could see plainly enough that the skewer had entered Rossi's back; there was the handle offering itself to be grasped much as had the sword in that picture of Excalibur in her childhood book about King Arthur. Rossi might, by a stretch of the imagination, fall forward onto the skewer he was handling, but not backward. Because of the body's position, death must have been instantaneous. Only a sudden, directly vertical collapse of an entirely flaccid body could account for the feet being together under the pelvis, while the knees splayed out to each side. The upper body bent directly forward, the right cheek resting on the flagstone. His eyes were open and perplexed, as if he had gotten himself stuck in this very awkward position and impatiently waited for someone to help him up. Donna stood, looking on in shock for moments before bringing herself back to the professional role that had brought her there.

She redirected her attention to the loose-limbed young man wearing the chef's apron. He seemed to have been guarding the body. Donna's next words were dictated straight—as well as she could remember—from the pages of the department's book of procedure under the heading, "In the event of a suspicious death."

"What is your name?"

"I'm Paul Treviso. I work in Mr. Rossi's kitchen."

"Has anyone touched anything here?" She swung her arm,

indicating the whole area around the terrace.

"No, not since I came down here, and I was the second person—that is the second person I know of—to see the body. My first thought—after I recovered from the initial shock—was to keep everyone away. No one has been allowed to come near . . . not even Gina."

"Gina?"

"Silvio's wife. When she learned what had happened she rushed down here and would have thrown herself on him. I had a helluva a time holding her back."

Donna held up her hand. "When did you last see him alive?"

"I'd say about ten minutes before Ann found him and started screaming. He'd come into the kitchen and told me he was going down to the terrace to check the charcoal and prepare to begin roasting the meat."

"Who is Ann?"

"One of the women who is serving. I sent her down to ask Silvio how his end of things, the barbecuing, was progressing."

"I see. So you were in the kitchen the entire time after he left the kitchen to go downstairs?"

"Yeah, sure."

"Anyone there with you?"

Paul laughed, "I'll say—Martha turning out hors d'oeuvres and Susan making dessert."

OK, thought Donna, this guy seems to have a pretty solid alibi. She believed she could trust him to keep an eye on the area until she'd get help.

"Any idea who did this?"

"Not a clue."

"Any trouble here today? Like quarrels?"

"Not that I know of."

I want to talk to you some more, but right now I've got to go upstairs. I want you to continue doing what you've been doing—not letting anyone near the body."

"Sure. By the way, I asked Frank Knowles to tell everyone to stay in the house, not leave. Frank is watching the front door."

"Good. Good thinking." Very good thinking, she thought.

Donna reached for her cell phone to call in to headquarters, but found she'd left it in the car. She didn't want the details of what had happened here to be broadcast on the radio where those who liked to listen to the police frequencies could hear them. She hurried back up to the parking area. She'd need all the available help to deal with this. Hoss was at least four and a half hours away. She had been first on the scene, so according to department protocol she became the one in charge. There were only two other deputies working her shift, David Wick and Becky McConnell. She'd need them both. Kate Shott, who had been waiting anxiously for a call from the Rossi place, got more news than she had hoped for. Donna made it clear that the other deputies were needed immediately.

"David is clear down at the other end of the county. It's going to take him forty-five minutes to get there," Kate told her.

"Tell him to hurry. Oh, and get hold of Don Silver to come and take pictures. And the forensic crew from the State Police Post in Acme, we need them too. Of course, we've got to reach Hoss as soon as possible." She paused to think, but nothing else came to mind. "Can you think of anything else, Kate?"

"Not right off, honey. How about if I tell Mr. Dreisbach what's happened?"

"Good idea, Kate. I gotta go."

Peter Dreisbach was the County Prosecutor and not usually part of the initial phases of an investigation, but she'd welcome

18

any suggestion on how she should proceed. She had never been the first deputy to arrive at a capital crime scene, never had to run the show by herself. She knew this was—Hoss had stressed it—the most important stage in a crime investigation. Evidence remained unaltered and the impressions and memories of the witnesses were still fresh.

Donna, still clutching her phone, walked again toward the imposing front entrance, scanning the large fieldstone boulders of the façade, and becoming aware, as she did, of the current of anxiety running through her. She was about to take on the responsibility for the investigation of this high-profile murder. With put-on confidence she strode through the front door. The low rumble of many, muted conversations ceased in a wave as each separate group became aware of the young woman deputy. Donna felt her role change from one of shocked spectator to the status of the one in charge.

Her voice firm, she announced, "I'm Deputy Roper of the Leelanau County Sheriff's Department. Soon other police officers will be here to take statements from all of you. In the meantime, I want you to stay where you are in this room."

Noticing that several people had been talking on cell phones when she came in, she added, "These will be statements we'll be taking from you, not interrogations, so you will not be allowed to avail yourselves of legal council at this time. You will make yourselves as comfortable as possible here and will not touch or dispose of any objects." She added then, while knowing there wasn't the manpower to back it up, "Your doing so will be noted."

Donna heard the stern quality of her voice and amended it. "I know that what has happened is a shock to you, but you must realize that what started out to be a party has become a very serious matter. You must resign yourselves to the inevitable inconvenience of an investigation." It occurred to her that none of the people in the room had seen Silvio Rossi—had no real idea of what had been done to him. She added, "An investigation of what is almost certainly murder."

She was right. Her confirmation of the rumor brought with it a crescendo of buzzing comment throughout the room.

OK, what next? She wanted to be downstairs to guard any evidence there might be at the murder scene, but at the same time it would be important to get at people's first, unguarded statements. She walked into the kitchen where all the staff had gathered.

"I want all of you to join those in the other room."

As they filed past her, she stopped a waitress. "Is Mrs. Rossi one of the people out there?"

"No, she's upstairs in her room with a couple of her friends." She indicated the curving stairway at the end of the kitchen and then her hand continued its motion toward the rear of the house that faced the bay.

Donna felt like a mother minding three toddlers in a crowd; could she afford to take her eye off any one of them?

This quandary was partially resolved when Becky McConnell, the other female deputy on the Sheriff's Patrol, walked through the door. Becky was a petite blonde on whose hip the holstered .357 magnum looked as strange as lipstick on a three-year-old. Donna drew Becky into the kitchen in order to explain the daunting task they faced.

"It's really true, then, Silvio Rossi's dead?"

"Very true, unfortunately—for a lot of people—including us."

"How did he die?"

"Someone ran a barbecue skewer through his back in the region of his heart. It's murder for certain."

"What?"

"Yeah, incredible, but true. Now, we've got to organize our procedure here. I've got a guy, who I think has a good alibi, watching the crime scene. One of us needs to talk to the wife and the other should start getting statements from all the guests and kitchen staff."

"I'll start getting the statements," Becky volunteered quickly, not eager to face a woman whose husband had just been murdered.

"At this point, we know there was a ten minute period between the time one of the chefs saw Rossi head downstairs and the moment the waitress screamed when she discovered the body. Maybe the initial object of our questioning is to ask each person if he or she witnessed anything to narrow that time period, or saw something suspicious. Ask all those who were on the rear deck if they saw anyone outside walking around on the grounds. The next thing we should establish is the whereabouts of each person—sort out those people who were together—three or more—during those ten minutes. In other words, those who have a fairly strong alibi from those who don't."

"Got it."

Donna climbed the stairs to face her difficult task. She glanced around the balcony study that overlooked the kitchen, a very cozy room. She noted the computer and it crossed her mind that one of her first tasks should be to secure it and its files. Computer files and e-mail records had become the current source of so much that's useful in an investigation. They had figured hugely in a rare, yet recent murder case in the county.

At the top of another set of stairs she found herself in a long hallway. The strong, unmistakable odor of vomit drew her eyes to the partially wiped-up stain on the carpet. She walked on along the hallway looking into each room she passed: bathroom, then an intersecting hall presumably leading to other bedrooms went off to the left. At this junction another stairway descended to the living room, and looking down it, Donna could see that, after the interruption of a landing on the first floor, it continued down to the house's lower level. Donna resumed walking along the first hall toward the rear of the house: bedroom, bedroom, a small sitting room and then, at the hall's end, a large bedroom with a grand view over Cathead Bay.

Donna wasn't noticed as she stood in the doorway. Three women were seated in the bedroom. A blond in her mid-thirties—Donna's age—perched on the arm of an easy chair that faced the view. Her arm lay across the shoulders of the woman in the chair. At that woman's side and leaning toward her, sat a gray-haired, older woman on a straight-backed chair. Their dress was smart-casual.

She knew instantly Gina Rossi was the woman in the easy chair. She also sensed that Gina seemed to be doing the consoling, patting the hand of the older woman and speaking to her in a reassuring tone. The moment arrived when standing there unobserved became eavesdropping. Donna said, "Excuse me."

Startled, the women looked around. Donna read irritation on the face of the blond. A familiar emotion for her, Donna surmised. The older woman became dismayed, as if the presence of the police made the tragedy real. These were only fleeting notions. Even if she hadn't been the person Donna had come to interview, the third woman's personality commanded her full attention. She was one of those rare individuals who, while knowing her own worth, seem to be ever cognizant of the needs of those around her. The perfect hostess. Donna felt herself being assessed at this moment to determine what support she required. The woman rose.

"Please come in," she said. She motioned toward a third chair. "Won't you sit down? I'm Gina Rossi."

Sitting down with these women, Donna thought, would put things on a more informal, social footing rather than the official interrogator's position, which she knew she should assume. On the other hand, to remain standing had become a decidedly awkward and unfriendly alternative given this woman's natural intimacy. Donna sat, and to re-establish the official relationship, flipped the cover of her notebook open to a clean page.

In an authoritative tone, she began, "I'm Deputy Roper of the Leelanau County Sheriff's Department." A necessary beginning, she thought, but she couldn't continue without adding quietly and sympathetically, "I'm very sorry Mrs. Rossi."

Gina couldn't meet her gaze after that. She covered her eyes with one hand and sobbed. She regained control and in a choked voice thanked Donna.

"I know it must be difficult to answer questions right now, but it's important," Donna said.

Gina nodded. "I understand. It's all right."

"I've been told you saw . . . your husband . . . outside on the terrace."

Gina answered evenly. "Yes, I saw him."

"This was a very brutal attack. Do you have any idea who would do such a thing?"

Gina again covered her eyes with her hand at the word, "brutal". She shook her head and sobbing said, "No."

The diamond on the hand Gina Rossi held over her eyes caught Donna's attention. With all the diamonds Donna had seen, she had never before witnessed such brilliance. Could there be something special about this northern light coming through the window?

Donna brought herself back to the issue. "Anyone at all with even the slightest motive?"

"No, everyone liked Silvio."

Donna waited until Gina gained command of her feelings and looked up at her. "At what time did you last see your husband alive?"

"I saw Silvio walk into the kitchen and leave again. I thought he was probably on his way to prepare the lamb he planned to serve."

"What time was that?"

"I don't know the time." She made a shrug only an Italian could make. "Maybe ten, fifteen minutes before we heard the woman scream."

"You were in the kitchen when you saw him?" Donna asked.

"No, we were in the little study above the kitchen. I was taking some friends to see the upstairs of the house."

The woman's English was fluent; Donna noted only a trace of an accent. Donna now sought to establish alibis as she had earlier suggested to Becky McConnell. An urgent need existed to sort out this crowd.

"How many were with you on this tour?"

"There was Rosa, here, and Marla and Judy Bombard."

"Just four of you then?"

"That's right."

Donna looked over at the older woman whom Gina had indicated. She nodded her head in agreement.

"I see, so you ladies were together until you heard the waitress scream."

"Yes . . . no, not exactly. Judy Bombard left us sometime before we got Marla into the bedroom."

Donna's questioning look pushed Gina to elaborate.

"You see, Marla got sick when we had climbed the stairs and she vomited there in the hall. When she felt better, we brought her to the bedroom across the hall to lie down, but Judy had gone by then."

"So, the three of you stayed together?" Donna looked at the two other women.

The blonde shook her head. "No, I'm Gloria Klein, Silvio's publicist. I came upstairs later."

"OK, so you, Mrs. Rossi, and Rosa . . . "

"DeSica," Gina added.

"Yes, and Marla?"

"Marla Phelps." Gina Rossi again supplied the name.

"So, the three of you were together from the time you saw your husband in the kitchen until the waitress screamed?"

Rosa DeSica answered. "That'sa right, but Marla wasa across the hall lying down. "

"Do you know exactly when this Judy Bombard left you?"

"No, you see officer, we were busy with Marla," Gina said.

Donna paused to make some notes.

She turned to Gloria Klein. "And, where were you during this time?"

Gloria Klein enjoyed the self-image of a fast thinking, self-contained New Yorker, at least one shelf up from any other American and several above this yokel deputy, who, she had to admit, was much better looking than anyone in this backwater deserved to be.

"I was talking to friends. I'm not aware of the beginning of the time segment you're asking about, because I didn't see Silvio go downstairs. I was talking to Jackson Baskin and Howard duMaurier until we heard the girl scream." Noticing Donna writing these names into her notebook, she added, "That's spelled small du capital M-a-u-r-i-e-r."

"Like the actor or the novelist, or . . . the cigarette," Donna returned.

The hint of a smile that appeared on the publicist's face said,

"Touché".

Donna closed her notebook. "Thank you for answering my questions," she said to Gina.

"Officer, is Silvio still . . . like I saw him?"

Donna nodded grimly. "Yes, until the forensic team has completed its work–but not any longer."

Gina winced.

"Excuse me," Donna said. "I have to go and get statements from your other guests."

She turned again and headed back along the hallway to the stairs.

4

Through the kitchen window Donna saw David Wick getting out of his patrol car in the parking area. Watching him approach the house, she identified apprehension in his expression and his movements. David had worked as a dispatcher before Hoss gave him patrol duty just a week ago. This was David's first contact with anything more serious than a fender-bender. Donna certainly had empathy for his feelings right now; she'd felt them herself those first days on patrol. She hurried toward the front entrance, glancing in the living room and noting that Becky had divided the guests into two groups, the few she'd talked to already, whom she'd sent out on the deck, and those yet to be questioned, who were sitting and standing around in the living room. Donna intercepted David outside the house on the entry walk.

"I'm glad you're here, David. We've got our hands full. The victim—it is Silvio Rossi—is at the side of the building. He's got a wicked-looking barbecue skewer through the back. Sure to be murder."

David's apprehension increased.

"I've asked one of the cooks to keep watch over the body until you got here. Why don't you go down and take over from him. Kate called the forensic guys. When they get here, we could use your help upstairs getting statements; there's a crowd of party guests."

"Right," he answered with a dry mouth and walked away toward the side terrace, not eager to see what awaited him.

Donna, now free to help Becky with the interviews, surveyed the situation. The guests, who had been charged with curiosity when she'd first arrived, were already beginning to show signs of restlessness. She discerned a few outright scowls of impatience. She decided to carry two chairs from the dining room into the kitchen where her questioning could not be overheard, and at the same time allow her to keep an eye on the crowd through the open kitchen doorway.

A long buffet table along one wall of the dining room held the silver serving dishes that had been intended for Silvio Rossi's feast. The sight arrested her. The waiting, empty platters starkly symbolized what had happened here.

She carried the chairs to the kitchen, and then signaled to one of the guests to come to her.

The dark haired, fine-featured woman who came and sat down opposite Donna appeared very nervous. One didn't have to be adept at reading subtle signs to see that.

"Your name is?"

"Karen Forbes."

Donna asked for and wrote down the woman's particulars in her notebook.

"Do you know who killed Mr. Rossi?" Donna asked bluntly.

"No," Forbes barked and then immediately modulated her voice. "No, I have no idea."

"Where were you Ms. Forbes, when the body was discovered?"

"In the living room, talking . . . No, I think I was on the deck looking out at the water."

"Being outside, the scream must have been loud."

"No, . . . I . . . I must have been inside mustn't I?"

"You can't remember whether you were inside the house or not when you heard the scream?" Donna pressed.

"It was so upsetting; I guess I'm confused."

So upsetting you can't remember where you were, Donna

wondered.

"How do you know Mr. Rossi?"

"I've known Silvio for several years. I met him first when I did a review of his restaurant. I am the restaurant reviewer for WNYX in New York."

Why is she so nervous, Donna wondered? Is it just the awfulness of the murder of a friend, or something more?

Donna smiled and said, "I take it the restaurant's review was positive." The attempt to relieve the woman's tension failed.

"All of Silvio's reviews have been positive," she replied, seriously.

"You came all the way here for this party?"

"Well, yes and no. Silvio made the invitation, but I also wanted a short vacation, so I drove here in a rented car. Most of the others came in the chartered plane."

"A plane was chartered for the party guests?"

"Yes, those in New York anyway."

"Were you a close friend?"

"You mean rather than a business acquaintance?" At Donna's nod, she said, "Maybe half way in between."

"According to other witnesses, Mr. Rossi went downstairs to make some cooking preparations and about ten minutes later the waitress discovered his body. Did you see Mr. Rossi go downstairs?"

"No, I didn't."

"After you came into the house, were you here on this floor the whole time?"

"Yes. Oh no, at one point I started to go down to the terrace to talk to Silvio about something, but decided he'd be busy and so I came back."

"Did you go out on the side terrace?"

"Oh, no," she hurried to emphasize, "I only went down a few steps."

"What did you want to talk to him about?"

"I wanted his advice about a restaurant review I was writing."

"You thought he'd be too busy to talk about that?"

"Yes, you see Silvio becomes totally occupied when he's cooking."

Donna had picked up a contradiction in Karen's account; she faced her with it now.

"How did you know Mr. Rossi was on the terrace cooking? You said you didn't see him go downstairs."

Sudden alarm showed on the woman's face. One could read her awareness of the misstep as clearly as if she'd declared it.

"Oh . . . well logically he'd be there. After all, he was barbecuing a portion of the dinner."

Donna was far from convinced.

"You and Mr. Rossi were having a problem, right?"

The question was leading, impertinent even. But it seemed right to Donna at that moment and she went with it.

"Problem? What problem?" she said, startled.

I'm right, Donna concluded. "Yes, that's the question."

"We had no problem. No problem at all."

Not any longer, Donna thought.

"That's all for now, Miss Forbes. Where are you staying?"

"At the Leland Lodge."

"How long do you intend to stay there?"

"Stay? I don't intend to stay. I'll fly back now."

"On the chartered plane." Donna stated.

"I don't think I'll wait; I have a lot to do back in New York."

"I thought you said you were here in part for a vacation."

"After what has happened, I don't, of course, feel like vacationing."

30

"I see." Donna didn't believe Karen Forbes had come here for a vacation. "You have a cell phone."

"Yes, of course."

"Please give me the number. I may need to talk to you before you leave for New York. Please go out to the deck and wait with the others until we are finished taking statements."

Donna looked into the living for the next person to question. She heard Becky saying, with restrained anger, "No one leaves until we're through. Interrupting me with your problems only delays our work!"

It seemed that people, who had come to spend the afternoon partying, suddenly had important appointments to keep.

Donna waved to the man who had met her at the door when she'd first arrived and who had been standing guard there earlier to prevent the party guests from leaving. She remembered that the chef standing watch over the body had called him Frank Knowles. She made him out to be about sixty, urbane and with the patient, amused smile of a philosopher. He had a graying beard and wore half-glasses perched midway on his nose.

"You say that all that time you were merely observing?"

"Let's say I was disengaged," Knowles replied. "I didn't feel like talking. Cocktail conversation is so . . . forced." He expected the questioning look he got from the beautiful deputy, whom he couldn't seriously think of as a real minion of the law. "I mean to say . . . Anyway, a crowd like this is difficult for me lately, because I can hear very little of what people say—especially women." He hurried to add, "I mean because of the higher frequency of their voices." He pointed toward his hearing aids.

"So you just lie back and cruise the pack?"

"Ah, yes, 'cruise the pack'. Thank you. I had the opportunity to inspect the room's objects d'art. Even though it's a new home,

Silvio saw to it that it was immediately well stocked with *art courant*. I imagine he simply called Paul Crecy at his gallery in New York and said, 'Send me your south and east walls.' As a matter of fact, I'm sure I saw these pictures there—hanging in the same order."

Donna couldn't help smiling.

"You had no conversation with anyone?

"No, not really. An occasional nodded acknowledgment, nothing more."

"And you were in the living room from the time you left your room upstairs until the moment the woman screamed?"

"Definitely."

"What was your relationship to Mr. Rossi?"

"Ah yes, was. I am the producer of his television show."

"What will happen to the show?"

"The show is no more, of course. It was the Silvio Rossi show. Without him, nothing."

"What will you do now?"

"The answer to that question ranks right along with: What is the meaning of life?"

"You seem to face this uncertainty with equanimity." Something about this guy made this word choice possible. Frank Knowles was pleased.

"The show's success has made it possible for me to accumulate at least several months rent in advance. And, in spite of producing a cooking show, I eat very little and simply. My kind of bachelor needs little for equanimity."

"So, you are saying that this is what you were doing the whole time after you arrived here–taking in the art work?"

"Actually, I had only come down from my room after the party was well under way. I'm staying here at the house. The flight from New York tired me so I went up to my room and took a nap. And yes, that is what I did the whole time—take in the art work."

"You spoke to no other guest during that period?"

Frank Knowles considered his answer before he said, "Oh yes, I remember now—I saw Karen Forbes. I noticed you interviewed her a while ago. I saw Karen coming up the stairs. I spoke to her briefly."

"Coming up from the terrace?" Donna pressed, remembering Forbes's claim that she'd only started down and then changed her mind.

"She was ascending the stairs; to say more would be speculation."

"But, you thought it likely she'd been down to the terrace..'""
He nodded.

"What did you talk to her about?"

"I don't recall, just social persiflage."

"Persiflage without content?"

"Exactly. 'You're looking well my dear,' that sort of thing."

"What was her manner?"

"Manner? Ah you mean emotionally. Did she seem to have just murdered her host? No, definitely not. A little preoccupied perhaps, nothing more."

"When was it you saw and spoke to her in relation to the waitress's scream?"

"Umm. Five minutes give or take."

"When are you planning on leaving our area?"

"Originally, in a couple of days with the chartered jet, but now I don't know."

"Thank you, Mr. Knowles."

"My pleasure."

5

As Donna stood up to motion to the next person to come to the kitchen, first Paul Treviso, then David Wick emerged from the stairwell.

"The State Police forensic unit is here," David told her.

"Good." Turning to Treviso, Donna said, "Thanks for helping out, but I still want to talk to you. There are a few more people we have to question then I'll be with you."

"These people must be getting pretty hungry; what about a couple of us putting a snack together?" Paul suggested.

"Right, good idea." This man is a real asset, Donna thought.

When Treviso left them, she told David the information she and Becky had been concentrating on. "What did they observe and do they have an alibi for the critical time?"

"I understand," David said.

"I'm going to run down and see what forensics are up to."

In front of Donna, at the bottom of the steps, a continuous glass wall faced the bay. A sliding glass door opened onto a flag-stone terrace. She turned to give the room a quick look before going outside. She saw a comfortable—what do they call them now she wondered—family room, recreation room? There was a pool table, so maybe game room. Leather furniture, shelves of books and a wet bar built into one wall. At the bar's end, the wall jogged back several feet before continuing on to meet the glass wall. This jog created a space behind the bar. Donna visualized a probable storage area for bar supplies. Still looking in the direction of the bar, she began moving again toward the open door to the terrace. From this new angle, she noticed something like the bottom step of a stairway. She walked over for a better look. There was no storage space here at all: she found, instead, a tightly spiraled staircase.

Something on the second step caught her attention. The glint of red light from one of its facets caught her eye. Donna almost picked it up before she reminded herself of proper procedure. She reached into the rear pocket of her uniform trousers and withdrew the plastic baggie she always carried. She scooped the earring up with the edge of the open bag and went to the window to look closely at her catch. Made for a pierced ear, the setting was of a finely filigreed gold. It looked to Donna to be an antique. She made the single stone out to be at least two carats. She was no gemologist, but she believed this to be a genuine ruby. It had the unusual quality of appearing to glow from within.

Donna went back and looked up the spiraling steps. The only light entering the shaft came from two stories above. She slipped the envelope in her pocket and began to climb. Half way up, a small landing and a closed door interrupted the spiral. She continued on up to where she heard voices through the circular opening above her. Her head emerged into the same bedroom where just a short time ago, she had left Gina Rossi with her two friends. They were still there and looked around surprised to see her.

"Hello again," Donna said, "I wondered where this stairway led. It's unusual."

"Yes," Gina answered. "Silvio wanted it that way. If I had guests on the main level, he could come and go as he pleased without having to stop and talk."

"I see." The burden of celebrity, Donna thought. She wanted to look at Gina's ears without appearing to do so and began telling her that the forensic crew would soon leave and her husband's body would be moved. Donna would usually notice the earrings another woman wore, particularly if they shone like the stone in her pocket. She could see now what she had not noticed earlier, because Gina had had her head turned when they were talking so that Donna only saw the right side of her face and in the right ear she wore no earring. What she saw now in Gina's left ear—and worked to not stare at—was the blazing deep red mate of the earring in her pocket. She thought of showing Gina the earring she'd found and to ask for her explanation of its presence on the stair tread, but something told her she'd better say nothing for the moment—wait until Hoss returned.

Donna turned to begin a descent of the stairs, saying a thank-you over her shoulder, and then she stopped and looked back toward Gina.

"Do you use this stairway much?"

The Italian shrug again. "Much? I use it when I go to the beach to swim. Mostly I go down the other way. The steps are easier."

"Did you use the stairway today?"

"Today? No . . . But waita. Yesa, I remember. When I finished dressing for the party. I went down to make sure there was charcoal."

Donna smiled, nodded and began to spiral down the steps. That no doubt explained the earring being on the stair. Still, Hoss might consider the earring to be evidence and she decided she was right to wait until he got back from his meeting before returning it to its owner. One sure thing; Gina Rossi owned and wore gemstones of the highest quality.

Any other thoughts were shouldered abruptly aside when she came onto the side terrace and once again confronted the corpse of Silvio Rossi. Flies, in quantity, had now discovered the corpse.

Don Silver, a fellow deputy and the designated department photographer stood to one side, packing his camera back into its case. Donna went over to him. They both stood in silence and observed the four State Police forensic technicians go about their work, fanning the corpse now and then to shoo away the flies. The corpse had been turned on its side. With this view, Donna could see that the skewer had entered the back a little below the left shoulder blade and exited the chest at a slightly higher point.

"Anything significant?" Donna asked Don.

"Prints on some of the handles of these skewers, and they found a thread on the handle of the skewer that killed him. It seems to match the fabric of these barbecue mitts. The guys say the prints on the handle of the weapon—sword really—are smudged. They doubt there will be anything useful. Yes, and Doc Bahle put in a very brief appearance. He said it looked to him as if the blade had penetrated the heart or aorta. He said and I quote, "Unless someone poisoned him as he fell, it's pretty obvious what killed him. I'll see him at the morgue.""

Don's calling it a sword caused Donna to walk over to the table where lay the five mates of the blade that protruded from Rossi's back. Don was right, swords they were, or rather rapiers. The blades gleamed and the points were razor sharp. She detected fingerprint dust on the handles. Each skewer had a State Police label affixed.

"Are you guys finished with these skewers?" she asked.

"Yep, we've lifted the few prints; you can have them now."

She picked one up and stroked the air like a kid playing Zorro. The blade was alive, bending slightly with the momentum of the stroke, but returning instantly to center. Engraved on the handle she read the name, "Wilkinson". Laying it back on the table she exclaimed, "Whew".

Two paramedics with an ambulance's stretcher had been standing apart waiting for the body to be released for transport to the morgue. "OK, we'll let you fellas get outta here," said one of the forensic technicians. He now grasped the hilt of the skewer in Rossi's back and with the other hand pushing down on the back of the corpse, pulled up and withdrew the blade. The technician's face paled as he completed the task. Another technician opened a cardboard box and held it out to receive what would become exhibit "A".

In less than five minutes, the ambulance drove slowly out the driveway of Silvio Rossi's new summer home.

The leader of the technical crew sidled up to Donna as the others were beginning to put away their paraphernalia.

"Where's Hoss?"

"At a meeting in Detroit."

"Son-of-a-gun. He missed the biggest crime this peninsula's ever likely to see."

"Did you find anything worthwhile?" asked Donna, purposely changing the subject.

"There are prints on the handles of two of the skewers, but no usable prints on the murder weapon. Maybe it was wiped. The guy who was down here with that other deputy—what's his name?"

"The deputy or the guy?"

"The deputy."

"David Wick. He worked as dispatcher for about a year."

"Yeah, that's right. Well, the guy with Wick when we got here said this famous sword company presented the skewers to Rossi. It seems Rossi had trouble one day on his TV show getting some pieces of meat on a very dull skewer. He made a comment about how great it would be if someone would make a decent set of barbecue skewers. This company heard about the remark and saw the PR potential in making a special set to give to him."

"You've heard the saying. 'Be careful what you wish for'," Donna remarked. "But, aside from possible prints, nothing else?"

she asked, her voice betraying disappointed hope.

"We've gone carefully over the immediate ground," he said indicating a wide area around the terrace. "We even put out the fires in the kettles and searched through the ash. It's possible something got thrown out there in the field. It would be worthwhile to take a sweep through it, but that's up to you and your gang."

He said he'd see Donna around and left with his crew, leaving her looking at the wide bloodstain on the stone terrace.

A wave of insecurity swept over her. The fact again announced itself; she was in charge of the investigation of a sensational murder the world would soon learn of and would then minutely scrutinize—minutely judge the actions she'd take. And, what had the forensic specialist just told her? They'd found no hard evidence! Would her boss have handled things here differently? What would he say to her if he were here right now? She imagined him saying, "Stay cool, young lady." She didn't feel very cool. She had been with the Sheriff's Patrol for almost two years, having left a good paying job as a sales-rep for Kellogg. That had been a good decision and she had grown confident that she had acquired most of the skills demanded by her new job. Still, the demands were pretty . . . "rural" came to her mind. Mostly she was called to ease people through problems. Murder was a rare event in the county, only one incident in ten years, but that had been a triple homicide. She'd been part of that investigation, but Hoss had led it. Now, here was her chance to lead and she didn't want to let the Department down.

"I'm going back upstairs, Don, to help get the rest of the statements."

"Want me to help out?"

"No, I think we have that part under control."

"OK, I think I'll get a hose to wash this blood away."

"Hey," Donna said with grim humor, "That's what Hoss tells us, we're a full-service Sheriff's Patrol."

He laughed. "When I'm finished, I'll start a search of the property beyond the area covered by the crime scene guys."

"Good idea, Don." Of course it was a good idea, and not one she had thought to tell him to do. "When you're through, come up and help us with a search of the house."

Becky McConnell saw Donna as she emerged from the stairs into the living room and interrupted the interrogation of one of the last guests.

"Here's what I have. First of all, no one on the deck noticed anyone walking around on the ground—back terrace or down toward the beach. You can't see the side terrace where Rossi barbecued from the deck. All of the people who had been in this room during that ten minute time period were in groups of three or more. A man and woman, John Seabold and Patrizia Nuvolari were alone together talking in a side room. Then there is this guy who is a chef in Rossi's New York restaurant, Vince DeSica, who claims he was taking a walk in the woods on the opposite side of the house from where Rossi was stabbed. He even denies he heard the waitress scream. Finally, one man . . . " Becky looked down at her notes. "A guy named Bruce Thomas claimed to be with a group of three others in the living room. But, when I questioned one of the others in that group, he mentioned off-hand that this Thomas had excused himself to go to the john for part of that time. The person felt sure Thomas had returned to the group before the scream. So, I talked to Thomas again. 'Oh, yes, slipped my mind,' he said, 'I was gone a couple of minutes'. He told me he'd used the bathroom in the game room downstairs, because the one on the main floor was occupied and he didn't want to wait.

Becky summarized. "That's the alibi angle. Everyone denies

going to the terrace at any time after they arrived at the party. And, everyone had been a GREAT friend of Rossi's, and on the best of terms. The waitresses are a special problem, since they were moving about and no one can vouch for them for the critical period with certainty. For instance, the waitress who screamed could have stabbed Rossi just before she screamed—unlikely, but possible."

Donna thought about Becky's report for a few moments.

"I've got two to add to the list. Frank Knowles and Karen Forbes. Also, did you question a woman named Judy Bombard?"

Becky began leafing through her notebook. "Yeah, she said she had been with a group of three others for at least ten minutes before the woman screamed. It's corroborated. Why?"

"I understand she began to go on a tour of the house with Rossi's wife, but after one of the women got sick, she disappeared. Which one is she?" Donna looked toward the group on the deck outside.

"She's wearing that light-green, matching slack and blouse outfit; sitting in that corner," she said, pointing.

"Why don't you talk to her again and find out what she did after she left Mrs. Rossi's house tour."

"Sure."

"We have everyone's address, right?"

"Right," Becky said.

Donna was reluctant to let people go. She wished she could make them all stay in this room until Hoss got back. Neither rationality nor legality backed her wish, only her insecurity.

"Then I guess we can let everyone go—talk to them again later if necessary. Legally, we can only hold them if there is 'probable cause'." Then she added, "If only that were true."

Donna then remembered the computer. "We should impound

the computer. Do you want to tackle that, Dave?"

"Sure, no problem. Where is it?"

"It's on a balcony overlooking the kitchen. There's a stairway. Take all the storage discs, of course."

Donna thought of the ruby earring again. She would hold on to it until Hoss got back. She'd record it among the other things taken from the house: the skewers, the computer.

She said to Becky, "Don Silver is taking a look around the property, but will be coming up here to help us do a search of the house. I haven't the faintest idea of what we should be looking for, but who knows. Right now, I want to go back upstairs. There are a few more questions I want to ask Mrs. Rossi and her two friends. "Tell you what, when you finish with Bombard and the party guests are gone, come up and interview the old lady. The other woman is someone I'd like to take on myself."

Becky laughed. "Do I detect ruffled feathers?"

"Only slightly."

6

The three women were still talking when Donna entered the Rossi's bedroom. The blond publicist, Gloria Klein, no longer perched on the arm of Gina's chair, but sat now in the chair Donna had sat in earlier. There were empty plates on a table from the snacks that Paul, the chef, had provided. The women's attention shifted immediately, apprehensively, to Donna.

She broke the tension with, "Mrs. Rossi, the ambulance just left with your husband. You'll be able to view his body at the Medical Examiner's Office"

"Thank you, officer."

"If you are able to, I'd like to ask you some questions now."

"Yes, yes."

"My colleague and I also want to talk to both of you ladies, so if you would wait in the next bedroom. "

"Come on, Rosa," the publicist said with weary resignation. "They've got their shtick."

Donna let it pass. She waited at the door until the two walked out, and then she closed it. As she sat down opposite Gina Rossi, it occurred to her that this could be a crucial interview. Maybe there was nothing to be learned from the wife, but on the other hand, learning anything of value depended on the questions she posed and how she interpreted Gina's answers. She wondered how her very good friend Derek Marsh, a psychiatrist, would proceed. Would he ask insightful, probing questions or just let the woman tell her story and listen carefully? No time to consider that now. Just as she began to speak, Donna noticed that Gina had removed the other earring. Who had noticed one missing, Gina or one of the other women?

"Again, I want to say how sorry I am."

Gina put out her hand and patted Donna's, just as Donna had seen her do with the older lady.

Donna decided to be direct. "Mrs. Rossi, who do you think killed your husband?"

"Killed? Yes, of course. It's so difficult to think of anyone wanting to kill Silvio. No enemies. He always treated people fairly."

"Mrs. Rossi, your husband ran a successful business. There are competitors. There are . . . "

"Yes, yes, of course, but Silvio always said to me that if he couldn't win while playing by the rules, there was no victory. He worked hard, but he hurt no one—believe me."

"The awful fact is someone wanted to kill him and did. If you let yourself, there must be a name that comes to you as the most likely. I'm not asking you to accuse, only to tell me a name that comes to your mind."

Gina stared out the window toward the empty beach. She clearly appeared to be sincerely trying to comply with Donna's request.

Donna studied her as she did this. She judged her to be close to her own age. Gina was beautiful, but the beauty wasn't built upon perfect features, even though they would pass in any classic sculptor's studio. Although understandably subdued in the present circumstance, one appreciated unusual life in her face: the lifting of an elegantly arched eyebrow, the pursing of her lips, the power of her eyes to hold your attention. Charismatic to anyone, Donna thought, but to those soaked in testosterone she would be irresistible.

Those eyes now engaged Donna. Her expression said in depth that her greatest wish would be to be helpful. "My dear, I'm sorry,

I simply can't think of anyone who would want to do this."

Donna could think of nothing to ask except go over Gina's movements during the morning and especially during the party. She listened once again to the description of Marla's sudden nausea and the abrupt cessation of the house tour. She learned that Gina had only patchy plans for the immediate future. She would close the house and return to New York as planned. She had given no thoughts to the restaurant; there would have to be discussions—decisions.

"Oh, by the way, Mrs. Rossi, would you have any objection to our taking your husband's computer and storage discs to head-quarters for examination? We'll return them as soon as we can."

"Silvio's computer?" She thought for a moment and then shrugged. "No, I have no objection."

"Thank you again for your cooperation."

In the hallway she saw Becky McConnell walking toward her. Donna nodded toward the open doorway to the bedroom where the two women were waiting. Becky went in and told the older woman she wanted to speak with her and Donna asked Gloria Klein to follow her into an adjoining guest bedroom.

Donna had been unsure of herself in the matter of procedure at a murder scene, but she had no qualms about going head to head with another woman who emanated hostility. Gloria Klein's attitude expressed the amused indulgence of an adult waiting for a two-year-old to deliver his or her best punch.

Donna looked her in the eye. "I get the impression you think our investigation is a big joke."

The statement visibly jarred the woman. Klein thought about it. "You could be right. Yes, you are right." The words were blunt, but the tone was even. "Yes, I admit that I'm guilty of chauvinism; you go about things differently here. Yours is a different pace, different syntax. If you'd like to have it, you can have my apology."

Donna hadn't expected this reply. They studied each other quietly for several seconds, each sizing-up the other.

"OK," Donna said. "Tell me—in your way—what happened here."

"As I told you earlier, Jackson Baskin and Paul duMaurier and I were talking. Jack did mention that he'd spoken to Silvio who had been going downstairs to start the barbecuing. A few minutes later—five, ten—we heard this scream. A lot of the people went out to the deck, but for some reason I remained standing there, so I saw Paul—Paul Treviso, one of the chefs from the restaurant—I saw him go down the stairs, then return a minute later. I went over to him and he said that Silvio had been stabbed and that he was dead. He started to leave to call the sheriff, but I caught his arm and asked him if he knew where Gina was. He said he saw her go upstairs earlier. At that moment I saw Marla Phelps come down the stairs. She looked unwell, very pale. I thought it was because she had just heard the news about Silvio and I asked her if Gina was upstairs and she nodded and continued on toward the front door. I went upstairs and noticed a puddle of vomit in the hallway in time to avoid it. When I got to the bedroom, I found Gina and Rosa. Gina stood looking out the window at the people crowding onto the deck below. Gina turned to me when I came to stand beside her and asked me what had happened."

Gloria Klein relaxed a bit and sat back in the chair. She'd been relating the story as if talking to another New Yorker speeding through her day. More slowly she went on, "I realized, then, that Gina didn't know about Silvio and I found myself in the unenviable position of having to inform her. When I finally managed to convince her I was telling the truth, she rushed out of the room and went down to the side terrace. I followed behind after I'd begged Rosa to stay there, telling her I was going to try to bring Gina back.

"Outside on the terrace, I saw Paul Treviso wrestling with Gina, trying to prevent her from falling on top of Silvio. I helped him . . . " Gloria pointed to a scratch on her arm she'd received in the fracas " . . . and we prevailed upon her to come back up to the bedroom. That's where you found us."

"What stairs did she—and you—use to go downstairs?" Donna asked.

"The main stairs, not the spiral stairs, if that's what you mean."

"I see. And the woman who got sick, Marla Phelps, is she staying here at this house?"

"No, only the people who are part of Silvio Rossi Enterprises are here. Silvio booked Marla into at a kind of private hotel south of Northport, The Bluewater Resort."

"You're staying here, right?"

"Yes."

"Are you one of those returning on the chartered plane?"

"Right again."

"Would you do me a favor and make a list of the people staying here and their official relationship with Mr. Rossi?"

Donna had a purpose in asking this, but she would have been hard pressed to put it into words—an intuitive action. By granting this favor, Gloria Klein would subtly begin to identify with Donna's purpose. It was just possible that Donna might get access to an insider's view. She added, smiling, "I also need to know the unofficial word on as many of the guests as you're willing to tell me about."

Gloria hadn't foreseen this request. "I see," she said. "What are we talking about here?"

"I'm talking motive."

"Ah."

"Surely you've had some ideas."

"You mean, I look to you like the suspicious type?"

"I think you see people's motives."

"Perhaps I do. You can't help but develop a healthy ability to scope the jungle if you want to stay alive in my business. But, that's only been for my own use; I'm not into character assassination."

"Neither am I," Donna said sincerely, "I'm only looking for help."

"Hmm. I'll have to think about it."

Donna returned to the first floor, reviewing her talk with the publicist. She began to lean on the hope that the woman would open up and confide information about the group surrounding Silvio Rossi, a view very difficult for her to acquire otherwise.

Everyone had been interviewed now except Marla Phelps. Klein had reported seeing her leave the house at the time the body had first been discovered. Donna planned to drive to The Bluewater Resort to get Phelps' story immediately after the other deputies and she completed a thorough search of the house.

"The first one who finds a confession note wins the prize," Becky quipped.

"Or a manual on fencing technique hidden under a mattress," added Don Silver.

"Something tells me we'd have more luck buying lottery tickets," summarized Donna.

And, she was right. After finding nothing they could identify as having any relevance to the murder, three of the deputies headed back to headquarters to await their boss's return. Even if Kate had managed to contact Hoss immediately with the news, it would still be some time before he got back from Detroit.

Donna lingered in the living room of the big house. What items did common sense dictate she should have thought to do? She felt much like a person standing with a suitcase in one hand and an airline ticket in the other, thinking: Did I stop the mail delivery, give my neighbor the key, turn down the thermostat? Well, she concluded, if she'd forgotten some glaring, big, fucking thing, she had and that was that. She jammed her notebook in her back pocket and started for the front door. Paul Treviso appeared at the entrance to the kitchen.

"Find anything?" he asked.

Donna hesitated. Something about this guy compelled an inclination toward friendship—something that moves one toward an intimacy outside the usual compartment of one's life, the stranger sitting next to you on the plane to whom you find yourself telling things you've told none of your friends. She trusted him.

"Unfortunately, no."

"Unfortunately?"

"Is there something to drink in there?" She motioned toward the kitchen.

"Anything your heart desires."

"How about a beer?"

Paul turned and walked over to the mammoth refrigerator. "Got some fancy Belgian beer."

"Sounds good."

Paul handed her a full glass and poured one for him.

"I don't mean this critically, but I thought you folks always turn down alcohol when on the job."

"We do."

Paul laughed. "OK. You were saying 'unfortunately, no'".

Donna leaned back against a counter.

"There's a lot at stake for us."

"Aren't you making it more personal than it is? You didn't commit the murder."

"Hmm." She drank some of the beer and put the glass on the counter beside her. "Perspectives. Seeing an issue from the other person's point-of-view. That's a big problem for us humans, isn't it? We think the other guy's perspective—even if acknowledged—is not the correct one or main one, not to be taken seriously."

"Whoa, I meant no offense."

"Don't worry, none taken. You see; this is a very big case for our little department. Since Rossi is such a big celebrity, the media will be looking over our shoulders 24/7. We'll be picked apart for any false step and blamed for any delay in arresting the killer. Remember the high school girl who disappeared in Aruba? What impression did you come away with concerning the Aruba police? If you recall, they were especially castigated for their handling of the early phase of the investigation." Donna pointed at her chest. "'The early phase'", that's me. As you've probably noticed, I've assumed the lead here. Not my choice. Our rule is, first on the scene takes command until the sheriff takes over—if he decides to. David Wick is starting his second week on active duty. Don Silver is our technical guy; he's got his things to do. Becky, while I love her, has made a life's decision to avoid taking the lead: do your duty if it means losing your life, but never take the lead. And, as you've no doubt heard, the sheriff's away."

"You're right, in your position I'd be feeling the pressure the same as you."

"Plus," Donna added, "While I love my work, it has been mainly because of the people I meet and the people I work with and being able to help when I'm needed. I don't get my pleasure from being a good cop technically. I can't bring myself to study the manuals. So . . . ."

50

"So, you're afraid that in a situation that calls for perfectly following protocol you're like a stand-in actor shoved on stage not having learned the script."

A short laugh of acquiescence came forth and she took a swallow of beer and looked at the glass. "This is pretty good beer. I'll have to look for it."

"If you can find it here. I'm sure Silvio had it flown in from New York."

"You'll be on your way there soon, I expect."

Paul shrugged, "I don't know about that."

"Really?"

"My wife and I would like to stay here."

Donna nodded understanding and approval. "Thanks for the beer and for listening to me."

Donna felt wrung-out as she closed the heavy front door behind her. She felt like going home and calling it a day, but she still had to find and question Marla Phelps.

Through the kitchen window, Paul watched Donna walk toward her patrol car. He liked the comely, dark-haired deputy. He liked her seeming lack of reverence for authority. Her outlook probably matched his own: get along, have fun, do your best not to hurt anyone, do what you say you'll do and screw the rest.

7

"I feel much better," Marla Phelps said, sipping from a glass of soda water in the sitting room of The Bluewater Resort.

Two couples sat together talking on the far side of the room, removed enough for Donna to feel comfortable that she and Marla could not be overheard. Large windows along the wall where they sat faced a dense planting of spruce trees creating a restricted, yet restful effect.

Marla Phelps was perhaps five years older than she, Donna guessed. She seemed a pleasant person with a ready, open smile. There had been no hesitation to Donna's request to speak with her.

"It happened very suddenly, similar to what I remembered during my pregnancies—nausea and then oops." She smiled at Donna and added sotto voce, "I'm not pregnant."

"And then what happened?"

"Gina took me to the bathroom and held my forehead as I retched. Then Rosa took her place as I continued to retch. Let's see . . . I felt a little better after vomiting and then I remember Gina cleaning me up and taking me to a bedroom to lie down. I did lie there for a short while, but then I thought of having to eat dinner. Food was the last thing I wanted or even wanted to hear about. I got up and went downstairs just as some sort of ruckus started. Everyone was running out onto the deck. I didn't care what had happened, I just wanted to come back to my room here and lie down . . . and I did. I know now the discovery of Silvio's body caused the disturbance. It's just unbelievable, I mean it's just too weird, like it must be a publicity stunt or something. I don't mean that, I know it happened, but . . . "

"But, you had no idea anyone would want to kill him?"

"That's right."

"I'm hearing that over and over. The fact remains, someone did and very decisively. What comes to your mind now, after you acknowledge that it did happen?"

"God, I don't know. What are the usual reasons? He reneged on a gambling debt? He was screwing someone's wife?"

"Did you know . . . "

"No! I'm just rattling on and I should stop. Look officer, there's nothing here. Zero. OK?"

"OK." Donna's tone became deliberately more casual. "What can you tell me about Rossi?"

"Maybe I'm not the one to ask. I didn't know him all that well," Marla demurred.

"Just your impressions, that's all I'm asking for."

"Well, let me see. I first met him when I did an article on his restaurant, Lucretius, for my magazine, *Gourmet*. That must have been half a dozen years ago when he had just opened. He can be very charming and he was on that occasion."

"That sounds like there were other less charming occasions."

"Not that I've witnessed, but I gathered from others that he had become very demanding of his staff and suppliers and could also be very critical and sarcastic. Maybe I held a special place in his thinking, because I was one of the first to recognize and publicize his work. He had this about him, even though he could be difficult, he never took credit for the work done by others—as many other principal chefs do. You got hell if you didn't perform up to his standards, but if you did, you and everyone else heard about it. He was very fair that way. I got the impression he became more short-tempered as time passed, maybe a bit of a bigger head also—if you know what I mean. That's not hard to understand; in recent times he has—rather he had—many people telling him how great he was. You could say he had more on his plate." She smiled at her unintended pun. "Or, so to speak."

"1 hear you saying no one should reasonably have taken offence to the point of committing murder. But what about the people at the party, guests and staff; are there among them, persons who might react unreasonably?"

"Number one, I didn't know everyone at the party, and number two, those I do know, I know only on a pretty superficial professional level. But I know of none who would be that floridly unstable."

"When are you planning to return to New York?"

Marla turned her head to look in the direction of a side room. "Jackson Baskin is calling right now to make a reservation on the first plane we can get."

"Not waiting for the chartered flight then?"

"I just want to go home to my family."

Donna wrote Marla's address and phone number into her notebook and stood up. "I'm glad you're feeling better and I appreciate your input. Thanks."

• • •

"They're all in Hoss's office," Kate Shott told Donna when she walked into headquarters. "Hoss just got back." She turned around to answer the phone, irritated and mumbling, "Reporters!"

Donna rolled one of the chairs from the waiting room into Hoss's private office. Becky and David had their notebooks open and Don Silver sat shuffling through pictures he'd downloaded from his camera and printed. Donna took out her notebook and sat down.

The sheriff of Leelanau County was a massive piece of humanity. His high school classmates had dubbed him Hoss, because he resembled the character in the old Bonanza TV series. He had been a three-letter, offensive tackle for Michigan State and All Big Ten in his senior year. This was his fifth term as sheriff. He looked disheveled and tired after the unexpected, urgent drive up from Detroit.

"It's uncanny," he said in disbelief. "I mean a celebrity like him being killed in this very unusual way. When Kate first told me about it on the phone, I expected her to start laughing and say, 'Just kidding'. Since I'm going to have to admit this really did happen, from what you guys are telling me, I also have to face up to another fact—we don't have the evidence we'd like to have."

Hoss greeted Donna with a nod. "Isn't that right, Donna?"

"Afraid so, Boss."

Looking from one to the other, he said, "Kate says the phone has been ringing without interruption for the past hour. Any minute we can expect the world's press corps to come pouring through the door. What are we gonna tell 'em?"

He got no answer to the rhetorical question.

Don said, "I wonder which of them will be the first to use the caption, 'Chef En Brochette'?"

Everyone groaned.

"That earns you the honor of being our designated Press Secretary," Hoss quipped. He got serious. "Let's go over what we have."

Just short of an hour later he looked at the notes he'd made.

"We've got five people—six including the guy who went to take a leak—without alibis for the critical period of time. We have the computer, which we haven't looked into yet. And we have yet to hear from the forensic squad, although from what you tell me we can't expect much help from them." He looked hard at the paper on which he'd made notes. "Oh, yeah, I wondered what word I'd written here—sword. A question came to me when you mentioned the skewers. How many people would know of the lethal nature of these particular skewers? I mean, you'd hardly think to use a standard barbecue skewer for this purpose unless you were pretty sure it would stand up to completing the work and not just give your victim a back-scratch."

"Good point," Becky said.

Donna remembered what she'd been told. "There is this about the skewers: they were presented to him on TV, so it might be widely known they existed. The question remains, how many knew Rossi had brought them here to Michigan?"

"Correct me if I'm wrong, but what I'm getting from all this is that we have no one we can legitimately regard as a hot suspect. First, no evidence ties the crime directly to anyone. Second, we have discovered no motive. All we have identified are several people who *may* have had opportunity." Hoss looked at the four deputies for a response. They stared soberly back at him.

Donna got up the courage to say, "Since I was the first one of us at the scene, I took command of the procedure. Do you believe there is something I neglected?"

Hoss Davis weighed his answer. "To be honest, Donna, I feel like we should have come away from that house with more. At the same time, I don't know what I might have done differently."

That's what Hoss said, but he wondered if his greater experience wouldn't have suggested on-site observations that his deputies missed. This led to a thought that showed on his face like a revelation.

"We've been talking about those at the party; would it have been possible for someone who wasn't at the party to sneak up on Rossi, stab him and then leave the scene without being observed?"

"Easily," Donna replied. "I guess we've only been talking about the guests, because they were the ones we were able to question. When I first walked up and saw the body, I first thought someone had likely come out of the woods next to the house and stabbed him. However, the forensic team went over some of that ground and found nothing to support that idea." She looked over at Don Silver.

"That's right. They looked carefully over maybe a fifty-yard radius and after they left I walked over the rest of the vacant field next to the terrace and maybe thirty yards into the woods. Altogether there are probably ten acres of woods."

"That's a dirt road there; did you look along it?" Hoss asked.

"Yes," Don answered. "I walked out onto the road from the woods and walked back to the drive leading to the house. A number of cars were parked along the drive, but there were no tracks made by any vehicle that had been parked there and had left. "

"What about someone approaching from the other side of the house—the west?"

"That would be difficult," Donna responded. "From there and from the bay side, a person would have to pass the rear deck on which people were standing and drinking. These people were specifically asked if they saw anyone on the grounds. No one had. Walking past the front of the house, the attacker would be in view of the large kitchen windows. Kitchen staff worked in front of those windows the whole time. At least it's fair to say that a person would have been taking a big risk to approach across the front of the house. Also, one guest, a chef from the New York restaurant, claims that while walking on that side of the house he saw nothing—if he's telling the truth."

Hoss glanced at his watch. "There are still several hours until it's dark. I'm going to have Kate call as many deputies . . . No wait,

I know what. We'll call that fellow who's on the tribal council—Robert something or other; it'll come to me. Anyway, he's the person who volunteers to lead groups on Conservancy nature walks. His hobby is tracking and I hear he's awesome. I'll call him and see if he's free this evening and willing to go out to the Rossi home. We'll give him a chance to examine those woods before we all go trooping through obliterating any evidence."

"Oh, there is something else," Donna said while digging into her back trouser pocket. She laid the plastic envelope containing the ruby earring on the table.

"I found it on one of the bottom steps of the stairway that leads from the Rossi bedroom to the lower-level game room. It belongs to the wife, Gina. She was still wearing its mate when I interviewed her. I thought it might be evidence when I picked it up, but now I believe that in itself it doesn't qualify as evidence."

"Why do you say 'in itself' it doesn't qualify?"

"Mrs. Rossi says she'd used the stairs earlier to go from her bedroom to the terrace to check on the cooking supplies before the guests started to arrive. Since it's reasonable for her to have dropped it at that time, its presence on the step becomes worthless as evidence."

"I follow you," said Hoss. "The fact that it's reasonable for her to have made that trip down to the terrace nullifies any significance of finding one of her earrings on the step. Besides, she's one of those who has an alibi." He paused for a moment and added, "So, you'll be giving it back to her."

"Of course."

• • •

Paul Treviso parked in the small parking area next to the

Trillium B&B in Northport where Silvio had booked him and his wife, Laura, for the past month. Laura ran up to the car before he could open the door. He'd called her with the news the first chance he'd had.

"It must have been awful." Her statement was also a question. She studied his face and saw that signs of stress had replaced his usual, carefree attitude.

"Let's go for a walk; I don't feel like being inside," Paul said, taking her hand.

The narrow, tree-shaded road led toward the center of the old village with which they had both fallen in love. Here there existed a quality of having stepped back into a gentler period in history, to a more humane time. Over the past days, they had talked of how great it would be if their kids, yet to be born, could grow up in such a place.

They had walked half a block, Laura waiting expectantly for his answer to her question, before he felt ready to redirect his thoughts to the murder.

"What did you say . . . oh yes, 'awful'. Yes, very awful," he said. "Did you know I've never seen a dead person before? The dead are so disturbingly inert. Especially so, when you're looking at someone you know well, knowing this inertness is permanent. I experienced a kid's sense of wonderment. I could stand there and watch for days, and Silvio would never move.

"Anyway, whoever did it, plunged this skewer right up to the hilt. You could tell this, because the whole blade was bloody. Silvio fell forward on it and pushed it back out part way." Paul mused on this a moment. "The guy must really have hated him."

"Who do you think did it?"

"There is no one that I think did it, but I know of three people who might be glad that Silvio is dead."

"Really? Who are they?"

"Just recently Silvio told me off-hand, while we were working together, that he'd learned—had proof—that a woman named Karen Forbes had been taking—let's call them contributions—from the restaurants she reviewed for her TV spot. Silvio didn't say he planned to do anything, but if he did make what he'd learned known, it would mean the end of her career."

"Funny, I've always half-way assumed there were kickbacks of some sort. Would this have been so damning?" Laura asked.

"You better believe it. Would you give her reviews any credence if you knew she took money for a good review?" He looked over at his wife and saw her nod of understanding. Paul laughed, "Besides, it's one thing to be involved in something shady, but quite another for it to become public knowledge. It's like a lot of dishonest behavior, many may be participating, but the one who gets caught is very, very bad."

"Who else?"

"Well, a lot of cookbooks, as I've suggested to you before, are plagiarized to some degree. You know the author didn't come up with or try out all those recipes. There is a certain amount of 'referencing' that goes on. Usually, at least one ingredient is changed. A couple of authors, however, were lazy. I'm talking about Seabold and Nuvolari; they didn't bother to alter anything from a 50's vintage Italian tome. It was a book that Silvio had used a lot when he started to get interested in cooking as a teenager. So when he looked into their new book to write a review for *Bon Appetit*, he experienced déjà vu. Again, he didn't say anything to me about exposing this theft. But he was mad."

"Did he let them know he had spotted the plagiarism?"

"Good question. Something about the way he told me the story made me think he had."

"I see what you mean. In each case, these people probably sighed with relief when they heard he was dead."

"I know I would have."

They walked in silence awhile.

"How is Gina doing?" asked Laura.

They had just turned the corner onto Nagonaba Street and were walking down the hill; the whole village lay in front of them clear out to the marina on Grand Traverse Bay.

"Very Italian at first. I decided I would stand watch over the body before the police arrived. She came charging onto the terrace and would have thrown herself on top of Silvio if I hadn't caught her and held her back. Before I left, I saw her and she seemed composed and concerned about everyone else's comfort as she always is."

"Poor Gina. What do you think is going to happen to the restaurant now?"

"I don't know. It's too successful to close its doors. The logical thing would be for Vince to take over the kitchen. Yeah, that's probably what's going to happen."

"What about us?"

Paul looked down into that upturned face that he loved so much. He smiled and wrapped his arms around her.

"Yeah, what about us? Do we have the nerve to do what we'd like to do?"

8

A wholesale exodus got underway from the shore of Cathead Bay to points east and west. Seats on the few daily flights from Traverse City were quickly booked.

Frank Knowles, finding out he couldn't get on a flight to Detroit with a connection to New York before the scheduled departure of the chartered plane two days hence, elected to rent a car and drive back east. He didn't want to be available for questioning. Karen Forbes left with him.

John Seabold and Patrizia Nuvolari drove immediately to the airport and took the first flight out, even though it was bound for Minneapolis. They'd make whatever arrangements they could from there.

Vince DeSica, the sous-chef at Lucretius, thought it would look better not to make an abrupt departure and hurry his mother away, since she wanted to stay with Gina Rossi. Rosa naturally saw Gina as requiring her motherly shoulder. He and his mother continued to reside in the Rossi home and wait for the chartered jet.

Bruce Thomas, the man who had no one to vouch for his claimed micturition, did not leave the area. He and his wife, Sandra, had a house at The Homestead Resort thirty-five miles to the south in Glen Arbor.

This comprised the group without witnesses to their whereabouts for the crucial time interval.

• • •

Robert Downs said he would be free that evening and be happy to help out the Sheriff's Department. He would leave the Ottawa/Chippewa Reservation immediately and meet Hoss at the murder site, fourteen miles to the north.

Robert, a handsome, physically fit man in his mid-fifties wore his black hair pulled back in a ponytail. His features and complexion spoke accurately of his heritage. Since early adulthood, he had sought out and received instruction on "tracking" from the elders in his and other tribes. He had also read everything he could find on the subject. In addition he also became an expert stalker. He enjoyed coming up to within feet of hikers walking along the nearby state forest trails and then fade away again without anyone being the wiser.

Hoss told Robert about the State Police crime unit's search of part of the vacant lot adjacent to the terrace. He stood now with Donna Roper and David Wick by Donna's patrol car and watched Robert, who, after a careful examination of the weed-filled vacant lot next to the terrace, disappeared into the woods.

"Do you get this feeling he has more rods and cones in his retina than we do?" David said.

"Know what you mean," Hoss replied. "I think it's simply a matter of paying attention, something I know I don't do as much as I should—lost the ability to do it perhaps."

Half an hour later, Robert Downs came walking toward them along the driveway. He gave Hoss a knowing smile.

"One of the men who searched this field also went into the woods. One of your men, Sheriff?"

Hoss blushed and laughed. "Touché, Robert. Yes, it was one of our deputies and he didn't find anything."

"Me neither. No one has been in those woods since the snow melted last spring."

What Robert had seen—apart from the evidence of Don Silver's having been there—interested him very much. He'd found fresh bear tracks. He'd heard of a bear being spotted down near Cedar, in the center of the peninsula, but not this far north. He wouldn't tell the sheriff. It would become Hoss's duty to mount a hunt. He didn't think Hoss wanted to do that and he didn't either. The bear was doing his best to mind his own business.

"Thanks, Robert. Let me know how I can repay the favor."

"You owe me nothing; I enjoyed it."

Hoss waited until Downs had driven away, then said, "I think we can rest assured that no one came at Rossi from the direction of the woods, but what we have to do now is fan out and make a pass through it, anyway."

"Really?" Donna queried.

"Can't you just imagine a defense attorney saying with dramatic disbelief, 'You mean to tell me, Sheriff, that you didn't examine that woods yourself. You accepted the opinion of an amateur Indian hobbyist?'"

The sun had fallen below the treetops, casting the mansion's façade into shadow as Hoss stood at the front door of the Rossi house with Donna at his side. David said he'd wait in the car. The three had already made the perfunctory sweep of the empty woods. Now, Hoss wanted to introduce himself to Gina Rossi and express his sympathy. He also wanted to see the inside of the house and meet Vince DeSica and Frank Knowles, two of the people Donna said had no alibi and who he understood were staying in the house.

DeSica answered the doorbell. He was momentarily taken aback by the size of the man he faced.

"I'm Sheriff Davis. We'd like to come in and look around the house and I want to speak to Mrs. Rossi if she's able to see me."

"Certainly Sheriff. I'm Vince DeSica. I worked for Mr. Rossi."
He moved aside and let Hoss and Donna enter.

De Sica, although of average height, seemed taller because he held himself erect and composed. Hoss sensed the man was habitually cautious about what he would reveal of himself. Even his best friends would never feel they knew him well.

"I've been told, Mr. DeSica, that you were outside the house at the time of the murder."

"Yes, that's true," he motioned in the direction of the western side of the house, the side opposite the recent search. "I was walking on the paths that Silvio had built into the woods."

"Can you tell me about that?"

"Not much to tell. I felt like getting away from the party for a while, and—"

"Why was that?"

"You mean getting away? I wanted to think about something."

"Some problem?"

How much should he say, Vince wondered. How much could this man learn of Silvio's plans? Would he be seen in a better light if he appeared to be open now? He decided to say nothing.

"No, no special problem. Just thoughts of heading back to the city and all the work there to be done.."

"You didn't hear the girl scream when she found the body?"

"No, I didn't."

"Who do you think did it?"

There was something about the size of the man and his lack of formality that had Vince off balance. It was like being interrogated by God. But DeSica believed even God wouldn't be able to find a chink in his armor.

"I'd like to be able to answer that question," he said shaking his head.

"Thanks. I'd like to speak to Frank Knowles before I speak to Mrs. Rossi. Can you tell me where he is?"

"Frank has already gone back to New York. He left a short time ago." Noticing Hoss's surprised look he added, "He went with Karen Forbes. She had a rented car."

"Got away pretty fast." Hoss commented. "Does that surprise you?"

Again, here was that penetrating style. "Surprised? Ah . . . " He gave a short laugh. "I don't know, Sheriff."

Hoss closed his eyes for a second. Something was going on here; DeSica was holding back—about himself and others. Hoss referred back in his mind to other situations where he'd encountered a group of people with a secret—a group secret. Hoss wondered how he could break into the conspiracy of silence he thought he'd identified. Gina Rossi came into the room and temporarily set those thoughts aside.

"You must be the sheriff," Gina said holding out her hand. "I'm Gina Rossi."

"Yes, I'm Sheriff Davis, Mrs. Rossi. I want to say how sorry I am and to tell you we'll do all we can to find out who did this."

"Thank you, Sheriff."

Donna watched the exchange with interest.

Gina led Hoss and Donna into a small study with a view towards Cathead Bay. The rest of the house featured contemporary Italianate furnishings, but not this room. The paneling and deep leather chairs reminded Hoss of magazine photos of celebrities' Aspen lodges. By their style, Hoss recognized two landscape paintings to be by local artists. The cherry orchard at sunset was certain to be by his friend Marti Jensen. There was also a portrait of Gina Rossi by the area's excellent portraitist.

Gina was polite and gracious, but Donna noticed her former

solicitousness was restrained. The content of the interview went no further than what Donna had already heard: Everyone loved Silvio. Silvio loved everyone. To this she added a new theme; "A crazy person must have done it, someone who has escaped from a psychiatric hospital."

Hoss agreed such a possibility needed to be checked out. He explained that he wanted to look around the house in order to fully understand the physical setting in which the tragedy had occurred. Donna immediately assured Gina that she knew the layout of the house and Gina need not trouble herself to lead them.

When they were alone Hoss said, "From what we've learned so far, it seems sure the killer did not come from outside the house. That leaves us with those inside. By what route could they get out to the side terrace and back again?"

"There are only three ways. Out the front door and risk being seen from the kitchen, down this stairway from the living room— the one Rossi himself used to go downstairs—and finally, the spiral stairway from the master bedroom to the lower level."

"Let's go downstairs and work our way up."

Donna led Hoss across the living room to the head of the stairs. He stopped and looked back toward the living room where the party guests had congregated. He saw that a living room wall extended like a screen, so that the stairway itself was not visible from much of the room. He turned and looked toward the kitchen. Here again the design made it possible for a person to come from the lower level and proceed on up to the second floor of the house without being seen by the kitchen staff.

"It's possible that someone walking around in the living room could wait for the right moment and slip down these stairs without being seen," Hoss surmised.

"That's what I thought too. This Bruce Thomas admits to going down and no one seems to have seen him do it," Donna said. "On the other hand, Frank Knowles saw Karen Forbes coming up the stairs."

"I wonder where he was standing? What do we know about the woman?"

"She has a weekly spot on the evening news show of a New York station. She reviews restaurants. Also the person who saw her, Frank Knowles, described her demeanor as, 'preoccupied'".

"Preoccupied as in, 'Am I sure I really killed him?' or as in, 'Do I have any overdue library books?'"

"Closer to the second."

"Let's go downstairs."

Once in the downstairs game room Hoss asked, "Where's that other stairway. I don't see it."

"It's behind that wall with the wet bar."

He went there and looked up the long, tight, cylindrical shaft.

"This where you found that earring?"

"Right. Second step."

"Is that a door I see up where that small landing is?"

"Yes. It goes into the room where we were just sitting with Mrs. Rossi. It's also the room where the authors, Seabold and Nuvolari, were sitting apart from the rest of the party, talking."

"So they—or one of them—could have skipped down this stairway unseen by the rest and done the deed?"

"Easily."

"Did we check for fingerprints on the door and knobs?"

"No."

Hoss shot a look at Donna.

"We didn't know there was a reason to before the forensic crew left."

"How about when you realized those two had no alibi except each other?"

Donna didn't have an answer. She said, "I'll have it done now."

Hoss said nothing, but thought that if that couple were guilty, they would likely have thought to wipe the knobs—but then again, maybe not.

"Nothing to lose," he commented. "I presume you have taken the prints of Mrs. Rossi, the household staff and the deceased."

"Got 'em all."

Hoss continued around the room until he came to the sliding door leading to the back terrace and stepped outside.

The sound of loud voices came from the direction of the side terrace and Donna walked to the corner of the house to take a look. Over her shoulder she said to Hoss, "Reporters! Half a dozen, a couple with minicams. Dave is marching them back up the hill."

"Just what we expected," Hoss said, staying back by the door and out of view. "Maybe worse than I imagined."

9

Lists of ingredients slid upward on the screen, ingredients and recipes like *Agnello brodettato* and *Salsiccia*. Don Silver had Silvio Rossi's computer operating in a basement room at Sheriff's Headquarters, where he searched through the document files for anything relevant to their investigation. He had found nothing so far, only recipes and texts relating to them and a number of short essays about wine, food and travel no doubt intended for magazines.

Don noticed several dozen files beginning with the letter "l". He soon found that the "l" designated document files of letters Rossi had written. Here Don came upon something of interest. After just half-an-hour of reading, he came to know the great chef as a man who could—when he wanted to—put together words that sizzled.

A letter to a seafood supplier: "We could do nothing with the allegedly fresh turbot you delivered on Tuesday except to put it in the alley for the cats. They took one whiff and began the trek toward Babbo to check out its garbage." A letter to the Editor-In-Chief of *New York Now:* "I'm very surprised, knowing of your own impeccable taste, that you hired *that* person for your food editor. As you must know in your last issue he described my *Crema di Cipolle alle Mandorle* as 'bland'. Sources tell me that the most sophisticated food he'd tasted before joining your magazine was macaroni and cheese in his college mess hall. God forbid my letter might cause you to reassign him as music critic. He would surely condemn Vivaldi's *Mass* as 'undanceable'."

Don smiled as he read through similar salvos from the Rossi

pen. They were cutting, but contained some humor. He came to a letter, however, that lacked any comedy. Addressed to a Random House editor, it read, "I regret that I must bring to your attention the fact that one of the books you recently published is plagiarized in its entirety. I am referring to *A Tuscan Table* by Patrizia Nuvolari and John Seabold. The book copied is well known to me by the title of *Da una Tabella Toscana* published in Milan in 1951. I believe the offense that disturbs me most is the theft of a creative work.

"Since yours is a reputable publishing house, I expect you will immediately take the appropriate action and withdraw the book from circulation along with making a public apology for what was an understandable mistake on your part. If, however, you disappoint my expectations, I will see to it that the public is not deceived."

Don printed this letter, then closed the document files and opened Outlook Express.

. . .

Dave Wick stayed behind at the Rossi house, after Hoss and Donna sped out of the driveway and away at a speed to have earned a speeding ticket for any reporter who attempted to follow.

Hoss took the back way to Sheriff's Headquarters instead of the main road back through Northport. The winding, undulating roads took them past cherry and apple orchards, century-old barns and views out over Lake Michigan where South Fox and the Manitou Islands were now dark shapes against a radiant sunset. As they neared the Highway M22/Carlson Road intersection, Hoss turned to Donna.

"Please get Kate on the phone and see if we've got a bunch of reporters waiting for us at headquarters."

Donna dialed and before she could ask, Kate began telling her that not only had the press arrived there in number, but a TV crew had also set up for an interview with Hoss when he returned.

They're not nice either," Kate declared. "They talk to me like I'm retarded."

Donna heard the wounded tone in Kate's voice. "Don't let it bother you, Kate; it's not your fault their mothers didn't teach them any better." Donna hung up and turned to Hoss. "As you feared."

Hoss made a spot decision and swung the patrol car sharply into the driveway of the Happy Hour Tavern and parked in the back out of sight of the road. He turned off the ignition but continued sitting.

"My problem with the media was tweaked last year during the Wilson murder case by that one TV reporter who was simply out to get me—discredit me and the Department. I believe most reporters are people with integrity aiming to get at the facts of a story, while observing the rules of common courtesy, but others are out to dig up something sensational to report with little regard for truth or context. They interpret "freedom of the press" to mean they have a license to do whatever it takes to get their story. I loathe this type of reporter. Problem is, how do you distinguish which of those types is now approaching you with a microphone?"

Hoss led Donna in through the kitchen entrance, greeting the surprised cook. When the owner of the tavern looked up from behind the bar seeing Hoss's huge shape fill the kitchen door, Hoss said, "Paul, we need a place where Donna and I can talk."

"Back room's empty."

"Thanks."

Hoss opened the door to the room used when overflow of the main room demanded it, waited for Donna to enter and closed the door again.

"Donna, you want some coffee or something?"

"Coffee would be good."

He opened the door again and caught the waitress as she passed. "Erin, could we have a coupla coffees back here, please?"

A few minutes later, he stirred sugar into his cup as he looked across the table at a deputy tired and stressed from her day's intensive work. He said, "We got us a three-ring circus, my friend."

"I know. I can't decide whether my sense of being at a loss is caused by the lack of evidence or the pressure I expect from the news media"

"It's both; they'll be pushing and we don't have the answers. We need to just focus on the investigation."

Now that he had been to the Rossi house, he wanted to place each suspect into the proper location there. "Tell me once again where exactly the six with opportunity were?"

Donna ran through the list again as Hoss ticked them off with his fingers.

"That's only five. Who are we forgetting?" Hoss said. "Oh I know, the guy who went to the john."

"From what you've told me, we haven't a whiff of a motive for any of these folks."

It was a question and Donna nodded.

"Looks like the only one still in the county for us to question is the cook."

"Yes, the chef, DeSica . . . and Thomas. He lives at The Homestead."

Hoss laughed. "Oh yeah, that guy again."

By way of defending herself, she added, "I had no evidence to detain them—still don't."

Hoss noticed her bristling. "Hey, no blame intended. But we gotta get more information about these six."

"There is a woman, the publicist, with whom I think I've got an understanding. I'm hoping she'll give me the benefit of her insider's view."

"She's still here then?"

"She told me she's returning to New York with the chartered plane on Tuesday. She's staying at Rossi's house."

"Good, maybe that will be the end of a thread that will lead somewhere. Why don't you take the patrol car and find her now? I'll call K.D. to come pick me up."

Hoss's cell phone rang. He listened and as he did a smile of satisfaction spread across his face for the first time since he'd heard of Silvio Rossi's death.

• • •

The phone call that caused Hoss to smile while sitting with Donna at the Happy Hour had come from Don Silver. Don had told Hoss he'd come upon some very interesting e-mail correspondence during his inventory of Silvio Rossi's computer. Among the recipients of Rossi's messages, Don had recognized the names of persons he'd heard Donna identify as being without an alibi.

Don had copied all of the "sent" and "incoming messages" and sat now opposite Hoss at the sheriff's kitchen table. K.D., Hoss's wife, poured coffee.

K.D. was a natural manager. She had easily assumed the responsibility for overseeing the raising of the couple's only child— now a sophomore at Michigan State— and the running of the home and the care of Hoss in all respects excepting his professional duties. When she could, she put her paddle in that water also. She had no wish to be in control, she just couldn't avoid her propensity to worry. She felt especially happy today to be in a position to take an active part in an investigation right here in her own kitchen, rather than, as usual, hearing a second-hand report from Hoss at dinner time.

"I've sorted the individual messages out according to time sent, so we can follow the course of the interaction," Don said.

Don usually sought the humor in a situation, but one would never know it by his deadpan expression—the same look Saint Peter must wear as he meets new arrivals at the pearly gates and says, "You can't be serious."

Hoss consulted his notes. "The people we're particularly interested in are, Frank Knowles, Karen Forbes, Vince DeSica and . . . let's see, Patrizia Nuvolari and John Seabold and also Bruce Thomas."

Don smiled broadly. "I think you'll find what I have here very interesting." He began reading aloud.

"Let's see now, Rossi sent this message two weeks ago. 'Karen dear, a little bird told me you've been making respectable additions to your bank account on a regular basis that coincides with your restaurant reviews. The old name for this kind of transaction was 'payola'. The birdie also told me that Gautier at the Oiseau Vert refused to make a contribution to the Karen Forbes retirement fund and his restaurant received a poor review. Not wise my dear; such action makes people angry and they talk. Perhaps I should tell you of my attitude toward this kind of deceit. It sickens me and it sets loose an uncontrollable need to expose the guilty party. For old times sake, I thought I'd let you know. Silvio.'"

"Well, well," said Hoss. K.D. sat down at the table, all ears. She gave part of her attention to the case itself, but the greater share was, as always, devoted to evaluating how the present news would play out for Hoss.

"Rossi received this the next day," Don said. "'Silvio, I can't think who has said this awful thing about me. I'm surprised you would have believed it for a minute. Please don't do anything until we have a chance to sit down face-to-face and talk. Fondly, Karen.'"

Don went on, "This was sent by Rossi three days later. 'Karen, dear, to do something reprehensible is one thing, but to lie to a friend is unforgivable. Your accepting money to give a good review on your television program was an offence to your employers and your public and not toward me directly, but I take lying to me as a personal offense. Sorry. Silvio.'"

"The same day. 'Are you sure of your facts? My attorney says I should remind you that a false accusation could be very costly for you. Karen'. "This is his answer four days later, 'Karen, dear, I'm sure.'"

Hoss observed, "Donna told me this woman didn't ride here in the chartered plane; now I understand why. But, she came to his party anyway probably hoping to talk him out of taking any action, and maybe *even* to silence him if he remained deaf to her appeal. Good work, Don, read on."

Don took up another paper. "Silvio, that short exchange we had this morning in the hall has left me in a daze. What did you mean when you said, 'So?', as the elevator doors closed and separated us? I had just said that a friend told me you'd been talking to that kid, Burgess. Did, 'So', mean that my friend was correct, or were you asking me for more information? Frank."

"He sent that on the sixteenth, so this reply came two days later," Don said and began to read.

"I don't know exactly what your friend said about Logan Burgess, but I've been telling you for months that the show has become stale. The fact that you didn't hear me underlines how out of touch you've become with new trends. It's all about leading the consumer and not being in a position where someone else is doing the leading and we're forced to guess the next dance step. If you'd be honest with yourself, Frank, you'll admit you really want to retire. Silvio."

"And the same day," Don said.

"Silvio, I know you've been burning the candle at both ends and in the middle for months now. We can sit down and have a quiet talk up there at your place in Michigan. See you up there. Frank."

"Frank Knowles is the producer of Rossi's TV show," Hoss explained to K.D.

K.D. got up to get the coffee carafe. She rose from the chair with the youthful ease of a person who works-out regularly.

"Sounds like ole Frank was unceremoniously being given his pink slip," K.D. observed.

"Can you believe all this?" Hoss chuckled. "When it rains it pours. Suddenly motives for murder are falling from the skies. I'm picturing Donna's face, when I tell her tomorrow. An interesting thing about e-mail, folks don't seem to regard their messages as documentation. Stuff they'd never consider putting into writing they put into their messages as if it all just goes out into cyber-space and disappears."

"And, not just e-mail, 'Word' documents also," Don said. "It's so easy to click on the 'save' button and forget you've got a copy of a letter you've written there among all the other saved documents."

Don, then, laid the copy of the letter Rossi had sent to Random House about Nuvolari and Seabold's book in front of Hoss, while giving a brief summary to K.D.

When he'd finished reading, Hoss said, "It indicates Rossi intended a copy to go to Nuvolari and Seabold.

"Incredible. Let's see, that only leaves that chef who walked in the woods and the guy with the full bladder. Don't tell me you've got something there that gives them motives, too. If you do, I'd begin to worry you are putting me on."

"Actually, there is an e-mail that concerns . . . Yes, here it is. I hadn't paid attention to it, because it didn't contain the same kind of threat as those others. It's a message sent to someone named Sam at the *New York Times*. 'Sam, Regarding our telephone conversation this morning; I want to emphasize the need to keep that information between us, since, as I said when we talked, there are delicate real estate negotiations going on. To have the fact that I'm planning to open a second restaurant made public may weaken my bargaining position. I will let you know as soon as the deal is closed. But, as I said, the name will be Ovid and Vince DeSica will be the Executive Chef. Thanks, Silvio.'"

"Scratch one name from the list of suspects," K.D. said. "One doesn't kill the man who is about to reward you with your own kitchen in one of New York's top restaurants."

Hoss considered her remark and agreed. "Yeah, we don't know for sure, but it would seem likely that these plans for a new restaurant would be cancelled now that Rossi is dead.

"Is that all, Don?" Hoss asked.

"I didn't find anything about Bruce Thomas, but there is another interesting letter." Don handed a sheet of copy paper to Hoss.

Hoss began reading a letter written by Rossi to the New York Federal Prosecutor's Office giving them the name and address of an employee named Jose Maria Flores who, Rossi said, he had only just learned was an illegal alien. He requested advice on how to proceed. This was six weeks ago.

Hoss opened a folder Becky McConnell had given him. She had made a list of all those who had been in the Rossi house at the time of the murder. He ran his finger down the list of those working and then the list of guests.

"This guy Flores wasn't at the party. I'm sure he'd like to kill

Rossi, but I think we can forget him."

An idea made Hoss go back to the letter about the two authors.

"This letter to the publishing house about Nuvolari and Seabold, I wonder if Rossi already mailed it. And, did he actually send the copy to the two authors?

"You see, what I'm thinking is this, with this Flores fella, Rossi had already done the damage. With Frank Knowles he had only alluded to the need to replace him. Also, in the e-mail to Karen Forbes, he only says that he knows what she's done; he doesn't say he has told anyone else. In other words, his death coming at the time it did could have prevented a problem for both of these people. The same goes for the two authors if Rossi had only mailed their copy of the letter. That needs to be checked."

"See what you mean," agreed Don Silver. "They would all have a motive to silence him before he acted."

The three sat looking at each other with that surprised awareness people can have when making an unexpected discovery.

"Let's be sure we're not racing ahead of logic," K.D. said. "Motives for being pissed-off aren't automatically motives for murder."

Hoss had some momentum going in the direction of solving the crime and his wife was suggesting in her usual, cautious way that they backtrack and walk slowly over the same ground. Grudgingly he agreed. He took a swallow of coffee and put the cup down with an attitude of readiness to re-work a problem.

"O.K., I'm a woman who's got herself a television program that must be paying the bills for some fancy New York living: lunches at the good restaurants, invitations to cocktail parties high above Central Park, good lookin' and important men want to cuddle up to me. I had to work damn hard to get where I am and if I'm brought down in a scandal I see no hope of regaining my position.

Now, would I kill to prevent that from happening?"

"In a New York minute," Don snapped.

K.D. nodded. "Possibly," she allowed.

"How about this one? I am the producer of a very successful show—again the money and the prestige. Then, I hear the star is displeased with me and has been talking to some young whipper-snapper about taking my place. How do I feel, mad enough to kill?"

"I don't know," Don answered. "The show's been running a while and Knowles must have a wad of money in the bank. I saw him; he looks old enough and tired enough to call it a day. I'd be angry, but I think I'd just say . . . " Don looked over at K.D.

"Go ahead, say it," she laughed.

"I'd just say screw it." Don said smiling.

"Is that really the word you were going to use?" teased K.D.

"You bet."

"Right! Anyway," Hoss continued, "I think you're leaving out an element—pride. It's one thing to have a show fold because the network wants to keep up with a new trend, like 'reality TV'. It would be much easier to say to your friends, 'You know, I'm actually happy the show ended, I was really tired of the pace.' It's another thing to be replaced by a younger person. I don't know what kind of guy this Frank Knowles is, but there are many who would kill to prevent the embarrassment and loss of face. Not a strong motive for murder, but real.

"OK now, my partner and I have published a book, which we represent as being original. We hope it will be a best seller and establish our names in this field. A famous chef who packs much clout is threatening to blow the whistle and expose us as plagiarists. Would I kill to prevent this from happening?"

"The public's reaction to plagiarism is a curious thing," K.D. said. "I thought about this just the other day when I read about a young woman being hailed as a genius for a debut novel she had

80

written; then it turned out she copied parts of it from another book. The literary world especially, and the public in general wanted to crucify her—much more so than the author she'd stolen from. It seems to me this strong feeling arises out of both a sense of betrayal—'You made a fool out of me for praising you'—and of jealousy. Everyone in the literary world would like to have written a novel that people are calling a work of genius. They have to swallow their envy and congratulate the lucky author, BUT when it turns out the work is a fake, a head must roll."

Hoss looked at his wife with surprise. She always looked much deeper into things than he. It caused him to re-experience a feeling from childhood when his parents would spell their messages aloud to each other. It caused a discomfiting awareness of another level of reality that usually passed right by him. He had to get back to the comfort of a practical, factual approach.

"Sounds like you're saying a person who anticipates that kind of hatred would be ready to commit murder to avoid it," he said.

"Possibly." Then, K.D. reminded them of a daunting fact. "But, in the absence of any evidence that implicates any one of these people, doesn't having many people with motives create its own problem? I mean, if only one person had a strong motive—along with opportunity and means—a prosecutor might consider a prosecution, but with four people having equal motives, opportunities and means, whom would he pick to prosecute?"

Hoss shook his head and began to laugh. "This reminds me of that old college drinking song that went like this, 'You meet the girl of your dreams. YEAH! But you're really just asleep and dreaming. BOO!'"

10

David Wick, who had stayed to guard the crime scene, was surprised to see a patrol car come down the driveway. Donna, having just left Hoss at the Happy Hour, parked and walked up to him.

"Anything happening here?"

"Not much. Had to shoo that bunch off the property a coupla times." He said this gesturing toward the reporters' cars, still parked along the road. Several had gotten out of their cars when Donna drove in, wondering if her arrival had any significance.

"Hoss is trying his best to avoid them, but I'm afraid he'll have to face them sometime soon," Donna said, "He sent me back to question Rossi's publicist. She's still here, I assume."

"Nobody has left since you did."

"Good. Better get your stick ready, I see one of the reporters coming our way."

The maid, who answered the door, told Donna she had heard Gloria Klein say she was going for a walk on the beach. Donna skirted the house, passing once again the spot where Silvio Rossi had applied his final marinade, and descended along a sandy path toward Cathead Bay. The brilliant display in the evening sky had slid down the spectrum to shades of plum and violet. A quarter of a mile along the curve of the beach, Donna spotted Gloria standing at the water's edge, looking out into the bay. Gloria started walking back toward the house, stopped and looked up at the sky, then resumed walking. Donna waited for her.

"Well, well, I didn't expect to see you again so soon," the bare-foot publicist said.

"I hope it's been long enough for you to have considered my request for your take on the party guests."

Nearby, was a semi-circular arrangement of Adirondack chairs. Gloria motioned toward them.

"Have a seat."

Gloria had changed into shorts and t-shirt. Sunglasses, a habitual part of her outdoor-wear, were planted atop her thick, blond hair.

"I did, as a matter-of-fact, give it some thought just now as I walked on the beach. Understand, what I can say about these people is my impression—and certainly not something I'd be willing to repeat in court, if you get my meaning." She gave Donna a significant look that awaited Donna's nod, and got it.

"OK, but there's another clause in this deal; if you want to hear it, I'll talk to you—with the understanding that what I say is between us. No one must know that you learned anything from me."

"Fair enough."

Gloria dug in her pocket for a bottle of Visine, and put a drop in each eye.

"Went swimming early this morning before the party. OK, where do you want to begin?"

Donna reflexively began to reach for the notebook she carried in her back pocket, then, remembering her pledge of confidentiality, relaxed into the chair.

"I have a few names, but first, why don't you tell me what comes to your mind about all this."

"You sound like a shrink. You're not married to one are you?"

A laugh burst from Donna and a smile that equaled a blush took over her face. "Close, but no cigar."

Gloria returned the smile. "I'll start with Silvio. There are two kinds of narcissist, the ones you detest and the ones you can't help liking even though you're offended from time to time by their exclusive self-interest. If this latter type happens to like you, you are treated as if you are almost as special as they are. They will be very generous, do surprising favors for you. You are included in a hallowed circle of 'the best and beautiful'. It feels good. You don't want to question the truth of it all. One drifts easily and obligingly along on a cloud of . . . worth. The continued lift that holds the cloud up, of course, is the narcissist, and knowing deep down that this is the case, the members of the group feed this governing ego, much as balloonists feed fuel to the fire of a hot air balloon to keep it aloft." Gloria paused as another thought inserted itself. "Yes, and if a person in the group, for whatever reason, falls out of the narcissist's favor—and this can happen so suddenly—then the others quickly comply with this turn of event in order to keep their places on the cloud." Gloria smiled wryly. "There you have Silvio Rossi."

"Strong feelings can result if you're one of those dropped from that cloud," Donna observed.

Gloria put out her hand and touched Donna's arm to interrupt her.

"Excuse me, but to round out a description of Silvio's personality another trait of his must be included. It played a large part in the direction Silvio turned his energy. I'm talking about his need to be better at anything that he noticed a rival doing. It was really transparent and patently childish. If a New York restaurant owner got an apartment on the twentieth floor Silvio had to have one higher up. If a top-ten chef bought a David Hockney painting, Silvio would buy two. That is what this house is all about. You know which New York chef bought a vacation home here a few years ago." She looked to Donna for confirmation.

"Yes, I know who you mean."

"Right. So, Silvio had to have a showplace to top it.

"As you just said," Klein continued, "being dropped by Silvio might generate murderous wishes, but I don't know of anyone here at the party who was soon to be in that category."

"Now I'll tell *you* something," Donna said, "that must remain between us. The people I'm particularly interested in are the ones who seem to have no alibi for the few minutes from the time Mr. Rossi went to his barbecue until he was found murdered: Frank Knowles, Karen Forbes, John Seabold and Patrizia Nuvolari and Vince DeSica. Oh yes, and Bruce Thomas."

"OK, Frank Knowles. I don't think he gets the recognition he should. He has really played a major part in the cooking show's success. Frank collects early American porcelain. It's a major leap from excitement over a bud vase to shoving a skewer into someone."

Gloria looked out over the water of the bay for several moments, and then looked down to where she began digging one foot into the sand before she went on.

"I don't know Seabold and Nuvolari. I understand they wrote an Italian cookbook and that's no doubt why they were invited. I know Karen Forbes from her TV show and that she is an old friend of Silvio's from the early days of his restaurant, but she is not an active member of his social group. I hear by the grapevine that she has trouble getting any man to be serious about her. On television she comes across very authoritatively, but in person she seems to be a timid soul and not my idea of a murderess, but you never know.

"Although I know nothing about this Bruce Thomas..." Gloria looked over at Donna, as if considering what she would say. She continued, "I do know something about his wife, Sandra. Sandra and Silvio. They had a thing going."

"Really? You mean an affair?"

"Uh huh. A summer thing. I'm pretty sure Silvio didn't know her before, and knowing Silvio, I'm sure it wouldn't have continued beyond his return to New York."

"Is their relationship well known?"

"No. I may be the only one who knows. I came upon them *in flagrante*, but they didn't know I had discovered them."

"When did this happen?"

"Oh, three weeks or so ago. I had flown out from New York to go over Silvio's schedule with him." Gloria rubbed her eyes. "Silvio was like that—many women, but very discreet—more than the women were." She looked sharply at Donna. "We never had it on, in case you're wondering. Silvio didn't mix business and pleasure—neither do I."

Donna paid no attention to what Gloria Klein said about her sexual life, she was thinking about Bruce Thomas, a man without an alibi.

"From what you just said, you don't know if the husband knew about his wife's affair."

"That's right; I don't know."

"Interesting."

"I can see you'd think so."

"And, Gina Rossi?"

"You mean did she know about Silvio's affairs, or this particular one?"

Donna had been thinking in the particular, but said, "Both."

Gloria shook her head as if the subject puzzled her. "Gina amazes me. I mean she must have known about his affairs—as I said, some of the women were very happy for people to know—but I never saw a hint of suspicion in Gina and she's one smart lady let me tell you. She acted as if she had the greatest respect for Silvio. Maybe she couldn't let herself know and denied it all. If that's so, she has to be the Queen of Denial. But, I don't think that's the case: I believe she tried to live above it all."

"Very interesting." After considering what she'd just been told, Donna said, "So, what you really meant to stay between the two of us is this affair you knew about."

"Particularly, yes, but you also have to understand that part of my job is keeping my finger on the pulse of my little world—which, by the way thinks itself to be the only world that counts. I have to know trends before they clearly form—have information before everyone else. That means I have to hear the latest gossip." She paused for emphasis. "People don't tell that kind of gossip to a person who they learn has blabbed to the police."

Donna had just had a glimpse into a world, which she could imagine, but one she wanted no part of. She got up and thanked Gloria for her help and at the same time thanked her lucky star that she was who she was.

• • •

The hour was late and Donna was bone-weary, but she had felt a strong need to share the experiences and concerns of the day with Derek before she went to bed. Also, except for the beer Paul Treviso had given her and two cups of coffee, she had ingested nothing since breakfast. They sat together on the outside deck a Scott's Harbor Grill, a place where they meet often because of its proximity to both Derek's office and her apartment. The air was warm off the bay and the city's lights across it appeared to be strings of party lanterns reflecting in the water.

Donna would not have an apartment if Derek could have it his way; she would be Mrs. Derek Marsh living at his house in pine-wooded seclusion ten miles west of the city. Derek, however, could not have his way. Donna was not ready to change a thing about her life . . . just yet.

After they ordered, she related the day's events in complete detail.

"What a day you've had," Derek observed. "You've given me the facts, but I could tell by the way you folded and refolded your napkin that there is another level—another story—that you didn't give me."

"Do you use that with your patients? Did they teach you there is a relationship between the folding of napkins and unconscious conflict?"

"Let's see, I think I do remember a course on the proper handling of the prickly patient."

"Sorry. I know you meant well in your simple way."

The waitress came at that moment with a bottle of wine.

When she'd gone, Derek said, "Ah yes, just as I prescribed, *Cotes du Luberon*." He poured some in her glass.

"What the doctor ordered?"

"Yes, to foster equanimity in lady deputies."

"Equanimity; I used that word today. I used it to describe a laid-back gentleman. I'd be happy to join him," she said raising the glass.

Derek tasted his wine and turning the glass in his hand appraisingly, said, "It comes from a region that is not renowned. Because of that it lacks self-confidence. But detect the notes of grapefruit, pineapple, herbs."

She picked up her glass and took a sip. "Um. I like it," she said putting the glass back on the table. "Personally I like my wine to taste like wine. Have you ever heard someone take a bite of grapefruit and say, 'Note the taste of *Cotes du Luberon*'?"

She leaned forward, her lips almost touching the bottle. In a stage whisper, she murmured sensually, "I like you. You shouldn't doubt yourself. You're really very good, you know."

Derek laughed. "How could we men have ever survived without women there to reassure us—even if lying a little?"

The arrival of the salads produced the break that signaled a change of mood.

"Come on, tell me what's bothering you," Derek nudged.

"As I told you on the phone, I was the first to arrive and so I took over the lead in the investigation. Hoss seems content to leave it with me . . . leave me holding the bag, I'm afraid."

"What's the problem?" Derek asked.

"No evidence is the problem. No evidence and the media and everybody else demanding an arrest."

"Ah yes, the media, bless its heart. In addition to wanting to know practical information about what is happening in our communities, we humans have a regular menu of desires, which we look to the media to satisfy, and the media is in the business of doing just that. If you think about it a moment, you can fill out the list: Something to be feared and opposing that a promised safety, some naughty story about our family or friends (displaced onto others, particularly celebrities) balanced with reassurance of the goodness of people. Add a story of heroism and one of cowardice, wealth gained and lost . . . and so on."

"That's what I'm afraid of. This story has something for everyone—famous, charismatic chef with an army of followers, brutally murdered in a manner worthy of an Oscar. A man with a Don Juan reputation and a houseful of rich and attractive guests who might play any imaginable role."

"Not only imagined in the case of the woman who lives at The Homestead," Derek added.

"Remember doctor; that was a privileged communication."

"That only applies between a doctor and a patient, but I'll make an exception in your case. Seriously though, I understand your concern about the case. I wish I could say you're worrying unnecessarily about the media, but I'd be lying. The best advice is to follow the course that most of the wise among the famous folk follow—don't read or watch anything about yourself or the case.."

"I hear you. What troubles me is that I know Hoss wants to show trust in me by giving me this responsibility and yet I know this case is very important to him. It reminds me of my learning to drive. My Dad sat next to me and tried to look very relaxed and cool—wanted to support my confidence—while all the time I could feel his impulse to reach over and grab the wheel. I'd like to tell Hoss, 'Thanks very much for trusting me, but *please* take the wheel any time you want to.'"

Derek understood the pressure she felt. "Come home with me tonight. You need some time away from this case—a little distance. Say, isn't tomorrow your day off anyway."

"Oh, I couldn't. I've got to go in. I need to review everything with Hoss."

Derek knew this was true. No way could she allow herself to take time off.

"I understand completely, but a few hours that completely take this case off your mind will enable you to look at the details afresh."

He could see that she was considering his suggestion.

"You can get to Headquarters just as quickly from my place as yours."

That did it.

Before heading out to Derek's home, Donna had gone to her apartment to get her uniform, which she was now wearing at the breakfast table. Derek came in from the kitchen wearing his bathrobe and carrying a skillet of scrambled eggs. The morning being chilly, he had started a fire in the dining-room fireplace after he'd put on the coffee. Before he sat down, he took up the poker and moved a log around.

"Watching you poke at the fire just now, I remembered a dream I had last night. I must have been Dorothy in the Wizard of Oz, because I wore ruby slippers and skipped down the road."

"Ah, you were off to see the Wizard. That must be me," Derek said.

"Wizard? It's clear that modesty isn't a problem here."

"It was worth a try," he said, leaning over and kissing her cheek. "How did you feel in your dream?"

"Light-hearted—looking forward to something good."

"As I remember," Derek mused, "Dorothy felt that way too. She was off to see the Wizard and he would solve her problem of getting back home."

"Are you going to analyze my dream?"

In a put-on, pedagogical tone, Derek corrected her. "I can but assist you in the analysis of your dream. You must do the work yourself, Miss."

"What a cop out."

"What comes to your mind about ruby slippers?"

"Ruby, let me think . . . oh my God, ruby earring!"

"Yes. You mentioned finding it. Do you still have it?"

"Yes, I do. Hey this dream analysis stuff works." Her voice expressed surprised wonder.

"Surely, you didn't doubt it?"

"Look, I'd doubt any guys who believe women suffer from penis envy."

"You've never heard me say that," Derek pointed out defensively.

"Because I'm never without my weapon," she said patting the holster on her belt.

"It must be comforting to have a weapon like that—a big one, too."

She almost agreed before she saw the trap and started to laugh and shake her finger at him.

"Yes, I have the earring and I should have returned it to Mrs. Rossi as I told Hoss I'd do."

"Why do you think you've held on to it?"

"Good question. I suspect the answer is that even though it can't help me a bit, it's still the only concrete thing I was able to come away with."

"Are you saying that possessing it means that your investigation wasn't . . . "

"A bust. Go ahead and say it."

"I wasn't going to say anything like that. And anyway, that's only the way you feel. But there is something I don't understand yet. You said that it was while watching me light the fire that you remembered your dream. What about that?"

"Fire? I can't think of . . . Wait, I had a thought . . . how did it go? Oh yes, Gina Rossi told me she had used the spiral stairs to go down to check that Silvio had enough charcoal. When she told me this, it seemed a reasonable thing for her to do. Any woman whose husband plans to barbecue for a large party would be inclined to check and make sure the poor dope hadn't forgotten some vital element—like the charcoal. But yesterday I had the thought that Silvio wasn't your average husband, he was a professional chef, one fully capable without his wife's help."

"But look at it this way," Derek said. "She no doubt knows he's capable of running his restaurant, but this was a different thing wasn't it; this was a party in *her* house. Just as we wouldn't be surprised if Silvio checks up on his restaurant staff to be sure food is being prepared in the way he thinks it should be—even though he knows they are all skilled professionals—don't you think his wife might have the same sense of responsibility about things running smoothly at her party?"

"So, Doctor, you're saying I have been stubbornly hoping my ruby earring would lead me to the happy solution of the murder just as Dorothy's ruby slippers led her to Oz?"

"Nice work, Deputy Roper."

"I'll give the earring back to her today."

He got up and went over to her and kissed her. Holding on to the earring was an independent act typical of her—a trait that made her attractive to him, but he didn't want to see it lead to trouble.

11

Paul Treviso slowly savored the espresso the hostess at the B&B made in her two-cup, stovetop brewer. After breakfast, he continued sitting at the large table in the dining room thinking about his plans for the day. He'd call Vince in a bit to see what he could do out at the Rossi place to help prepare some of the kitchen equipment for shipment back to New York. He thought of poor Gina getting up and realizing that Silvio really wasn't there in bed with her—would never be again He decided to delay his call to the house for a while.

The image of Silvio's crumpled and bloody body seemed impossible on this dazzling morning. Laura's smiling entrance into the room helped him suppress the memory of that image. She was excited about something.

"There's a store I want you to see down in the village. It's pretty unique, especially in a small and remote village like this."

Paul carried his empty cup to the kitchen and thanked the woman for taking the extra trouble to make him espresso and then joined Laura. She led him down Nagonaba Street toward the heart of the town. As they came abreast of the Ace Hardware, Laura couldn't restrain her eagerness and pointed to a building up ahead. Above the door on the clapboard siding ran a sign as wide as the store's façade. Bold, blue letters spelled INDIGENOUS DESIGN. It reverberated in Paul's vision, because the "GEN-US" portion of the word was outlined in bright red with a red "I" superimposed over the "O" of INDIGENOUS.

"Indigenous plus genius," Paul exclaimed.

"Wait'll you see what's inside. The owner or manager was busy with other customers yesterday and I didn't get a chance to ask the questions I wanted to."

"Such as?"

"Such as, 'How's business?' Or, more to the point, can a person operate a gallery in this town and also eat?"

Paul squeezed Laura's shoulder. "Or even more to the point: Can two easterners run a restaurant here and eat more than the scrapings from the plates?"

The man behind a desk in the center of the room looked up and greeted them when they entered. The Trevisos had no doubt about his being Native American.

"Hi, come on in and look around." He recognized that Laura had been there earlier and added, "I saw you here yesterday. I'm sorry I didn't get a chance to talk to you. My name's Harry Swifthawk."

"Pleased to meet you," answered Paul. "Paul and Laura Treviso. Laura told me I had to see this place."

Harry Swifthawk shot a look of approval toward Laura.

"Let me take you on a little tour," he said. The eagerness in his voice affirmed that after having taken visitors on the rounds of his store for several months he was as excited about it as the day he and his wife and sister had opened the door and waited for their first customer.

"What we have here is a collection of Native American art from what we judge to be the best artists across the country—and a few miles across the border into Mexico. This bowl, for example was made by Enrique Lopez from the Mexican village of Mata Ortiz."

Harry Swifthawk smiled with satisfaction when an expression of growing awe showed on Paul's face as he turned the bowl in his hands.

"This is great! It's hard to imagine how a person could make this. Such intricate detail," Paul said.

"I know what you mean, man," Harry replied. "How about this knife, the handle is made from deer antler and amber. Look at that carving!"

And so the tour went for the next half hour. Paul had also noted the prices of the objects he'd admired and a question had to be asked.

"These things are pretty pricey and this store is a long distance from many with that kind of . . . "

"You are wondering how we make ends meet. Am I right?"

"Well, that's one way to put it."

"To tell you the truth, I had serious doubts about that problem, but I gave in to my sister, Marti, and my wife, Mary. My sister claimed that if you have something that is really good and unique, people would come. My sister's an artist, who's had shows in New York. Marti Jensen. That's one of her paintings there." Harry pointed to a landscape that Paul recognized as the local terrain.

"The 'better mousetrap principle'," put in Laura.

"Right. It's been slow, but we're beginning to see the light at the end . . . of the month," Harry said. "In the meantime, it's been great fun learning about the different artists and talking them into letting us have some pieces."

"I imagine that job becomes easier as the reputation of your gallery grows," Laura said. "Any artist would like to be included in a collection touted as the 'best Native-American artists'."

As they progressed around the shop an idea ran through the Trevisos' minds: "Build a better mousetrap"—run a better restaurant. After they had seen and admired the objects in the collection, each seemingly more amazing than the preceding one, Paul was ready with his question.

"You're banking on customers driving the extra miles to the tip of the peninsula to buy your art. Do you think they would do the same to dine-out? What has been the history of restaurants in the village?"

"Not outstanding," Harry answered. "Mostly—except for a couple—they've gone belly up."

"How about a world-class gourmet restaurant: Has anyone attempted that?"

"I don't know if you'd call it gourmet, but a few years back, someone opened a restaurant in that house on the corner with the big beech tree. I never ate there, and I think they only served lunch. Closed down after a year as I remember."

"What's there now? The house with the big beech tree?"

"It's empty."

"Where is it exactly?" Laura asked, her excitement evident.

Harry pointed in a general southwest direction. "Turn left at the corner, Waukazoo Street, walk on by Dog Ears Books and then you should be able to see the beech tree at the end of the block. You can't miss it; it must be the biggest in the county."

Paul and Laura's eyes locked on each other's. They were sharing the same thought.

12

The jetliner had just been cleared to land at Traverse City's Cherry Capitol Airport. Dan Pollock looked out of his window in first class, down at the sunlit expanse of Grand Traverse Bay, dotted this perfect sailing morning with dozens of white sails. It would be nice if he had come here to enjoy the bucolic offerings of the region, but this was far from the truth: His was a desperate personal mission. There's a story, an oft-repeated one, of a man or woman who had enjoyed success, even fame, but had been unable to sustain the journey to a comfortably honored retirement, because of a stumble near the end of that voyage. The renowned actor, for instance, whose last pictures had been resounding flops, the legendary quarterback with an embarrassingly bad season, the novelist, once compared to Hemmingway, whose latest effort clutters a table in front of Borders: This was Dan Pollock's plight.

The plane's course while taxiing toward the terminal gate went unheeded by Pollock. Unselected memories pushed forward, joined to one another by an invisible yet related thread.

Pollock had put in long hours on the journalistic ladder before that lucky evening in 1995. An Adirondack hotel had been the site of a summer New York Press Club meeting. Pollock and a woman reporter had driven up together for the deductible get-away from the heat of the city. That first night, on his way to the bedroom he shared with his traveling companion, some TV types, wanting another hand for poker, yelled to him as he passed the open door of their room. He was not interested in joining the group, or at least he was more interested in what awaited him in his own bedroom, but the man-to-man cajoling mounted by the card players made it difficult to walk on by. He would sit in for a few hands.

It became, of course, much more than a few hands and he lost a month's salary. On top of this, his bedfellow became very angry and that aspect of the weekend was a washout. Very sorry that he had given in to the cajoling, he was lecturing himself the next morning on the need to stiffen his backbone when one of the poker players called him. The guy was a producer who had an idea for a new show, prime time investigative journalism. The guy said Dan's looks and style of speech fit the model he had in mind for the show's anchor and lead investigator. Was Dan interested?

Pollock had thought often about the course his advancement might take, but the scenario had never involved television and certainly not the star of a prime time program. Was he interested? That wasn't the word that described what Pollock felt that day with the phone to his ear. He was thrilled. Dazzled. And, scared. Could he really be a successful broadcaster? Could this guy be wrong about him? Dan had witnessed so many others make abortive attempts to break into television. How many sport stars had had brief careers as "color" analysts, only to be pulled off stage abruptly as it became clear they lacked the chemistry the tube demanded. What would making a flop of this opportunity mean to his future in journalism? Overriding all of these serious concerns was the certain knowledge that if he declined this offer he would likely never hear another like it.

"Yes, I'm very interested," had been his reply that morning.

The hour-long show was called The People's Bureau of Investigation, or PBI, the name by which it became known to anyone in the nation owning a TV. It aimed to create the notion that Dan Pollock and his team of investigators represented the no-holds-barred demand of the public to know the truth. It turned out

Pollock perfectly fit the role of the common man's surrogate, asking the questions everyone liked to think they would have asked in his place.

The rapid success of the show surprised its creators. Soon it dominated the prime time hour it occupied on Sunday night, pulling audiences away from the other networks. No face or voice in America became more recognized than Dan Pollock's.

The format of the show settled into a familiar expectation for the viewer. Invariably, Pollock had a "bad guy" cornered, Pollock likely peering through the crack in a barely open doorway asking questions of a briefly visible subject who did his or her best to not be photographed. Pollock cared not if he got an answer. If not and when the door finally slammed shut in Pollock's face, He would face the camera and, with a smirk that filled in all the blanks for the viewer at home, conclude with a remark such as, "Now why wouldn't this guy want to answer that simple question?" The audience ate it up at first. Viewers, hurrying to pay the pizza boy before the show's next victim was introduced, never stopped to consider that these stories were carefully selected. The production staff put in long hours to find situations where the subject of the investigation could not respond with a clear defense. The staff also had to be careful to identify cases that were not likely to result in lawsuits—the subject hadn't the money for lawyers or had other dirty linen that he or she feared would be aired in court. In short, PBI's object was showbiz and not journalism.

Before the cracks began to appear in the perfect, unblemished surface of PBI, ten years had passed and Dan Pollock became famous and would have been rich too, if not for his two divorces.

Pollock interrupted his memories and got up from his seat. The flight attendant retrieved his briefcase and handed it to him with the admiring smile he expected. Immediately inside the terminal awaited the advance man who had flown out the day before to make preparations for Pollock's arrival. Dan saw him and walked over.

"Hi, Jim, found us a decent place to sleep?"

"Better than decent actually. Also, I think you'll be as surprised as I was with the beauty of this countryside. Pretty neat. It's clear why Rossi built here."

"Oh?"

"I rented a house on a lake about halfway up this peninsula. It's close to the Sheriff's Department."

"How far from the Rossi House?"

"Maybe a twenty minute drive, but I can't see you'll have much need to go there after the first location shots."

"And also the interview with the bereaved widow," Pollock threw in.

"Right. The house I got has four bedrooms. I'm having the furniture removed from one for a communications center. The living room makes a good conference room. A restaurant in a town called Suttons Bay will cater."

"Right. Joan's coming on the next plane, did you get the message?"

"Yes, she called me and I've got a work space set up for her. I've hired two local kids to chauffeur. One of them will pick her up."

Pollock followed Jim Johnson to the baggage area, and then went out of the terminal to have a cigarette while Jim waited at the carousel for Pollock's two bags.

Dan's thoughts drifted back along the path they'd been taking as the plane landed: What had gone wrong? The first signs that the show had a problem were denied—normal vacillations in viewer numbers due to events on other channels: playoffs, award shows and the like. It took those higher up in the network management—those uninvolved with the weekly production—to take seriously the slow, but steady angle of decline in the show's ratings.

Eventually, it was the network's president, Martin Bondi, who put his finger on the subtle cause: the very reason, which had propelled the show's early success, had now become the reason for its loss of viewers. The opportunity to participate in a quasi-lynching can be exciting. However, after being a party to a few such humiliations of fellow humans, the average person begins to feel very unwell and no longer wishes to participate. With many there follows a vehement rejection of what had previously been enjoyed.

Marketing pollsters brought back further and depressing news that a steadily increasing percentage of those left in the audience belonged to an economic segment that had little spare cash to spend on the sponsors' luxury products.

Hearing this appraisal by the network president, and anticipating the network was readying the axe, the show's producers recognized the need for an emergency change of direction.

They decided to raise the aim and go hunting for bigger game; they would target nationally known political and entertainment figures, even though this was chancy, because of the increased danger of lawsuits. Luck was with them. Acting on a tip, the academic credentials of the president of a large state university were investigated and the viewer at home was treated to Dan Pollock entering the man's office with smiles and handshakes and then sitting across the desk from him and asking why it was that the files of the university from which the president claimed to have received his PhD. had failed to produce a record of his ever having been a student there.

The response to this show was very positive and PBI immediately regained some of its former ratings. The network axe went back on the shelf. The producers had stumbled upon an interesting psychological phenomenon: being the passive participant in the chasing, catching and pillorying of petty thieves soon caused most normal viewers to feel as shabby as the thief, but being a party to exposing the misbehavior of one's "superiors" produced a most satisfying self-righteousness.

But luck quickly showed its fickle nature. Again acting on a tip, and basing the exposé on hotel records supplied by a snitch, the show's producers went after a senior U.S. Senator, the Chairman of the Senate Ethics Committee. At an interview, in which the producers claimed rules of senatorial ethics were to be discussed, Dan planned to confront the unwary lawmaker with the charge that, while supposedly at a conference (paid for at public expense) the senator really had been holed up with a young bimbo.

Dan was welcomed into the office in the Senate Office Building and given coffee by a secretary. The senator, whose face Americans knew as well as that of Colonel Sanders, arrived and shook Dan's hand, and favored Pollock with that kindly, fatherly smile which had helped him get re-elected six times.

"Now, son, I understand you want to talk about the rules of ethics that we senators try to live by."

"Exactly, Senator." And then Pollock, with the cameras running, proceeded to bluntly state his accusation about the Senator's alleged, tropical island caper.

At first, the old man looked at Dan with surprise and wonder, as if he were just being shown a rare breed of toad. Then he burst into laughter.

"My wife will get a kick out of this, young fella. Where did you get such a silly idea?"

While not being altogether a silly idea in essence, the venerable lawmaker meant that the dalliance ascribed to him reached beyond his current capability. More to the painful point, the senator had the unimpeachable support of others that he had indeed been at the conference where he should have been. *The Washington Post*, which then did their own investigation, revealed that the incriminating hotel records were forgeries.

Dan Pollock looked foolish and the audience that had willingly taken part in this bogus witch-hunt felt embarrassed and angry. Yet another debacle soon followed—this time with a whopping lawsuit. PBI and Dan Pollock were in great trouble. Just then a blessing seemed to come from the blue in the shape of the Rossi murder. Dan could go to the site in this remote Michigan county much as Truman Capote had gone to the plains of Kansas. No expose was involved, so they were safe from lawsuits. There was even an easy victim for Dan's patented sarcasm—the local sheriff and his likely band of clown deputies.

As the car followed the southern shore of Grand Traverse Bay, Jim, the advance man, chattered on about the arrangements he had made, but Pollock only half listened. He looked out at the narrow park that lay between the road and the water and the many joggers, skaters and volleyball players. These people seemed so removed from Pollock's reality that he could have been watching a travel-ogue. Would he ever again have the inclination, or the time, or energy to hit a volleyball? He couldn't imagine it. He had but one thing on his mind—survival. Survival until a dignified exit could be managed. After that, he'd see what else might be possible for him.

Jim said, "Suttons Bay," as they came to a busy, three-block-long village. He pointed. "That deli will do our catering."

A quarter-of-an-hour later they turned north on a road called Lake Leelanau Drive, and soon afterward Jim slowed and entered a long, gravel driveway that ended at a rambling lakeside house.

"And away we go," thought Pollock. First off, he'd get an appointment with the widow. He opened the car door and stepped into the next phase of his life.

13

"She says no."

"What do you mean, 'No'?"

"She told me, 'I have no need to talk to the press.'"

"I'm not the press."

"I explained, of course, and she said, 'Whatever.'"

"Whatever?" Suddenly Dan Pollock realized he faced an unfamiliar situation. Having the subject refuse to talk to him was common, almost welcome, because he could then resort to an accusing innuendo without fear of intelligent rebuttal. Dan had merely to stand on the subject's doorstep and gesture toward the door that had just been slammed and make his closing, snide comment, but not in this case. What could he say or imply after knocking on the widow's door and getting a "no". He'd surely be shooting himself in the foot to make any negative remark.

"She just needs to be convinced we are here to praise her husband and that we'll do what we can to see that the guilty party ... etcetera, etcetera. Call her . . . no wait, better let Art do it. He's coming this afternoon. Line me up for an interview with the sheriff. Two cameras so we'll have a good back-and-forth edit."

Art Brock, the show's executive producer, was a consummate charmer. It was he who had called Pollock after the poker game at the Adirondack hotel. Even those who were not fond of him conceded that he could charm the pitchfork out of the devil's hand. Dan Pollock had used and relied upon Art's charm until he had come to think of it as partly his own, like the sweater two sisters share until the borrower comes to believe it's hers.

Art Brock, however, was also a realist and detached enough to view the show's problems with an emotionally undistorted perspective. He knew the show had run its course. Even if this current attempt at photojournalism succeeded, where could PBI go afterward? Each week couldn't be counted on to furnish a celebrity murder. Art, like Dan, needed a good closing number. It was the finale that people remembered.

The moment his plane landed, Art called Dan to be brought up to date and learned of the problem with Rossi's widow.

"What do we know about her?" he asked Dan.

Dan looked over the report the show's research staff had compiled on Rossi. "Not much. She was born in Italy, on the Riviera, city of Savona. Silvio met and married her there. There's a lot on his public life, but no mention of her participation with him. Spends time volunteering at a children's home. No children of her own. Married sixteen years. That's about it."

"So," Art said, "Private person. Follows her own interests. This might be difficult. We can rely on most people to want their 'fifteen minutes of fame': They're happy to be on camera. Others want to tell their side of an issue. Some hate the world and want to tell all of us off—makes for good shots. But, 'no need for the press' sounds difficult."

"OK, so it's an exercise with a ten point difficulty. You'll stick the landing and you know it."

"I'll see what I can do. Give me her number."

• • •

Kate Schott, taking a break from the dispatcher's desk, looked out the front window of Sheriff's Headquarters into the parking area, then said to Shorty McQueen, a retired deputy who had stopped by to shoot the breeze with his old buddies, "The television people are here, Shorty. We've been warned that Dan Pollock was coming. Run back and tell Hoss."

"The bearer of bad news. Is that any way to treat a friend, Kate?"

"Better you than me."

"Shorty!" Hoss exclaimed when the man knocked as he walked into his office. "How's life among the idle rich?"

"Tolerable, except I'm afraid the damned media has followed me here to get my opinion about the situation in the Middle East. They're just coming into the building now. Got a shit-load of equipment."

"I wish your reading of their purpose in coming here were true. I dread this, but I know I've gotta talk to them. All those damn fool questions. And if you dare to give them a short, 'No statement' kind of answer, they'll get rough, like, 'Your Department hasn't had experience with this kind of investigation, have you?' or how about, 'When are you calling in the State Police?'"

"Have you stopped beating your wife?"

"Exactly."

Over the intercom, Hoss told Kate to have the press set up in the conference room, and then he said to Shorty, "Stick around for the interview, ole buddy, for moral support."

"I'd better not. I might get mad and start kicking over the light stands."

Hoss looked into Shorty's craggy face and started to laugh. "Yeah, I can see it happening."

"You see, Hoss, there was a time I cared what people thought of me. Then came the time when I didn't care any longer, but I cared that I didn't care. Now, I don't care that I don't care."

"Come back and see us more often, ole buddy. Right now I've gotta go act like I *care* about this interview."

108

Hoss called Kate and asked her to tell him when the crew had finished and the interviewer was in the room. He did not want to be sitting there waiting for the man to make his appearance. Ironically, Dan had given the same directions to the producer of this interview segment and was waiting in the parking lot. The standoff continued for a quarter of an hour, until Dan's impatience got the better of him and he charged into the conference room like a miffed Napoleon not being given a proper reception by those he'd just defeated.

Hoss let him wait a few more minutes then walked into the room with an affable welcome sans apology. This irritated Pollock even more.

Hoss maintained a friendly, serious expression throughout the interview, but didn't once go beyond, "Like I said before, all factors are considered in an investigation, and we will do what we think necessary to identify the person who killed Mr. Rossi."

At one point, recognizing that he wasn't going to force Hoss out of the comfortable stance he'd taken, Pollock decided to do what Hoss had anticipated and nettle him by casting the members of the Leelanau County Sheriff's Department in the role of country rubes.

"You may be unaware, Sheriff, of the professional standing Silvio Rossi had. Many think he was America's best chef. Did you know that?"

"Yes, I've heard that."

"And he was also a very popular television star. I'm sure you must have been aware of that."

"So I've heard."

"You never saw his show? You must have television here."

"I don't watch cooking shows much."

"I don't think you appreciate Silvio Rossi's importance, Sheriff. Do you realize how serious his murder is?"

"Well sir, we tend to give a great deal of importance to a person getting murdered in our county. It doesn't matter who he or she is. I'd like to think you'd do the same."

"Yes. Yes, of course I would." This wasn't going the way Pollock had planned. He tried quickly to think of his next point of attack.

Hoss had no wish to stay around until the guy got around to suggesting the State Police should be brought in. "Good, then we see eye to eye on this problem. I guess that about covers everything. Glad you could stop by."

Hoss's six foot four frame unfolded like a time-lapse photo of the growth of a giant redwood. He put out his huge hand, which Dan was forced to take, and then he left the room.

• • •

Art Brock wouldn't make the mistake of approaching Gina Rossi in a way where he could be rejected before even talking to her, so no telephone call, no ringing her doorbell. He would go about it the correct, old-fashioned way, through a proper introduction. He first called one of the show's research staff and directed her to dig into Gina's personal life more closely. Among the bits of information reported to him two hours later was the seemingly—to the researcher—incidental fact that Gina Rossi actively painted with a small group of artists who, borrowing from Leonardo, playfully called themselves, "Ladies without Ermines". Art had heard of the group; his wife in fact was an administrator at the art school where the "Ladies" met once a week. Art laughed to himself; he'd possessed the needed introduction all along.

Art called his wife. She felt reluctant to impose on Gina in her grief, but gave in finally and made the call Art wanted her to make.

Art stood now for a moment and admired the Rossi house. The architect, a local man, had achieved some national recognition to go along with his considerable imagination. Art had seen Gina's picture before—always standing just behind Silvio. So, Art was prepared to see an attractive enough brunette when the door opened. He was surprised and thrown off balance by the forceful effect the real Gina had on him. Here stood a most beautiful woman. She was complete: looks, obvious intelligence, savoir-faire and what perhaps surprised him most, she evinced an open offer of friendliness. He was to discover the offer would be withdrawn quickly if not met with honesty.

She invited him to follow her to the study. Art made some remarks about the house and then reminded himself that he was with a recent widow.

"I want you to know I'm very sad about your husband's death," he began. "Both my wife and I want you to know that we sympathize with your loss."

"Thank you, Mr. Brock. Your wife, Jean, has been such a friend to our small group." With a laugh in her voice, she added, "She has given us a home."

Gina's manner changed slightly to one that said: Now that the required pleasantries have been said, what is your business?

"I understand from your wife that you wanted to talk to me, Mr. Brock."

The "Mr. Brock" was too formal and built a barrier, which Art hoped to dismantle.

"Please call me Art."

Gina smiled but made no reply.

Art detected that a subtle change had occurred in her attitude since they began their conversation. The opening warmth had changed into only qualified warmth—no longer the "friend of a friend" who'd be extended all possible help. It had been his empty condolences that had led to this change.

Uncomfortably, Art continued, "Of course, you know that the whole country has sympathy for you at this time. They would like to hear your account of this tragedy. I happen to be a producer for the television program I'm sure you're familiar with, The People's Bureau of Investigation or PBI. We would like to assist you in connecting with all those people who have come to love your husband through his show. We could set up an interview right here in the comfort of your beautiful home and the viewers in their homes could witness your warmth and friendliness just as I am now. You could share your reactions and grief with this large group of friends."

Gina had listened with interest to Art's speech. She smiled at him in the way a professor might who had just heard a student make the pitch of how it would be to the professor's great advantage to give the student a passing rather than a failing grade.

"That's silly, Mr. Brock. Those people are not my friends. They are people wasting time they could spend much more creatively say, working in their gardens, going for a walk or reading a book. And, what, Mr. Brock do you imagine I would gain from telling strangers about my life?"

"Mrs. Rossi," He acutely felt the need to be able to call her Gina, but she hadn't invited it. "You are a public figure. There exist a tremendous number of people who looked to your husband as a model, an inspiration even. A public figure owes something to that audience. Your husband's mantle, as it were, has now been passed to you. There exists a kind of responsibility to meet with his followers and through that conversation help them with their loss, just as knowing of their interest and love for Silvio should help you."

Again Gina followed every word with keen interest, nodding

her head as she did. Art thought he might have accomplished his mission.

"You know, Mr. Brock, I think you really believe that nonsense about owing something to an audience. I hope you do, otherwise that was a very deceitful speech."

Her amused smile told Art that either way, she didn't care at all. She went on, "Whatever each individual in an audience gets out of spending their time listening or watching a performer is what they have coming to them. They may in addition build their own fantasies about that performer and want the performer to behave in a way that supports that fiction, but that is of their own doing and imposes no real obligation on the performer. Silvio may have gotten satisfaction knowing he had a large audience. That would be his fantasy and may or may not have been important to him. Important to him, or any performer for that matter, is that a large audience means one can then ask larger fees from sponsors. A large audience means a cook at home believes he or she must buy the chef's latest cookbook and the many gadgets he endorses. And, of course, if a New York businessperson wants to make an impression on a client, then it becomes necessary to take that client to Lucretius and pay whatever is asked. That, Mr. Brock, is what show business is all about . . . and you know it, and why shouldn't it be? But, it has nothing to do with me. I never watch television. I only saw Silvio's show once."

Art knew he wasn't going to get the interview Dan Pollock wanted. He was also aware that his "deceitful" seduction had been identified and he'd been scolded, but he felt excited nevertheless, because he was in possession of a delicious quote. "I only saw Silvio's show once."

Gina Rossi knew what he thought and never would have said any of these things if she hadn't known how she was going to close this meeting.

"Mr. Brock, I agreed to see you this afternoon as a favor to your wife based on our friendship. If one word of what I have told you is made public, I will consider it a breach of that friendship and I will make sure your wife knows it."

That evening Art told Dan Pollock that the interview wouldn't fly.

Dan said, "A smart, hostile bitch eh?"

"Not at all. Actually, I think she's just too dumb to be interesting and also afraid to be interviewed. A real hausfrau," Art lied.

"That so? Figures. I understand he brought her over from the old country."

14

He figured he could sit at one of the outside tables at Kejara's Bridge without having to buy any food, so he sat there through three cigarettes before he made up his mind to go ahead with his plan. He had information he thought he could sell to this Dan Pollock. He felt cruddy doing it, but he was broke and hungry and knew a kind of desperation he'd only read about before. If he didn't get some money, his next step to survive would be picking through garbage cans. The past month of living hand-to-mouth had brought a deepening decline in his self-image, which hadn't been much to start with. He now thought of himself as a piece of human waste and he expected to be treated as such by others. At times he became angry without much provocation toward those whom he imagined rejecting him and would yell out, "Asshole!", at a surprised person who, otherwise, hadn't noticed him. This was the problem he now faced: How could he expect Dan Pollock to listen to him?

He had learned where the television people were staying—a two-mile walk from Kejara's. He got up, dropped the cigarette butt from his nicotine-stained fingers and started out. Along the way he went through alternating periods of despair, then rage, then fear as he reviewed in his mind the reception he'd get when he finally got to his destination. These ruminations were interrupted abruptly on the driveway leading to the house by a white Ford Explorer, which sped by forcing him into the weeds at the side of the driveway. The car hadn't even slowed down for him.

He shouted, "Asshole!" But the driver's indifference made him feel small and lonely and afraid. He thought of turning and hurrying back to the shelter of the abandoned sugar shack that he'd found to sleep in. His hunger reminded him he must go on and give this idea a chance.

Parked by the house was another Explorer like the one he'd just encountered. He stood at the door of the house looking in vain for a doorbell. A doorknocker in the shape of a stag's head seemed to be the only way to announce himself. He didn't like it. He wouldn't know how hard to knock. He searched again for the bell. Finally, he made a couple of tentative strokes of the knocker. No one came. Faintly, he could hear music in the house. They can't hear me, he thought; then he took hold of the stag's horns and hammered it against the striking plate. Fear seized him. He had done what he'd feared—called attention to his anger.

A heavily muscled man opened the door. He wore jeans, a t-shirt with PBI printed on it in large letters and a look of irritation. The knock had been very loud. The man appraised the dirty, shabbily dressed person, who had now retreated a couple of yards from the door. He saw a bum—a bum to be dismissed but also to be sounded. Bums could be trouble. The man in the house was a cameraman who had been with Pollock's staff from the beginning. He, because of his size, had also served in the role of security. There were always weirdos who wanted to get attention, wanted to get an autograph, or were just plain nuts. The guy facing him looked to be in the last category.

"Yeah, what can I do for you?" the man said.

He had thought of what he would say to Dan Pollock when he met him, but had not gone over in his mind what to say in this situation.

He squeaked out, "Dan Pollock," and stopped.

"What about Dan Pollock?"

"I want to talk to him."

"Sorry, he's not here." The cameraman began to close the door.

"It's important."

"What's important?"

"That I talk to him. I know something he would want to pay me for."

Oh boy, thought the cameraman, one of those.

"You've got the wrong idea, buddy. We don't buy information." This time he did close the door.

What should he do now? He still thought that Pollock would want the information he had—would pay for it. He didn't dare knock again. He walked back to the edge of the parking area and stood looking at the house.

The cameraman watched him through the window. He had to get rid of the guy. Dan would be back soon and get real pissed if he saw the guy standing around out there. He opened the door decisively, charged outside and strode menacingly toward the man who now retreated down the driveway.

"That's right, get your butt outta here. If I see you again, you're gonna be damned sorry."

Stumbling hurriedly back out the drive to the road, the would-be informer muttered just softly enough so the big man couldn't hear him, "asshole."

He walked nearly an hour in the direction of the shack where he'd found shelter before he again confronted himself with the unavoidable fact that he was very hungry and knew of no way to get money for food apart from the plan he'd formed earlier. He turned and started trudging back toward the house he'd been chased away from.

"Isn't that the same guy whom we passed in the driveway when we drove out coupla hours ago?" commented Dan Pollock.

The young driver who had chauffeured Pollock and another cameraman to the State Police Post in Traverse City and back had just turned into the driveway of their rented house.

"Looks like him," the driver answered.

"I don't like the looks of him. Call the Sheriff's Department to pick him up. That big doofus of a sheriff thinks he can brush us off, but he can't avoid answering a call for protection." Pollock laughed at the thought.

Once inside the house, Pollock went into the communications room that had been set up to ask his secretary, Joan, if there was any news. The young driver came in and made the call he'd been told to make. The camera/security man who had answered the door to the vagrant's knock overheard the call.

"Hey, that must be the same bum I chased outta here."

"What's that?" Dan said, and had the man tell him of his encounter.

"You say he told you he had information I'd be willing to pay for?"

"That's right; you know what those crazies are like."

Pollock turned suddenly to the young driver. "Go get the guy. Tell him I want to talk to him."

"But, I've just called the sheriff. Should I call them back?"

Dan laughed. "No, let them hunt up and down the road. They've got nothing better to do."

15

Alone on the deck facing the bay, Gina Rossi went over in her mind the many details she must attend to. She lifted a glass of white wine to her lips and took a sip. She had already made arrangements with a local funeral home to have the body cremated once the police released it and to have the ashes shipped directly to Silvio's mother in Bologna. She had spoken to Vince DeSica a short time ago to ask him to assume the position of executive chef at Lucretius . . . until she could sell it. She would give him first refusal and enough time to find backers when that time came. It would be soon. The house, of course, would have to be sold. She did think the beach was beautiful, with its knee-high grass and pristine sand shaped by the wind into dunes and valleys. Yes, it was beautiful here, but no longer a part of her life.

Gina drank some of the wine and placed the glass down on the railing. There was the matter of the earring. She had not been able to find it anywhere. The police had searched the house thoroughly. Surely they would have said so if they had found it. She could have lost it at any time, from getting dressed for the party, until Gloria had pointed out that it was missing. She didn't like to think it, but the possibility that someone at the party had found it and pocketed it seemed likely. The ruby earrings had been her mother's and therefore irreplaceable and the loss saddened her. If she didn't find it before she left for New York, she would tell her insurance agent to go ahead with a claim. Since she wasn't saying it had been stolen, he'd already told her there was no need to file a police report. "Mysterious disappearance" was the phrase he had used.

She picked up the glass and finished off the wine in one long swallow then turned and went into the house.

． ． ．

It took some persuading to convince the man out on the road that he'd be safe to return to the house from which he had been chased away, but he finally climbed into the large SUV to be driven back. Inside the house, the driver led him to the conference room and told him to sit down. Almost immediately Dan came into the room exuding his friendliest manner and, simultaneously noticing the man's agitation and his stained fingers, offered him a cigarette. Intuitively Dan gave the man some room and instead of taking a chair next to him, sat across from him.

"I'm told you have some information that I'd be interested in."

The man nodded while taking a deep drag on the cigarette. Dan waited.

"I know something. I'll tell you for a hundred dollars."

Dan feigned surprise. "That's a lot of money. What's this about?"

"It's about that chef who was killed."

Dan noticed that the man had become calmer. He did feel more confident, in fact, because he believed he possessed something of worth to Pollock.

"How do I know this is worth paying for?" Dan asked, keeping his tone friendly.

"Don't worry—it is."

"I don't usually pay for information," Dan lied, "but I'll make an exception this time. I'll give you twenty bucks."

"A hundred," the man barked as if he clutched a bomb he

would set off if crossed.

Dan sensed he was dealing with a fragile psyche.

"OK, I'll give you a hundred. What have you got for me?"

"The money first."

Pollock only hesitated a moment and then reached in his rear pocket for his wallet and took out two fifty dollar bills and held them out. The man snatched them. They represented food!

The man smiled now triumphantly as if he had just won a contest.

"Maybe we should start with you telling me your name," Dan said easily.

The man considered this as if it might be some kind of trick and then said, "Gregory."

Pollock thought of asking if this was his first or last name, but again, intuitively he let it ride. Actually, Gregory had heard his last name but few times in recent years. He thought of himself as a one-name person.

"Well, Gregory, I'm waiting to hear what I paid for."

"I saw them fucking."

Unexpected, the word slapped Pollock.

"You say . . . you saw them?"

"The chef and the woman."

Dan's attention riveted on Gregory's words. "The chef?"

"Yeah, the guy who was killed and a blond woman. They had pulled off the road onto the dirt track that leads to . . . " He hesitated. "That's near where I stay. I had been walking back to my place and I saw the car and thought it was empty at first, so I went to look it over and saw them inside going at it. They never saw me."

"How did you know it was the chef?"

"I've seen him lots of times on TV. We watched a lot of TV at the place where I lived before."

"What about the woman, the blond?"

"Don't know her."

"Then it could have been the chef's wife for all you know."

"No way. Why would a guy who's got a fancy house fuck his wife in a car out in a field?"

"What kind of car was it?"

"New looking black Mercedes sedan. Michigan license number QFK114."

Suddenly Dan became suspicious that he was being stiffed. In a situation such as the one the guy described, who would bother to memorize the license number?

"You memorized the number?"

Gregory's expression became defensive, his posture rigid. Dan thought it was because he'd caught him in a lie, but this wasn't the case. Dan had just singled out a trait that Gregory knew to be odd, something that set him apart from others. Gregory correctly discerned the distrust in Dan's eyes. He had seen it many times before.

"It's something I do without trying," he said, as if confessing a character flaw. "I memorize license numbers. I know thousands."

Dan couldn't believe what'd he'd heard. "What do you mean?"

"I memorize every license number I see. I always have."

"Come on!" Dan burst out.

"It's true."

From where he sat, Pollock could see the rear of one of the two Explorers parked outside. "OK, there are two cars in the parking area. You have seen both of them. One has been parked here and I just drove up in one. What are the numbers?"

"XZA196, and the car you were in is 709ZKZ."

Pollock looked out the window at the plate of the car he had just been in. 709ZKZ.

122

"Son-of-a-bitch." Pollock mumbled. He had heard of people who could perform unusual feats of memory. He understood they often weren't all of one piece in other areas of their functioning. That would certainly apply here. His interest in Gregory's story sharpened

"So, what happened then?"

"I watched at a distance until they drove away. The woman was driving."

Pollock believed the story. He also felt sure Gregory knew no more. He started to dismiss him, then hesitated. He had to be able to contact him if the story needed to be corroborated, but there was something else. Pollock sensed he faced a drowning man and to walk away would be equivalent to watching him struggle in the water and turn one's back. This man and he were worlds apart in material circumstances, yet in his current emotional state, Pollock identified their similar fight to survive.

"You know, I meant it when I said we didn't buy information. We do have a research staff that digs into cases, however. I can't have you on the payroll, but I'd like to have you on a retainer as a consultant for as long as we're working on this story. I may need to ask you more questions. That OK with you?"

"You'll pay me?"

"Of course. Two hundred a week. OK?"

"Yeah, yeah sure."

"Then I'll need your full name and social security number."

"Gregory Abbott. The number is . . ."

"Wait. Hold on a minute. I'll never remember it. You can give it to my secretary. Stay here and I'll send her in. After she's talked to you, you can go, but call in every day to see if we need you. She'll give you the number."

Pollock went into the communications room and whispered to

his secretary that he wanted her to question Gregory and get as much information as she could: past jobs, addresses, schooling, everything. He also wanted her to call their contact in the Michigan State Police and get the name and address of the owner of the car with the QFK114 plate. Once he'd done this, Dan went in search of Art Brock. They needed to discuss how to use what Dan had just learned.

• • •

"Have you ever shipped ashes to Italy?"

"No, why?" answered the funeral director.

"That chef, Rossi, his wife wants him cremated and shipped home to his mother," replied his assistant.

"Nice touch."

Laughing, "I guess so, but I thought it was also like a joke; 'You never wanted me to have him; now he's all yours.' But, I'm serious when I ask if you've ever done this before. I can imagine red tape up to the armpits getting permits to import human remains to Italy."

"Trouble with you; you're always thinking inside the box. I'll drop into Leelanau Books and get one of their shipping labels. We'll ship the great chef home 'book rate'."

• • •

Art Brock had been sitting on a bench at the end of the dock that extended into Lake Leelanau reading the *Times* when he'd looked up and seen a 1920's vintage motor launch capped with a blue and white striped and scalloped awning cruising by close to shore. The half dozen passengers were having a grand time munching on appetizers and drinking white wine. The skipper, a gentleman sporting a magnificent, white Uncle Sam beard, raised his glass to Art as they passed and Art returned a salute.

Dan Pollock came trotting down the dock to tell Art what he'd just heard about Rossi's backseat lovemaking.

Art only took a moment before stating, "We need to know who that car belongs to."

"I've got Joan on it now. And, my friend, we're the only ones who know about this juicy bit."

"Great. We need a break. I've just been outlining your 'on the scene' for the six-o'clock news. So far we haven't any film footage worth showing. We've got the sheriff telling you to butt-out and a shot of the State Police Commander telling you the sheriff's got everything in hand. And, since the sheriff isn't talking, we know nothing about suspects and I don't have to tell you that our life's blood is the suspect. We need pictures of suspects. And, we can't even speculate about motive. I've been going over the list of guests at Rossi's party given to me by our research staff. Some familiar names on it, but none we've any reason to think had it in for Rossi. Let's pray there's a jealous boyfriend or husband involved with this back-seat bit. If so, we have someone with a very hot motive."

Both men turned at the sound of Joan's rapid steps on the planking of the dock. She handed Dan a sheet of paper with the manner of one bearing valuable news.

"This is the name of the person the car is registered to, Bruce Thomas. He's on the list of the party guests. There is also a Sandra Thomas on the list. They are locals. They have a house at The Homestead in Glen Arbor, a village south of here on Lake Michigan."

It took only a couple of beats for the significance of this information to register with the two men.

"The woman in the back seat must have been Sandra Thomas,"

Dan said.

"Which gives us a jealous husband at the party. We've got to find a guest who will talk to us, tell us about the possibility of Bruce Thomas having an opportunity at the party to kill Rossi."

The three of them pondered the question. Joan came up with a suggestion. "The publicist for the Rossi TV show, Gloria Klein, has been a useful contact for us for New York gossip in the past. She's on the party's guest list."

"Perfect," Art asserted. "Gloria is one who knows that one hand washes the other. Find out where she is and I'll call her."

Art said, "I've got a feeling that, finally, my guardian angel got off her butt and started earning her pay."

When he returned to the house, Joan called Dan aside. He listened without interruption to the tale she told him about Gregory, the informer. She had found out that he stayed in an abandoned, wooden building originally constructed to boil down maple sap to make syrup. When he'd first ventured up into the peninsula he'd hitched a ride with an Indian who'd told him about the shack when it became clear to him that Gregory had no place to stay. The shack had neither water nor heat. Gregory had come north after he'd been released from a halfway house in Bay City a month ago. His original home had been in Livonia, Michigan. For ten years, he'd worked at a tool-and-die company that did job work for the auto industry. The nosedive of the industry caused the company to close its doors and Gregory to be unemployed. Up until then, he had worked in the warehouse managing inventory. It had been the only job he'd ever had. He was a high school graduate.

"I'll bet his father knew someone to get him that job. My nose tells me he is one of life's square pegs." Dan got up. "Thanks Joan." He stopped at the door and turned to her adding, "He must be on the state's case-load. Let's go one step further and see if we can get the whole story. When you have time, call the appropriate state office—Human Services or whatever it's called here."

"May I ask a question," Joan asked.

Dan cocked his head to one side, inviting her to ask.

"Why the interest in this person?"

Dan thought about it. "Don't really know. I only know I'll feel bad if I drop this guy right now." He saw that this puzzled her even more. "Or something like that," he said and left the room.

Gloria Klein recognized in Art Brock's tone that his opening chatter was a prologue to the business of secret sharing and she prepared herself. Still, she was surprised when he said, "We know that Rossi was screwing Sandra Thomas. I need to know if her husband—you know he was at the party—had an opportunity to skewer Rossi."

"Where did you hear this about Silvio and the Thomas woman?"

"The way you asked that question says that you knew it too. I can't name names, but I can tell you it is eye-witness stuff."

Pretty careless of Silvio, Gloria thought. She said, "This is between us?"

"Naturally."

"His name is Bruce, and I don't know if he knew about his wife and Rossi."

"Too bad. If he knew, he'd be a prime suspect. We badly need a suspect right now, my friend."

"Maybe this would help; I heard his name mentioned as being among those without an alibi for the critical time."

"There were others, then?"

"Yes, but no motives that I know of," she answered.

"Who are they?"

Gloria wasn't giving away all she had to barter. "When you know some motives, call me."

"So, you're telling me Thomas had opportunity and is a police suspect?"

"I believe the phrase is 'Everyone is a suspect until proven otherwise'."

"You're being too clever, Gloria; you know I have to earn a living."

"OK, how's this, I think there's a good chance Sheriff Davis doesn't yet know about Silvio and Mrs. Thomas."

"I owe you one, my dear."

• • •

His tattered backpack bulged with bread, cheese, salami and a two-liter bottle of Coke. A young man from Dan Pollock's crew had given him a ride to a grocery near the house in one of the SUVs, the one with the 709ZKZ plate. Gregory had then chanced to catch a small bus that ran around the peninsula to a spot three miles from the abandoned shack and walked from there. An overgrown track led from the paved road up a hill to a dense copse of sugar maples that covered the hill's top. Out of sight from below stood a weathered, but strongly built single-room building sided in two-inch planks of native cedar. Gregory had earlier discerned signs that someone else had stayed there in the past. A plastic bag still containing food appeared to have been left by the previous occupant. Animals had scavenged and only the torn remnants of food wrappings remained. Gregory swung the backpack off his shoulders and onto the long table built along one wall. He immediately made himself a sandwich with thick chunks of salami and cheese he'd loped-off with his pocketknife. He carried his sandwich and the bottle of Coke out to the edge of the stand of maples and looked out from his high perch. It was late afternoon, but some men still worked down in a vineyard off to the southwest. Gregory wondered what they were doing, surely not picking grapes yet. The previous day, while walking he had passed a group working in an apple orchard and wondered briefly if he could get a job. He'd decided it would be a waste of time to inquire, because the men seemed to belong to a crew and were all Latinos, probably Mexicans.

Standing there, surveying the beautiful and varied landscape, a cloud of doubt and morbid futility came over him. Was this place to be the end of the line for him? He didn't think this "consulting" gig with the TV guy would last longer than a week. That would give him two hundred dollars more. He could stretch the money to buy food for a month. It would be cold soon. The shack had no heat, no water. He would have to go south. Tired and dejected, he had no energy to set out alone across the country. To have a job and live in this place was his idea of paradise, but who would hire him? He had heard "no" so many times, he shied from asking any question that would prompt it.

The sandwich tasted good. The sunshine felt good. He lit a cigarette. These things would be enough today.

• • •

Hoss Davis sank into the large easy chair that had become molded to his body. He had a can of Bud Lite in one hand and the TV remote in the other. K.D. came into the room from the kitchen, where she had just spread pizza dough onto a pan, and stood behind Hoss's chair. Hoss had been told that Pollock would be doing an "on location" spot on the network's six-o-clock news and he and K.D. were both curious about how Pollock might use the interview he'd had with Hoss. The Rossi murder, apparently judged by those who decide what things were important to the nation, had been given the second spot.

"This is Dan Pollock. I'm standing in front of the magnificent home built by Silvio Rossi in this remote setting. [Scanning shots of house from water, fading into a telephoto of the barbecue area] Tragically, he had only been able to use it this one summer before being struck down in the prime of his career. He was murdered, as you've heard, at the party that was to be the last before he and many of his guests returned to New York to begin a busy autumn season.

"There has been no progress reported by the local Sheriff's Department in the Rossi murder. [Front of Sheriff's Headquarters and an uncomplimentary still of Hoss squinting edited out of Dan's interview with him.] PBI, however, has discovered a significant fact. One, we judge, that will lead to the arrest of the killer. It concerns an extra-marital sexual relationship formed by Silvio Rossi while here on vacation. I am not going to reveal the details tonight, because it is our civic duty to first, and immediately, give this information to the local sheriff. I will certainly reveal our information to you tomorrow night on the regular broadcast of PBI. This is Dan Pollock in Leelanau County, Michigan."

"'Extra-marital sexual relationship', 'Share this information with the local sheriff', What in the world?" Hoss experienced the exact same sensation he had known many times while playing football, the shock of being blind-sided—and the kind of embarrassment that went with it.

130

16

"Did any of you catch Dan Pollock on the six-o-clock news yesterday?" asked Deputy Russ Preva.

Almost everyone in the conference room at headquarters for the morning briefing had heard Pollock's claim of having information about Rossi's alleged sexual antics and his inference that this would prove to be the motive for the murder.

Russ hadn't finished. "Pollock made it clear he thought we are a bunch of bumpkins who wouldn't know a clue if it had a label on it while his gang, on the other hand, hardly hit town before solving the case."

"I heard him too, Russ." Hoss looked around the room. They were all nodding their heads except Donna, who hadn't watched the news.

"The part I liked best," Russ went on, "was when he talked about it being his civic duty to immediately notify the local yokels before he could tell the nation. Kate," he nodded toward the dispatcher's room, "said they hadn't yet called with our doggie biscuit."

Experiencing the feeling of the poker player who has just seen his bet met and raised, Hoss sighed, "Maybe Pollock's got the real thing."

What she had just heard troubled Donna. Was the sexual affair Gloria Klein had told her about—and she hadn't reported to Hoss—the same one referred to by Pollock? Klein had stipulated that the information must be Donna's alone. Donna had agreed to Klein's deal with the intention of personally learning more about Bruce Thomas. She had only just begun her inquiry.

"I have a hunch they're waiting for us to call them. They're going to make us sit up and beg for the biscuit," Becky McConnell put in.

"And if we don't call, they can say they offered to share information and we ignored the offer," Russ said.

"Beautiful," Hoss commented. "Russ, would you . . . "

"Make the call? Right now?"

"If we're going to do it, let's not have them say we delayed."

Russ got up and went into the dispatcher's room to have Kate find the number for him.

Hoss went on talking as Russ left the room, "Although these guys are going to use us if they can to make themselves look good, I hope they do have solid evidence to break this case. We sure don't have any leads ourselves and I'll be glad to get this case closed and have the media and the 'nation' leave town."

Russ came back into the room. "I called the house Pollock is using, but the woman who answered said he would be away for a short time. I gave her our number."

The meeting broke up and Hoss drew another cup of coffee out of the brewer in the conference room and ambled down the hall to his office. His cell phone rang.

"This is Sheriff Davis."

"Good morning, Sheriff. I imagine you called about the statement I made on the news last night that we had uncovered vital evidence in the Rossi murder."

It surprised Hoss that Pollock had called him on his cell phone. The number was unlisted. Surely Russ would have left the main office number.

"Yes, you said you were going to let us in on your information, 'immediately'".

Pollock ignored Hoss's implication that he had failed to do as he'd promised his viewers. But, he knew from the quote that Hoss had listened to the broadcast with undivided attention.

"Yes, we made a sure discovery and the more we've learned as we've expanded our investigation, the more certain we've become that we have the name of the killer."

Hoss suspected the man intended to make him feel as if he, Hoss, were but a bystander with a marginal role in the investigation. It worked. That's exactly how he felt.

Before Hoss could respond, Pollock went on, "Of course, you can understand that this information is quite a scoop for PBI. We intend to make the revelation tonight on the show. It is imperative that no other news media knows of this until we break it tonight. This means, Sheriff, I have to have your promise that you will say nothing about this, nor take any action until after our show. Not even your deputies can be told, since, as you must know very well, there is little likelihood of a secret being kept in that case."

Hoss had not expected this. He could, however, appreciate the malicious intent in Pollock's offer. Pollock's offer of supposedly important information, hinged on Hoss behaving in a way that negated his role as sheriff. To respond appropriately in the performance of his duty to the people who had elected him, Hoss needed to put his force to work immediately in the direction the new evidence pointed. If he refused to agree to Pollock's terms, then the man could, and no doubt would, say that the offer to share the information had been made and had been turned down. Hoss saw clearly that the claim Pollock had made about it being his "civic duty" to inform the local sheriff was pure deceit! Pollock only wanted a plausible reason to delay revealing his scoop in order to tweak the viewers' curiosity—create a large audience for tonight's broadcast.

What Hoss said next was off the top of his head rather than thought out. "That's not the way we work here, Mr. Pollock. We try to use all of our force in the most effective way. If you really intend to do 'your civic duty' then you will relate the information you have with no strings attached. It is understood by my deputies that information concerning an active case is confidential. If you want to tell me what you have 'discovered', I welcome it, but I'm not willing to withhold it from my deputies just because of your show."

The ball definitely had been returned to Pollock's court. He faced a difficult decision. He could refuse to divulge the name of Rossi's lover and run the risk of this hippopotamus of a sheriff claiming he had withheld vital information, or he could tell Davis what he knew and run the risk of another network getting and using it before he did. Hell, Pollock thought, there was really no choice; both he and the show needed this break. All television sets would be tuned to PBI tonight to hear what he had promised the audience. If this sheriff did go claiming that he, Dan Pollock, had withheld vital information, he could simply lie and say the sheriff had been told, but obviously didn't know what to do with it. Whom would the public believe, Dan Pollock or the backwater sheriff? Besides, Davis couldn't prove otherwise. Knowing that all calls to and from a sheriff's office are recorded, Dan had deliberately called Hoss at his cell phone number. Getting that number had been child's play for his research staff.

"I'm sorry, Sheriff, that you can't accept what I'm offering you. My conditions are very fair I believe, conditions, which many other law enforcement agencies have been very willing to accept—to their advantage—over the years. Well, anyway, after tonight's show the information will be yours. I'm being called away, Sheriff Davis. Be sure to watch the show. Nine o'clock."

"Before you rush off," Hoss said, "Having and withholding information that would aid a law enforcement agency in performing its duty is known as obstruction of justice. Think about it."

The words, "obstruction of justice", produced a jolt and it did cause Dan to think. He reminded himself that Hoss had no proof of the content of this call. At worst, the network's legal department might have to work it through, as they had many times before. He needed this scoop.

"Goodbye, Sheriff."

"There's something I have to tell you, Hoss." Donna had followed Hoss to his office and waited outside until she saw he'd finished the conversation on his cell.

Hoss heard something serious in her tone. He went over and closed the office door and came back to sit at his desk. He motioned to a vacant chair.

"What's on your mind?"

"I might know what Pollock is referring to about Rossi's Leelanau sex life."

"Oh?"

"Rossi's publicist, Gloria Klein, told me in confidence that she had come upon Rossi and Bruce Thomas's wife, Sandra, doing the thing. I didn't tell you, because Klein said she'd talk to me about her take on the various suspects as long as our conversation remained between us. I figured it was better to have the information and look into it myself, rather than not have her views at all."

She stopped and checked her boss's reaction.

He nodded. "Rossi and Sandra Thomas, you say?"

Hoss mulled this over a moment then realized he'd passed over her appeal for him to understand the problem she'd had in withholding this information.

"Yes, that's the way I'd play it in your situation." He said. "I understand your not saying anything to me."

Donna felt better. She said, "What particularly concerns Gloria

Klein is that those she has to work with in her business not see her as having a loose tongue. I see now that I could have—and should have told you. There'd be no way for Klein's colleagues to know that our information came from her."

"I guess we'll have to wait until their show tonight to see if he names Sandra Thomas," Hoss said. "What do we know about her?"

"She was on the guest list. David Wick interviewed her. I looked at his report: she has an alibi. Her husband was there, too. Bruce. He's the guy who left his conversation group to go to the john. I've already done some inquiring about him. Thomas lives at the Homestead in Glen Arbor, so I thought there was a good chance he played some golf at King's Challenge. I know that one of Kate Schott's brothers is a pro there. It turns out he has given Thomas lessons and has played a few rounds with him. Kate's brother said he's a nice guy, takes the ups and downs of his game with humor. That's not much, but it's all I know so far."

"Not a hot head," commented Hoss.

"At least not on the golf course. Barbecue kettles might just set him off."

Hoss laughed, then said, "If that's all Pollock has, this sexcapade with the Thomas woman, then he doesn't have much. It only gives Thomas a motive. We've got lots of folks with motives; it's evidence we lack."

"I think the television viewers will believe he has more than that—more than we have, anyway," Donna said.

Hoss sat pensively tapping a pencil on the edge of his desk. "I said that I hoped he had the evidence to break the case. I still mean it. Maybe he is on the right track with Thomas. "

Hoss thought they should take a look at Thomas, possibly bring the guy into headquarters for interrogation, but he didn't want to appear to step-in and take over.

"What do you think we should do?" he asked.

"I think we should bring him in for questioning."

If they did bring Thomas to headquarters for questioning, Dan Pollock would know of it, Donna surmised. She pictured Pollock crowing to his audience that he had propelled the Leelanau County Sheriff's Department into some useful action. She didn't like the picture.

"Maybe we can do it without that TV bunch knowing about it," she added wishfully.

"Fat chance with them camped on our doorstep." He tapped the pencil a few more times ending with an emphatic drumbeat. "Do you want to do the interview?"

"No way. I'm not the right person"

Donna imagined herself in Thomas's place. She cast Hoss in the role of interrogator. That wouldn't do; although big and imposing, he was naturally too easygoing, too likeable. Hoss could play the part of "good cop" well, but not "bad cop". If they were going to precipitate a confession from Thomas, first there had to be a very "bad cop". Immediately one deputy came to mind, Don Silver. Don played a double role in the department. He had trained with the State Police crime lab in order to supervise a crime scene until the full crime lab crew could arrive from the State Police post at Acme. He also filled the role of the department's photographer. What had come to Donna's mind, however, was the stony, poker face this otherwise affable friend could adopt. She hadn't witnessed a single adult-baiting teenager who had been capable of standing up to Don's icy stare.

"Don Silver," she said. "Followed by you."

"Ah yes, the old one-two." Hoss laughed as he saw the role she'd chosen for him. "OK. And you and Becky can go and pick him up. A ride here with two women who won't talk to him should set him up nicely for Don. Becky just went out on patrol; have Kate bring her back. I'll brief Don."

Donna stood up and put into motion what felt to her a little like an elaborate practical joke.

Donna could now appreciate Hoss's insight into the male psyche when he'd told her and Becky to drive to the Thomas home and bring him to headquarters. In the first place, Donna standing at the door had been less threatening to Thomas. So much so, that he hadn't even thought of calling his attorney or leaving a note for his wife. Once he had been placed in the back seat of the patrol car, his natural inclination had been to begin a casual conversation tinged with the playful remarks of a man talking to two nice-looking women playing at what he saw to be a man's role. What he got back were terse one-word responses to only some of his questions and no responses to any of his remarks. There was no doubt that his confidence had been shaken during the ride in. Don Silver awaited him.

Becky mutely led Thomas to one of the interrogation rooms, motioned to a seat and then left him. Bright fluorescent light saturated the room. Facing him, a mirror made up most of the opposite wall. He glanced at the mirror, suspecting he was being observed. But, then, maybe he wasn't. Maybe he was alone. Time passed. Had they forgotten him? Sandra didn't know where he was.

Had he been able to think about the experience objectively, he might have seen that the set up was pretty typical, nothing he hadn't seen many times in films. But, this wasn't a film, and objectivity abandoned him.

Don Silver opened the door to the room as if he were coming in and then, leaving it ajar, went back down the hallway to engage in a conversation with another deputy, a conversation that Bruce Thomas could only catch bits of, seemingly concerning duck hunting. The speaking stopped and Thomas thought he was finally going to get some attention. Nothing happened. He got up from the chair and looked out the partially open doorway into the hall. No one was around. He thought of walking out, until he suddenly again felt he was being watched, and turned and looked into the wall of mirror behind him. Had someone been on the other side of that glass all this time? He thought of saying something to the mirror: What's going on here? Instead, he sat again. His gaze traveled to an upper corner of the room, where the lens of a camera stared down at him. He felt sure it had been recording him all the time. Footsteps in the hall. The door opened and Don Silver came in and closed the door. Without speaking he sat opposite Thomas. His expression spoke of distaste for the task of talking to someone who disgusted him. He suddenly looked intensely into Thomas's eyes.

"She was in on it, wasn't she?"

"No . . . I mean, in on what?"

Don made no reply to the question, but chuckled to himself, "You gave yourself away, pal; it's plain she was."

"No, That is she . . . we didn't do anything."

Don seemed to pay no attention to what Thomas said, but continued, "You went down to the barbecue area to confront him— tell him you knew he was screwing her." Don paused. "He laughed at you."

"No, that's wrong. That's not the way it was."

"Correct me."

Suddenly Bruce Thomas saw a yawning pit open up, one he could easily step into and never be able to climb out of. He looked into the mirror and said to it, "I'm not saying anything more without my attorney present."

He had been right about the mirror. In the small room behind it, Hoss, Becky and Donna had been observing and listening to the interrogation.

Don continued in a cold, indifferent tone, "You know you lied about going to the downstairs bathroom. You must have done that before you came to the party. No one else had that need!" he stated unequivocally. "It's a lie to cover what you really did."

Thomas's confidence grew with each passing second. If he said nothing, they could do nothing to him. This wasn't the C.I.A. he was dealing with.

"What do you think your attorney can do to help you?" Don said mockingly, "He can't reverse what you did to Silvio Rossi."

The three beyond the glass listened carefully for Thomas's reply. The majority of persons would be compelled to deny again that they'd done anything to Rossi. Instead, Thomas seemed to be in solid control. He felt safe in his silence.

"I imagine Rossi taunted you, maybe he threatened you. His taunting made you pick up that skewer like any other man would do." Don was offering Thomas an acceptable explanation for his action, tempting Thomas to grasp at it.

Thomas fixed his eyes on the tabletop. The way he held himself said, "We can spend the rest of the year here, but I'm not going to say another word."

Hoss looked at his two deputies and they both nodded recognition of defeat. Hoss got up and noiselessly left the room and opened the door to the interrogation room interrupting yet another futile attempt to dislodge Thomas.

"OK, Deputy Silver, I'd like to talk to Mr. Thomas. You can go." He said this dismissively, as if he were the proprietor replacing a rude and incompetent salesperson in order to give the customer the respect he deserved.

Hoss settled into the chair Don had sat in and asked Thomas if he'd like some coffee. Thomas declined.

"Well, I'd like some," Hoss said in a casual tone. He leaned over to the wall and pressed one of the buttons on an intercom and told Kate that he could, "Sure do with a cup of hot coffee." He looked over at Thomas. "You sure you don't want some?"

Bruce had resolved to say nothing else, but found himself on the point of giving Hoss a positive answer. He really would like the coffee and without a doubt, this big guy was a horse of an entirely different color than that other . . . prick.

Hoss discerned Thomas begin to loosen-up and then regain his resolve to decline any interaction with the police.

"One of the hardest things a guy could have to face," Hoss said, "is finding out his wife is screwing another guy." Hoss noticed Thomas wince. "It could push a guy to impulsively do a thing he'd never for the life of him do normally. Spur-of-the-moment. People understand that."

It was hard for Thomas to resist the "good cop". His natural instincts wanted a good relationship with this giant who epito-mized solid, gentle manliness. To decline this offer of friendship seemed, at the moment, to be forever turning his back on mem-bership in a circle of the right kind of guys. On the other hand, his survival instincts said he must not forget for a moment to keep his mouth shut.

Hoss believed the man's determination. The moment had come when he must back off and gracefully segue into a respectful and friendly termination of the interrogation.

Donna and Becky, in the observation room, recognized this change of direction and left to go to the building entrance to deliver Bruce Thomas back home.

Reporters had set up a regular camp in the parking area out

front. A van belonging to one of the networks even supplied hot coffee for one and all. When the two deputies emerged from the building with Thomas, they began filming and throwing out questions.

"Where are you taking him?"

"Is he being charged?"

"Sir. Do you want to make a statement?"

Donna didn't act on it, but had the impulse, once in the car and moving, to apologize to their passenger. They rode in silence for several minutes, letting the effect of the assault recede.

Becky broke the ice by offering Thomas a stick of gum.

He hesitated, but then took it. "Thanks."

Tension between Thomas and the two women eased after this so that by the time Donna turned into the wide, curving entrance to the Homestead Resort where Thomas lived, he was thinking of the two deputies as pretty good guys just doing their job.

Somehow the reporters had learned Bruce Thomas was the man they'd seen the two women take into Sheriff's Headquarters and were waiting now at his home.

Becky got out and opened his door and he trotted to his house, holding his forearm in front of his face. A man with a microphone trotted beside him shouting questions.

Becky got back into the patrol car and Donna drove slowly away, both looking back in awe at the scene.

17

"Bruce Thomas is now the center of a feeding frenzy," Becky announced when she and Donna returned to headquarters.

Don Silver and Hoss were waiting for them, so they could all discuss the interrogation.

Hoss clasped his hands behind his head and leaned back in his swivel chair. This maneuver always made Donna nervous. She couldn't understand what kept the chair from giving up and totally collapsing under the stress of his weight.

"The media certainly creates a reality of its own," Hoss mused none too happily. He swiveled the chair around to face the others.

"OK, guys, what shall we make of Mr. Bruce Thomas?" He looked at Don Silver. "Don?"

"My reasoning before the interrogation went like this: If he was guilty, he'd be expecting me to accuse him directly. I thought I might catch him off base if I opened by implicating his wife. At the beginning, I thought it had worked and I had my fish on the line. When I said, 'She was in on it?' and he answered, 'No.'; I thought I had him. That answer usually means the subject is unintentionally admitting there was something to be in on. Thomas saw his error and corrected it to, 'I mean, in on what?' When I pressed on and said I could see by his reaction that his wife did help him murder Rossi, he quickly denied it, 'She didn't,' he said. That answer, of course, again leaves out the immediate denial that either of them killed Rossi that he should have made if innocent, it only denies that she helped. Seeing his error again, he changed it, to 'We didn't do anything.' The point at which I really thought I had him landed was when I suggested how he had gone down to the barbecue area and skewered Rossi and he snapped back, 'That's not the way it was.'

"'Was' is the important word here. He is admitting that there 'was' something connected to skewering Rossi, only it wasn't what I accused him of. I felt pretty confident after his answer. But, after he said, 'That's not the way it was.', I made a mistake and said, 'correct me.' That's when he slipped off the hook. I think I may have used the wrong word. I should have said, 'Tell me about it.' in a sympathetic tone. 'Correct me' is too . . . like working on a problem . . . too impersonal like."

"Confrontational?" Becky suggested.

"More like too challenging, like I was a teacher and we were in a classroom. I think I blew it, friends."

Hoss nodded thoughtfully. "So, it's your opinion that he is guilty, near to breaking down and confessing, but then got control of himself?"

"That's about it— got control with my help."

Hoss swiveled the chair toward Becky. "What say you, Becky?"

"That's an interesting issue Don raises—about the effect just one word can have in an interview—but I disagree that his saying, 'correct me', did any damage. I think we can make too much of this guy's opening, 'No', to the question of whether his wife was, 'in on it'. Once you start thinking the guy is guilty, you can read all his responses as confirming your bias. But if we understand that this had to be a very mentally confusing situation being hauled into a police station and put into isolation, you can understand his responses as those an innocent—but stressed—person might make. It's a close call, but my gut feeling says the guy was telling the truth."

"Do I understand that you're making a challenge to the official's decision on the field?" Hoss joked.

"Even the best officials can make mistakes," Becky returned, giving Don an elbow nudge.

"Donna?" Hoss indicated by tone of voice that since the lead in the investigation belonged to her, her reading of what the interrogation could tell them carried the most weight.

Donna had listened to the exchanges between her friends with interest. Their views had helped her sort out her own observations while watching Don and Bruce Thomas.

"I'd say his responses were too equivocal to draw a conclusion. He's still a viable suspect in my opinion. Perhaps his level of potential has been raised from yellow to yellowish orange."

The three deputies then looked to Hoss for the last word.

"I see it like this," he said thoughtfully, "Maybe Don is right and Thomas is guilty, but lacking a confession, there is no action for us to take where he's concerned. I believe that puts him where Donna indicated—worth looking at more closely."

"How about if I have a go at the wife?" Don said. "Of course, she is forewarned now, but she may still rattle easier than her husband."

"There may be another factor operating here," Donna said. "I think we've been assuming Thomas knew about the affair his wife was having in order for him to have a motive to kill Rossi. What if Thomas didn't know about his wife and Rossi?" Donna let that thought sink in for a moment. "In that case, we enter the scene in the midst of a marital meltdown. She'd be rattled for a different reason."

Don put in, "The more she's shook up, the more likely she is to talk without control. And, here's another reason to tackle her. Suppose she knows her hubby killed her glamorous boyfriend; she might be so angry she'd like to hand him to us."

"So you're both thinking she might be vulnerable and might say things she otherwise wouldn't. I, too, think we should bring her in for questioning. There are a couple of ways we could do it. Have Russ Preva drive out there now and get her. She would have little time to prepare what she'll say. Or, we let her know that we intend to come pick her up in the morning. Let her stew over it all night. What's your feeling about that?" He looked at each of them.

Becky spoke first. "I'd say, wait until morning. But, I don't feel strongly about it."

"I'll go along with that," agreed Don Silver.

"If we tell her we're picking her up in the morning, I'm willing to bet she doesn't sleep a wink. She'll be spent by the time Don confronts her," said Donna.

"OK then, first thing in the morning before she even has her coffee," Hoss concluded..

As the deputies left his office, Hoss had the uncomfortable feeling that he was only doing Dan Pollock's bidding.

• • •

Pollock sat alone on the porch facing the lake. He had gone there after the conversation with the Leelanau Sheriff to think about how to tell his audience about the guy's unwillingness to cooperate. On other, earlier occasions he'd seen the reaction of locals to his hints that their city's elected officials were incompetent. In one case, the result had been the recall of a mayor. This sheriff should know that. Art Brock interrupted Pollock's rumination, as he came out on the porch and took a rocking chair beside him.

"I just talked to the boss." Art Brock said to Pollock. "Bondi wanted to know if what you said about Rossi's sex life is true, or if you were bluffing to build an audience for the next show? He was pleased when I told him our plan."

"Our plan?"

"We will question both the Thomas woman and her husband on camera and play what breaks by ear."

"Thanks for telling me."

"I made it up as I talked to him. By the way, one of our guys just called in to say a couple of deputies picked up Bruce Thomas and brought him to their headquarters. He was there for an hour and then they took him back to his house."

Dan pondered this development. "What do you think it means that they only held him an hour?"

"Probably just routine questioning."

"Yeah, but it could mean they've learned of Rossi and the Thomas woman. In that case, we'd better get cracking with 'our plan.'" Pollock jumped to his feet like a hunter heading for the field.

• • •

Like that uneasy sense of having forgotten an appointment, Donna was nagged by the feeling there was something she had intended to do that first day at the Rossi House but had forgotten. Several times she'd attempted to catch the fleeting thought off-guard and capture it, but without success. Now, while leaving Hoss's office with Becky after the debriefing on Bruce Thomas, it came to her .

"Becky, the other day when we were at the Rossi house, I asked you to go back and question a woman named Judy Bombard about what she did after she left the group with Gina Rossi. Did you get a chance to do it?"

"Sure. I wrote out a note and put it in your mail box."

"Oh Lord, I've been so preoccupied I haven't gathered my mail."

"Do you want me to tell you what I remember of it?"

"That's OK, there's no reason to take up your time; I can read the note," Donna said.

"That's better anyway. I wrote it right after I talked to her. I might forget some detail now. I talked to a lot of people that day."

Donna went back inside the building to the squad room and sorted through her mail and found Becky's note. She had written it hurriedly, but it was legible.

"Judy Bombard—addition to her first statement. JB says Mrs. Rossi asked her if she would like to see the rest of the house. JB was curious, said OK. R had already asked the mother of one of the chefs.

After JB, R asked Marla Phelps to go on the tour. So, there were the old lady, MP, JB and R. They went into the kitchen, where R added champagne to 4 glasses already containing a red liquid called casease (sp) in order to make a drink called keer."

Cassis, thought Donna, the currant liquor, and *kir,* or rather kir *royale,* because of the champagne instead of white wine. She read on.

"Each woman took a glass and followed R up to a balcony that overlooked the kitchen, where she proposed a toast to good cooking or something like that.

"They went on upstairs and were walking along the hall, when MP suddenly became sick and vomited right there in the hall. R hustled her into a bathroom and at that point JB made herself scarce. She has a great problem with vomit and vomiting—makes her sick to see it—and had to get away. She went back downstairs and sought out some people to talk to in order to take her mind off

MP getting sick. Continued talking to those people until she heard the scream. It checks out with the other guests she named."

Sounds like a real phobia, Donna thought as she pocketed the note. Anyway, that completed the unfinished business with Judy Bombard.

· · ·

The van transporting Dan and Art and a camera crew were nearing The Homestead Resort, when Art Brock's cell phone rang. A reporter assigned, along with a cameraman, to watch the Thomas house told him the couple had left and gone into the village of Glen Arbor, where he'd followed them. Sandra Thomas had entered Steffen's Market, while Bruce had gone into Art's Tavern. Art Brock told the van's driver to change destinations.

Bruce Thomas had told his wife, when Becky and Donna brought him home from the interrogation, that it had been routine; all the guests at the Rossi party were being asked general questions about their recollections of that afternoon. Sandra had not seen Pollock's appearance on the evening news and knew nothing of Pollock's claim that Silvio Rossi had been having a sexual fling during his vacation.

Therefore, it was an unsuspecting Sandra Thomas who found herself confronted by Dan and a cameraman as she came out of the market. She, of course, recognized his famous face and was thinking more of the fact of his celebrity than of what he might ask her. His first questions were innocuous and the ones she would have expected: "Mrs Thomas, I understand you were at the party when Silvio Rossi was killed. Have you and your husband known Silvio Rossi long?" (This would be edited for the broadcast to, "have you known Silvio Rossi long?") "Did the two of you like him very much?" would change to, "Did you like him very much?" "Were you and your husband going to see him in New York?" to, "Were you going to see him in New York?"

Her replies didn't need editing. "Were you at the party?"—"Yes, I was at the party." "Did you like him?"—"Yes, very much." "Were you going to see him in New York?" was followed by, "Yes, of course."

Dan then hit her with the statement, "We have learned that you and Silvio Rossi were having a sexual affair. Did your husband know about it?"

A stunned woman looked into the camera. She began to cry, put her hands over her face and ran to her car, dropping the bag of groceries she'd just bought. Pollock couldn't have wished for a better response.

The footage of Bruce Thomas was shot a short time later. One of Dan's staff had traced him to Art's Tavern where he waited, talking to friends, while Sandra shopped. Dan and the cameraman waited outside until they got a sign that Thomas was paying his bill and would be coming out of the tavern. When he saw the camera, Thomas reacted much differently than had his wife. He put up a hand to shield his face and stepped back into the Tavern. When Dan and the cameraman attempted to follow, they became entangled with customers coming out of the tavern and Thomas made good his escape through a back exit. Discovering this, Dan hurried back toward the Thomas's car, where Sandra was waiting. Pollock got there in time to film Bruce jumping into the driver's seat and speeding away—familiar footage for PBI.

18

A sanguine Dan Pollock sat with other members of the crew in the former living room of the rented house on Lake Leelanau. Broadcast time approached for the show they had put together and taped earlier. Dan was happy because he had a real scoop. He even imagined, as he sat expectantly, that he would be given credit for cracking the case.

The broadcast started. All in the room were silent as Dan began developing the background story of the murder: Silvio's rise to fame, his building the magnificent vacation home, the fateful and tragic party. Dan dramatically described the party and the New York guests as if he were describing the ballroom of the Titanic. Now came the big revelation: Silvio Rossi and Sandra Thomas were involved sexually. His delivery of this big surprise had a cadence that should have been accompanied by kettledrums. Next came the scene of the encounter with Sandra outside the store and her bursting into tears when Dan confronted her with the affair. Immediately the audience was treated to the desperate effort of Bruce Thomas to avoid Dan and the camera. Could there be any doubt in the viewers' minds about the lay of the land?

A light chatter started up among the PBI staff, such as one might hear in any living room as the home team scores the touchdown that puts the game on ice.

Now came the footage of Becky and Donna leading Bruce Thomas into Sheriff's Headquarters, giving the false impression that this event followed the previous one. Dan's narration all but stated as fact that Thomas would soon be charged.

"We lit a bonfire under the Leelanau County Sheriff," Pollock didn't actually wink at the audience, but the gloating in his voice amounted to the same thing.

Dan began the wrap-up with a shot of the Rossi house in the background, intoning, "Silvio Rossi invited his lover and her husband to this house for the final party of the summer. Rossi and she planned to continue their affair in New York after his departure from here, but Silvio Rossi never made it to New York for that rendezvous. Most of those at the party had an alibi for the time when it would have been possible to go down to the barbecue area and kill America's favorite chef. [telephoto shot of the side terrace] One man at the party had no alibi for this critical time . . . and his wife was sexually involved with the murdered man.

"This information was totally unknown to the local sheriff before we informed him. Don't be surprised if this case now comes to a speedy close.

"This is Dan Pollock broadcasting from Leelanau County, Michigan" A pause and then the signature close, "Americans deserve to know. We are your watchmen, America."

As Dan's face with its serious, concerned expression was replaced on the screen by an SUV charging up an impossibly steep and rutted trail everyone in the room cheered and those next to Dan gave him fives. They were all sure PBI had climbed back to a respectable position. There was, of course, the problem of where the program would go from here. Courtroom coverage was a daytime production and not suited to the show. This might well be PBI's last stand, but it was a way to bow out that would leave them all welcome guests, be it professionally or socially, from then on.

• • •

152

Barclay Scott, the owner of the Riverside Inn in Leland, turned from looking at the TV screen to address the man sitting across the bar from him. "Puke," Scott said and sighed.

Deputy David Wick smiled. "You're ornery and unappreciative. That man works hard to represent America—asks the questions you want to have asked. You must not be an American."

Barclay responded with a growl. "What's this he's claiming about the Thomas guy, Dave?"

"Don't know for sure. I wasn't there when Thomas was brought in for questioning but I've not heard anything about charging him."

"Pollock's just blowing smoke then?"

David shrugged. "Who knows? I suppose I've always had this idea the big media, the networks, have access to information the rest of us don't get."

Barclay said, "I know what you mean." He pulled a draft for another patron, took it to him and returned. Coming back he added, "We feel that way about most authority don't we? We're sure our President or military is on top of things, acting on good information unavailable to us and then we learn differently."

Wick laughed, "A guy I know, who lives up here now, but was once a top engineer for one of the big three auto companies, gave me the definition of an expert—a bullshitter from out-of-town."

"That makes Dan Pollock an expert for sure. Every time I see Hoss, I tell him that life's all done with mirrors," Scott said.

"Tell you what, Barclay, draw me another *real* glass of beer."

• • •

"DAN POLLOCK POINTS TO KILLER" So read the banner headline of The Leelanau Clarion.

"Dan Pollock disclosed on his regular show, PBI, last night that he had informed the Leelanau County Sheriff's Department early in the day of information his staff had acquired about the murder of Silvio Rossi. Pollock said the Sheriff's Department had not known that Sandra Thomas, one of the guests at the party where Mr. Rossi died, was his lover. Pollock further stated that the woman's husband, Bruce Thomas, was one of the few people at the party who had no alibi for his whereabouts for the critical few minutes in which the famous chef was murdered.

Bruce and Sandra Thomas live in The Homestead Resort complex near Glen Arbor. Thomas, a computer software designer, and his wife moved to this area two years ago when the Thomas's twin daughters entered the high school at the Interlochen Center for the Arts.

"When reached by this paper last night for a statement, the Leelanau Sheriff's Department declined to comment."

• • •

"One of those TV reporters outside came up to me as I came in the building just now and asked if we would do them a favor and let them know when we were going to arrest Thomas. They would be able to get better pictures if they had a little lead time to set up their equipment." Russ Preva said this to the group as they assembled for the morning briefing.

"I know," returned Hoss in a grumble, standing at the blackboard at the front of the room. "Tell me this kind of pressure from the media doesn't influence a lot of police action. Mistakes are made, interrogations do not follow proper procedure to the point that evidence becomes inadmissible in court and the names of witnesses who have asked to remain anonymous become known."

154

Hoss had written assignments on the board before the deputies came in. He turned and pointed to the first item.

"Russ, I want you to go to the Homestead and pick up Sandra Thomas. She was told last night we would come for her first thing this morning. If the reporters try to follow you when you're going there, try to shake them by making it look like a routine patrol."

"He means stop for coffee at The Stone House."

Hoss would usually have joined in the laugh, but bothering him once again was the idea that he and the department were acting out a script written for them by Dan Pollock.

"Donna, Becky, I want you to wait until Russ gets . . ."

The phone rang in the room. All calls were normally held until after the morning briefing. They all watched Hoss answer.

"Oh God," he said in a voice out of which the bottom had dropped. "Who reported this? Is he still on the line? No? Was he sure?"

Hoss listened, said something inaudible into the phone, hung-up and turned to the group.

"Sandra Thomas hanged herself. Her husband just found her in the garage."

19

There was absolute stillness in the room. What he'd just heard on the phone hit Hoss especially hard. She'd been told that she'd be questioned in the morning. Had this precipitated her suicide? He took a deep breath and reminded himself there were actions that must be immediately taken. He picked up the phone again.

"Kate, first call the Glen Arbor Fire Department, then the State Police and have the crime-scene unit go to the Thomas place—that's Bruce Thomas at the Homestead. Notify Doc Bahle. Call Thomas and tell him not to leave the house or talk to anyone. Tell him we're on our way."

"Don, get your camera and other stuff. When we get there, Russ, tape off an area that keeps the goddamn media a block away—so far away even their telescopic lens won't be able to get a picture of the Thomas home. C'mon everyone, we're all going to the Homestead."

The life support vehicle from the Glen Arbor Fire Department arrived first. The several reporters and the single camera crew, who had spent the night at the bottom of the steep driveway, followed the truck up to the house like a bunch of seals following a bucket of fish. A guy with a minicam was actually trying to get a shot through the window of the house when Russ Preva's face appeared in his viewfinder.

Russ, the first deputy to arrive, tried to get the reporters to leave the Thomas property. They ignored him until he arrested one recalcitrant member of their lot and locked him in the patrol car.

He yelled to those remaining, "Obstructing the police in the course of their duty. Who wants to be next?"

They reluctantly retreated. A barrier was finally set up at the bottom of the hill where the road leading to the Thomas driveway intersected the main resort road. Only those who lived on the road were permitted to pass. Threats were shouted at Preva that his actions violated the freedom of the press and the network would take legal action. Russ told them they were making too much noise—disturbing the peace.

Hoss had waited for Don Silver to gather his equipment before leaving headquarters with Becky and Donna in a van. He paused a moment on the asphalt apron in front of the Thomas home before entering. From the hilltop site, one could see the shore of Lake Michigan through a gap in the thickly surrounding woods. Sided in cedar left to gray naturally, the house projected the image of home . . . and comfort.

"OK if I go down and give Russ a hand?" asked Becky.

"Good idea," agreed Hoss.

He turned and entered the open front door. Don and Donna followed, knowing there was no way to prepare for what awaited them.

From the entrance hall, Hoss noticed Bruce Thomas sitting in a sunroom off the main living room, sitting and staring at the floor.

"Donna, go and talk to him. Let him tell his story."

A paramedic stood waiting in the kitchen for the police to arrive. Seeing Hoss, he turned and led them through the utility room into the garage.

Another paramedic was standing near the back wall of the garage. Sandra Thomas's body lay alongside a black Mercedes sedan in the narrow space between the car and the garage wall. Her face was deep, mottled purple above the rope ligature around her neck.

"We haven't touched her beyond determining that she was dead. Rigor has begun in the arm muscles," the man offered. He pointed toward the car's hood. "Her husband cut her down. Looks like she climbed onto the hood, tied the rope to the ceiling joist, put the noose around her neck, and stepped off the hood."

Scanning the hood of the Mercedes, while the man talked, Hoss could see bare footprints in the dust on the metal.

"The stage of rigor means five or six hours—She did it in the middle of the night," he murmured. He spoke then to the paramedic. "You fellas can go. The State Police will have to examine her. A county van can take the body to the morgue."

The man clearly had distaste for the scene and was happy to be excused.

Hoss thought about the meaning of the suicide. Sandra Thomas had been called the night before and told that the police would be at her home the next morning to bring her to headquarters for questioning. The obvious conclusion was that she couldn't face the interrogation. Did it mean she knew her husband had killed Rossi and blamed herself? Did she not want to go through all which that entailed—a trial, a conviction, and a life sentence for the man she had caused to become so enraged that he killed in order to expunge his humiliation? She probably thought she couldn't live through her own guilt for bringing on the degradation attending the events the next months would hold for her and her children. Better to end it right here in the family garage. Not that that would do her children much good, Hoss thought, but when a person has reached the desperation necessary for suicide his or her judgment tends to jump the tracks. It occurred to him that there was likely to be a suicide note, a note in which Sandra Thomas must have repeated these same thoughts. She would have left it in a place where her husband would be sure to find it. Hoss wondered if Donna knew of a note—had been given it to read. He had an impulse to break in on the conversation she was having with Thomas and satisfy his curiosity, but he held back. Better to let Donna handle it her way without interruption.

Don Silver had returned to the utility room to unpack his photographic equipment. Hoss, left alone, looked over the body of Sandra Thomas more carefully. He had never seen her before. She must have been an attractive woman. Silvio Rossi, by the reports he'd recently heard, was a connoisseur and collector of beautiful women. No trace of Sandra's beauty remained now except her long, blond hair spread over the concrete floor. What a total tragedy, he thought.

Hoss left the garage and went through the utility room to the kitchen. He passed Don Silver and a State Police trooper who had just arrived. Hoss picked up an empty glass he saw on the kitchen counter and filled it at the sink. He barely nodded at the crime unit as they passed through into the garage. He stood with his back to the counter and took a couple of swallows of the water. He pictured Dan Pollock crowing into the camera about how he had solved the case, a case which may have gone unsolved had it not been for the acuteness of PBI's staff.

Donna had heard Hoss come into the kitchen. She excused herself, telling Bruce Thomas she would be back immediately. She had an envelope in her hand, which she held out to Hoss.

"There were two suicide notes, one she left for her husband and children, which he still has. This one is sealed and is addressed, Leelanau County Sheriff. I've got to get back to him so I don't lose the rapport." She turned to leave.

"Wait a minute. Do you know what the other letter says?"

"What he's told me. She's deeply sorry, but she can't go on, knowing she has ruined her home. He said that she's been depressed for almost a year. Took antidepressants. Gotta go back."

Hoss looked at the letter in his hand. Would it be a repetition of her morbid self-accusing thoughts she'd expressed to her husband? Might it also say that she blamed herself for her husband's action?

Hoss slipped the letter out of the envelope and laid the envelope on the counter. The letter had been written on a word processor and printed. He began to read.

"September 3, 2007   4 A.M.

Sheriff,

I am writing this note to you, because you must understand some facts about my marriage, which will help you to see that the accusation that man Pollock made about my husband last night on television is totally false. A year ago, Bruce and I reached an amicable agreement to divorce as soon as our daughters graduated from high school. We had recognized that we'd become different people now and with different interests than those we shared twenty years ago when we married. My husband had met a more compatible woman through his work whom he plans to marry as soon as we get our divorce. I am perfectly in agreement with this. In addition, my husband knew of my relationship with Silvio and didn't object as long as I was discreet. He was very—as am I—concerned that our daughters' lives not be disturbed unnecessarily by our attempts to work out our own lives.

My point is my husband had no motive for killing Silvio. Not only is it completely unlike him to do such a thing, but he also saw that my relationship with Silvio made me happy. Bruce's worry about my emotional problem was relieved when he saw the hope

160

that my love for Silvio gave me.

I am going to take my life, as soon as I finish this letter, because I have lost that hope that I briefly had. I have destroyed my daughters' lives. I cry when I think of the humiliation they must now feel. They can no longer love me. Bruce no longer loves me and I can't live without Silvio's love.

Please understand that Bruce is innocent. I have no idea who killed the man I loved, but if I did, please believe that I would tell you.

Goodbye"

The signature, Sandra Thomas, was written with a ballpoint pen.

Stunned, Hoss reread the woman's farewell. The note had not been what he was prepared for. "That poor unhappy woman," he murmured. Tears came to his eyes. What a fragile base for her hope, a love for this man who, Donna was sure, would have returned to New York and shrugged off any attempts she made to see or talk to him. Hoss wondered if her husband knew of Rossi's reputation with women. Actively now, Hoss directed his attention to the part of the letter that bore on his main interest, the denial of Bruce Thomas's guilt. The case she made in the letter was certainly convincing. If what she claimed about her marriage was true, Bruce Thomas's motive for murder had evaporated.

Hoss's thoughts skipped back to a question he had just asked himself: Did Bruce Thomas know about Rossi's reputation? If he did, wouldn't he expect his wife to be dumped by Rossi? Wouldn't he foresee this as a potential blow to his wife and her emotional stability? Was it possible that believing she could handle her lover's death easier than his betrayal, Thomas had chosen to act and kill Silvio Rossi?

He reconsidered. OK, it made some sense, but it was a stretch—far out actually. Most likely Thomas knew nothing of the chef's love life beyond the affair with his wife. Thomas was a busy man, a software consultant. He probably knew or cared nothing about TV chefs. And, murder to prevent depression? He rubbed his broad forehead, surprised by his unusual flight of imagination.

Donna came into the kitchen. She had the other suicide letter in her hand and held it out silently toward Hoss. He could tell she did not trust herself to speak without crying. Hoss read the letter. He felt the same sadness, but he also objectively discerned how distorted Sandra Thomas's judgment had become, how distorted the judgment of a very depressed, suicidal person can be. Her certainty of her worthlessness was based on such unimportant and meaningless evidence. He wanted to reach back and shake her.

An angry declaration from Donna broke into his rumination. "Her death is Dan Pollock's fault!"

Her vehemence startled him so that it took seconds before he considered her words. Yes, what Donna said was no doubt true. If Pollock hadn't made Sandra's affair with Rossi public, hadn't broadcast it to the nation, the woman would only have suffered the loss of a man she loved and not the additional burden of having thought she had brought shame to her daughters.

Hoss said nothing, but handed Donna the letter that had been addressed to him and watched as she absorbed its meaning.

"That son-of-a-bitch," she spit out as she'd finished reading. Involuntarily her hands formed claws that were meant for Pollock's face. Hoss had never seen his beautiful deputy so angry. He watched as she passed through the steps to regain her control.

"What are you going to do, Hoss?"

"I'm going to hold a press conference."

Hoss followed Donna into the room where Bruce Thomas sat

alone. Hoss sat down opposite him and handed him the note Sandra had addressed to the Sheriff. Thomas nodded as he read, until he came to the final paragraph and here he began to sob.

Hoss waited in silence until the other man wiped his eyes and looked at him again.

"Mr. Thomas, I plan to give copies of this letter to the press. I'm doing this for several reasons, but before I do, I think it is important to go over all this with your daughters. They should read this letter—a copy of it—before it's made public."

"I agree. After that guy broadcast the fact that Sandra and Rossi were involved with each other, both of us talked to the girls on the phone last night and promised we would sit down together this weekend and discuss it completely. After I called you, when I found Sandra, I phoned them and told them what had happened. I was afraid the press would find out and immediately broadcast it. I did not want my daughters to learn about their mother's death on television. I'm going to drive down to the school now. I'll give them a copy of this letter."

Bruce Thomas took them into his office and made a copy of the suicide note, and as he did, he began to imagine the effect its being made public would have on Dan Pollock. He began to feel a little better.

He handed the copy to Hoss and said, "I think I know what one of your reasons is for going public."

Hoss smiled and brought his huge hand down on the man's shoulder.

"Take care."

20

As soon as Dan Pollock heard that Hoss had announced a press conference, he had no doubt he'd scored. He'd already been told about the suicide, so, the announcement, coming as it did immediately after the sheriff had been to the Thomas's home, could only mean one thing; a suicide note had been found, in which the dead woman named her husband as her lover's killer and explained her suicide as a result of her guilt for having precipitated his jealous rage. Pollock called the news editor of his network and convinced him that a live, on-the-scene news-break was in order. The timing of the press conference coincided with a time when a good share of American housewives watched their favorite soap. What could be more fascinating than a news-break concerning real-life melodrama?

Pollock, Art Brock and members of the show's staff who weren't involved in the live broadcast, sat in the living room of the rented house watching the afternoon soap, "Days of Destiny". They were all in high spirit. Joking remarks, mostly sexually tinged, were being flung-out toward the show's characters. Pollock popped the tab on a beer and filled his glass.

"Hey quiet! Here it is," shouted one of the staff.

The serious faced man behind a New York "news-desk" looked into the camera and announced that the regularly scheduled program was being interrupted to bring viewers a breaking story.

"We now go live to a news conference that has been hurriedly called by the sheriff of the county in which the famous chef, Silvio Rossi, was murdered."

The face of the on-the-scene reporter appeared. In a hushed voice, he said he was inside a conference room in the Leelanau County Sheriff's Department, where, shortly, they expected Sheriff Davis to make an announcement of the arrest of the man who had murdered Silvio Rossi. Noise of footsteps and voices filled in the background and the television screen now showed a very tall heavily built man in uniform preparing to seat himself at a table facing several cameras. Everyone fell silent.

His expression deadly serious, Hoss placed a sheet of paper on the table and looked into the camera.

"I have decided to hold this press conference in order to correct misleading speculation reported on television and by the press that, in my opinion, has led to tragic consequences. I want to share the information we now have in the hope further hurt may be halted."

Dan Pollock had poured beer into a glass, but the act of lifting the glass stopped halfway to his mouth. Where the hell was this guy going with this preamble? Misleading speculation? What the hell did that mean?

Hoss took his reading glasses from the breast pocket of his shirt. Before putting them on he said, "At approximately four a.m. this morning Mrs. Sandra Thomas committed suicide at her house in Glen Arbor. Mrs. Thomas and her husband were the subjects of the speculation I just mentioned. I am going to read the suicide note that Mrs. Thomas addressed to me."

Hoss put his glasses on, cleared his throat and mentally prepared himself to read through the whole note without giving in to the emotions that overcame him during his first reading.

No one breathed in the living room of the house on Lake Leelanau. Pollock's beer-glass remained a few inches from his lips. When Hoss read the final, "Goodbye", an involuntary, "Oh, shit," escaped from Art Brock.

Brock, the realist, knew instantly that it was all over for PBI. Dan Pollock instinctively began to search for a defense, but the fear he felt meant he knew the same truth. He wasn't yet able to let himself form the simple sentence that had already flashed in neon in Brock's awareness: Our hasty and stupid need to win led to a woman's suicide. Brock also knew what must follow as well as he knew the line that comes after, "To be or not to be." Tomorrow's op-ed columns across the country would be devoted to the evils of irresponsible journalism. He got up and walked outside. He didn't want to be there to answer the call he expected would come any moment from New York.

21

Hoss walked into his office to find that the deputies who had been working on the Rossi case, had naturally gathered there. They stood looking toward him, waiting for some direction. Inwardly they sensed that the case, which for a time seemed to have been taken from them by Dan Pollock, had been returned to their hands. Hoss recognized their need for leadership. He needed to give it, but at the same time he wanted to avoid seeming to preempt Donna. It wouldn't be fair after allowing her to bear the burden of responsibility through these past difficult days.

"I think Dan Pollock and his bunch got their fingers burned badly enough so we won't be bothered by them any longer," he ventured. "Others are still going to be here appraising our progress daily—hourly. We've got to ignore them and concentrate on our investigation."

It is remarkable how a group experiencing a weakening of cohesion and confidence can be reunited and given purpose by a few words from a leader it respects.

Hoss leaned over and took two sheets of paper from the drawer of his desk and handed them to Donna.

"As we've already suspected," Hoss said, "we didn't get much help from the forensic unit. I got their report this morning. I'll summarize: fingerprints on murder weapon smudged and unidentifiable, prints on two of the other skewers, Silvio Rossi's and two unidentified others, but Rossi's are superimposed, meaning he handled the skewers last—possibly even at the time they were presented to him. Only Rossi's prints are on the kettle handles.

Donna asked the techs to go back and see if they could lift prints on the handle of the door leading from the small study onto the spiral stairs. The only clear prints were Donna's.

"There is a another fact they pointed out. The angle of the sword thrust was upward. It entered the back two inches to the left of the spine and between the seventh and eight ribs and exited four inches to the left of the midline, between the fourth and fifth. According to the autopsy report by Doc Bahle, the blade passed through the left ventricle of the heart and nicked the fifth rib on exit."

Hoss went to the blackboard and quickly sketched the outline of a man and indicated the path of the skewer.

"Doc qualified his report with a lot of ifs-and-buts. As I make it out, it comes down to this: doubt is thrown on a very short or a very tall person having done it. He reasons this way: most people would thrust forward at waist level and aim toward the heart upward at about a forty-degree angle. A person of the same height as Rossi, five-nine, would perfectly fit the requirement of the angle if Rossi was standing erect. However, and this is likely, if Rossi had been leaning forward over his work, then the thrust would have entered between lower ribs. However a taller person's thrust would then enter at the point it did on the corpse. The significance of the angle is further blurred when you consider a lunge originating, not at the waist, but at shoulder height, much as a fencer would execute."

Hoss smiled at the group just as a teacher might after having just explained the reasoning behind Einstein's General Theory of Relativity.

"I've studied your descriptions of our suspects, and I've concluded each of them physically comes within the limits of possibility. Vince DeSica, described as 'over six foot' in Becky's report nudges the top of that limit."

"Rules out Donna, too," quipped Russ Preva.

168

"Thanks, Russ," Donna replied.

"DeSica," Hoss went on, "although he has no alibi, is not a serious suspect: He has no motive. Rossi's death, we've learned from Rossi's emails, actually hurt him. Almost certainly Bruce Thomas has now been removed from the list. That leaves us with: Karen Forbes, the woman Rossi threatened to expose for taking side money for her restaurant reviews, Frank Knowles, Rossi's producer, whom it seems he was about to replace and the two plagiarist authors Rossi threatened to expose.

"Donna, what do you think our next step should be?

Hoss seemed determined to maintain her position as lead investigator. She both liked and disliked this. What could she do but try her best to soldier on.

She replied, "We now know of motives for this group that we didn't have when they were first questioned. We need to question them again using the information we now have."

Hoss nodded. "My take on this Karen Forbes is she's a shrinking violet. She would be likely to whine and plead with Rossi, but wouldn't have the gumption to run him through with a barbecue skewer. The authors? No one we've questioned seems to know much about either him or her. Finally we have Frank Knowles. Rossi's publicist told Donna that Knowles is a guy who collects antique porcelain—not the profile of your average killer.

"Like Donna said, we faced an unusual situation at the time of the initial interviews. Party guests from out of town had very sound reasons for going home. Normally, suspects are still in the area, or become very conspicuous if they leave town. If we question these three again, it means someone has to take a trip to New York. With our barebones budget and tax payers like Ben Petoskey attending every County Commission meeting studying our expenditures as if the cost of every paper clip we use came out of their pocket alone,

I hate to have to spend the money to send someone to New York—but I must."

Hoss knew whom he wanted to send. Donna, with her experience as a sales rep for Kellogg, had more of the polish he associated with a New York appearance. Like a good parent, he had to avoid seeming to have a favorite, since they would all see this assignment as out of the ordinary.

"Don, you're our designated interrogator, but I can't spare you. You are also our liaison guy with the state lab. To make sure we spend as little of Petoskey's money as possible, I guess it comes down to which one of you best knows your way around New York." Hoss already knew the answer.

"Becky, how about you?"

"Senior trip in high school."

"Well, that's a start. Russ?"

"For our tenth anniversary, Julie and I had a big weekend. Saw 'Cats'."

"David?"

"I couldn't make the senior trip—strep throat."

Hoss looked at Donna.

"I guess I fit the job profile; worked there for a year when I got out of college and my college roommate lives in Manhattan. She'll put me up for a few nights. That would make one less item on the expense account for Petoskey to complain about."

"You're hired. I want you to leave as soon as possible. Better prepare yourself by learning all you can about the backgrounds of these four: published books and so on, where the authors are concerned and as much as you can about the producer's and TV reviewer's bios. Anything else you can think of that would help you?"

"How about a syringe of 'truth serum'?"

"Truth serum? You must have been watching old movies."

22

It had been five years since Donna had been in the city. Walking along Madison Avenue now, she thought it looked much the same. If anything, less busy, but that was probably the hour, a quarter past ten in the morning. A current of cooler air had slipped into the city overnight like a calling card for autumn. The day was clear but the temperature had caused a number of those Donna passed on the sidewalk to have put on sweaters and light jackets.

Earlier in the morning, she had sat down with a cup of coffee at a "Post-It" plastered table with her friend, April's, two kids and their nanny. April and her husband, Josh, had already departed for their long day as officers in that army of finely tuned and highly energized professionals who made New York hum..

"This is yours," Giselle, the nanny, said as she selected one of the notes and, as if she were a card dealer, stuck it down again in front of Donna.

"T ballet cls doing SLk Ask." Donna stared at the cryptic message. She knew then how much had changed in her life, since the time when she'd had to face this level of challenge before morning coffee.

Teresa, April's nine-year old, said, "She means that my ballet class is putting on Swan Lake and you should ask me about it. I'm going to be one of the cygnets."

"You are? I mean that's wonderful," Donna burst out with genuine enthusiasm. She sensed immediately that her response was out-of-line in this home where the mother was Associate Editor of Rolling Stone and the father the foreign currency manager for Goldman Sachs. For Teresa to be picked to dance the short but classic role of one of the young swans in Swan Lake meant only the accomplishment of what was expected of her, a mere indication that she remained "on track"—not worthy of an accolade. For Teresa to have responded to Donna's excitement in kind would be to have admitted that she also regarded her accomplishment as special. She believed her parents held higher goals for her.

Donna felt sad for the little girl, but then reminded herself that life-styles came in different sizes. Teresa gave no indication of thinking she was missing out on the simple pleasures.

Soon Sheridan, the seven-year old brother, had adjusted his iPod and the nanny and the two kids were off by taxi to their private school.

Donna, left alone, finished her coffee. She had done her home-work assignment on the bios of the cookbook authors, Nuvolari and Seabold, and on Karen Forbes and Frank Knowles. She had found fairly legitimate and predictable material. Nuvolari was Italian. She had a doctor's degree from the University of London in economics. Following this she had been on the faculty of that school and now held a faculty position at NYU. Seabold was New York born, bred and schooled with a bachelor's degree in English from Cornell and an MBA from Columbia. He'd worked for years for a big publishing house and was now retired. Neither had much experience as far as Donna could uncover in food preparation. This seemed to support their plagiarizing a cookbook.

Frank Knowles's career had followed a straight line from a BA in communications from Northwestern through an entry-level position at an Indianapolis TV station, moving on to New York in 1975 where he held various production-related jobs, culminating with Cucina da Silvio. He'd divorced at thirty-four and never remarried.

Karen Forbes had gone to Barnard majoring in journalism. She wrote restaurant reviews for a magazine, then for the *Post* and then on to her TV spot.

Donna had managed to set up appointments with Forbes, Nuvolari and Knowles on the first full day she'd be in the city, but Seabold insisted he couldn't find time to see her until two days later—a good thing for the Sheriff's Department's budget that April and Josh had taken her in.

Karen Forbes stipulated that her attorney must be present at the interview. At nine-thirty Donna was shown into the lawyer's office. A sober appearing man and a hostile looking restaurant reviewer faced Donna. At first, Donna posed innocuous questions about Forbes's relationship with the murdered man. Forbes represented the friendship with Silvio to be without blemish. Donna then confronted her with the e-mail evidence. It was clear to Donna that this was the first the attorney had heard this information, but before he could respond in his professional capacity, Forbes vehemently denied the allegation that she had taken money for good reviews.

"Marcel Gautier told Silvio a lie. I panned Oiseau Verte because it deserved it. I am a reviewer; naturally there are times I must give a negative review. I was—"

"Karen, I believe I would like to review this matter with . . . "

"No, I have nothing to hide. They can look at my bank records and see if there are deposits that coincide with my good reviews. Silvio was way off base by making such an accusation and I went to Michigan with the purpose of setting him straight. When I saw him go downstairs to begin cooking, I thought it might be a good time to talk to him alone. But, one can never tell what is—what was—a good time to talk to Silvio. He could be receptive, or quite otherwise. I got cold feet and decided to wait until later. That is all there is to this whole nonsense."

And, that concluded the whole interview. Any attempt to open the issue again was either blocked by the attorney, who repeated that his client had already answered the question, or by Forbes's reiteration that Donna had been told the truth.

Hoss would certainly have had to alter his opinion of her as a "shrinking violet" if he'd been here, Donna thought.

Donna had no time to mull over the meaning of the meeting before she had to hurry to her appointment with Patrizia Nuvolari. Donna had set-up the meeting by taking the direct route of calling the author at her home, the unlisted number having been supplied by the NYPD. Nuvolari sounded surprised to hear who was calling and that Donna requested an interview with her. She didn't hesitate for long to suggest to Donna they meet for this talk at the office of Nuvolari's literary agent. Donna suspected Nuvolari wanted a witness. She entered the agent's building, now, wondering if the author would take the same rigid stance as Karen Forbes.

Donna identified herself to the agent's secretary, who took her straightway to an office, where both author and agent awaited her, a quizzical expression on the face of each.

"Thank you for arranging to see me so promptly," Donna began, "I have come to New York to further our investigation of the murder of Mr. Rossi, as I'm sure you've guessed."

"Yes," replied the author, who retained a strong Italian accent in spite of her years in England and the U.S. "We thought so, but I can't imagine why you'd want to talk to me."

"It's your relationship with Mr. Rossi that interests us. How did you come to know him and for how long?"

Nuvolari made the Italian shrug, shoulders drawn together, chin thrust forward and up. "Silvio? I've known Silvio many years. Not well, understand. Not close friends, but we are, after all, both Italian. I eat at his restaurant half dozen times a year." Another shrug. "That's all."

"And yet, he invited you to his party in Michigan."

"Well, yes, but that was something else."

"Something else? What do you mean?" Donna asked, recognizing a possible entry into the subject of plagiarism.

Nulvolari looked to be in a quandary. She looked over to her agent, who listened as an attorney might. The author made a motion with her hands signifying she could only answer by going into a long explanation.

"It was Silvio's way to apologize and I, that is John Seabold and I, thought we had better go along with this or Silvio . . . Well, we wanted to be on good terms with Silvio. He had much influence, of course, in the field of our new book—Italian cooking."

Silvio apologize? Donna was puzzled. "I don't understand, Ms. Nuvolari."

"It was nothing really. A misunderstanding."

Donna decided to play some of her cards. "We have a copy of correspondence between Mr. Rossi and your publisher. In it Mr. Rossi threatens to reveal a fact about your new book."

"You have . . . you have that letter?"

"Yes, we do."

At this point the lawyer in the agent kicked in. "My client is unprepared to continue this interview without the benefit of legal council. I suggest . . . "

"No, Kirby, it's all right. I begin to understand why Deputy Roper is here, why they think . . . Yes, I understand now." She had turned toward the agent as she said this and now faced Donna again. "First, have you spoken to John Seabold yet?"

"No I haven't. I thought I would talk to you first."

"That's good. Maybe what I tell you will satisfy you and you won't have to involve John. You see John is the father of my daughter's husband. I asked him to help me with this book project, because he had experience in publishing. He said he'd be happy to advise me and told me to feel free to call him. I then faced up to how much of his time this would likely involve if I really did make use of his know-how every time I needed it. I knew I'd feel guilty and end up not asking for his advice when I really should. But, if he were a co-author, he'd be paid and I hoped he would also see the book as his project. He was reluctant at first, but in the end, I convinced him. It has worked out well, but I would not want to involve him with the police. I don't want him to be sorry he agreed to work with me."

There was nothing in what the woman had just said that spoke to the issue of plagiarism.

Patrizia Nuvolari continued. "We were all shocked when Silvio sent that letter to the editor at Random House. The editor then called Kirby, and she called John and me. It was decided that since I knew Silvio, it would be less formal, and less embarrassing for Silvio if I talked to him."

You mean, pleaded with him not to expose the plagiarism, thought Donna. Embarrassing for Silvio?

"He agreed to see me, she continued, but told me it would do no good to ask him to change his mind. He was short with me and I could say nothing to him on the phone, so I went to his restaurant where he said he would give me a minute of his time. I sat down in his office and he frowned and looked at me cold as a stone. I told him I understood the reason for his anger. I told him I would be angry also, but that the problem had arisen because, busy as he always was, he had not taken time to look at the whole book. And then, I opened the book I had brought with me to the forward page and asked him to take a moment to read the first couple of paragraphs."

Patrizia Nuvolari smiled at the memory of that moment. She reached for and took a copy of her cookbook off the agent's desk.

"First of all, the book was in the public domain as far as the United States is concerned. The author did not renew his copyright. Now, what Silvio read, and I have to add, what you would also have read if you had taken the time, is this," she began to read. " 'We have undertaken to bring today's lovers of Italian cuisine a classic book on the subject. We have included the equivalent measure by volume used in the United States along with the measure by weight as used in Italy. In addition we suggest alternate ingredients that are more available to America's cooks. We hope in this way we can truly revive this incomparable work by Regio Ricci and reawaken this treasure of Italian cuisine.' "

Contritely, she said, "I can't blame Silvio entirely for misunderstanding our purpose. On the dust jacket—see here—there is the title, *A Tuscan Table,* and below this in large print it says, 'A Revival of the Italian Classic, *Da una Tabella Toscana* by Regio Ricci'. Unfortunately, on the advance reader's copy of the book, the printer had made an error on the color of the subtitle. It was close to the background color of the dust jacket and, therefore, very difficult to read. The error was caught almost immediately and corrected, and the advance reader's copies that had been sent out were replaced. Unfortunately, Silvio happened to get and read one of the early books with the error.

"Silvio had opened the book and scanned through it, recognized Ricci's recipes and became furious. Like I told Silvio, I would have also . . . if I had not then given a friend some benefit of the doubt and looked into the book more carefully. Well, Silvio was very embarrassed when he realized his mistake. He made an appointment with the Random House editor and went in person to apologize." She smiled at Donna, "And, he invited me and John Seabold to his party—and we decided to go."

Donna sat quietly for several moments. She hadn't looked at

the book at all. She figured she'd have no way of comparing the recipes without the original book and had taken Silvio Rossi's word for the plagiarism.

She shook her head and with chagrin said, "I . . . I seem to owe you an apology also. I didn't read the forward either. I'm sorry I wasted your time."

Donna thanked the two women for clearing up a point that had been important to their investigation. She got up to leave and started toward the office door. She had intended to ask another question of the author, but the surprising and embarrassing outcome of the interview had erased the question. She couldn't remember what it was.

Over a lunch of cold sesame noodles in a small Chinese restaurant in SOHO, she reviewed her morning. The authors' motive had evaporated and common sense said they were no longer suspects. Karen Forbes's denial of the truth of Rossi's e-mail accusation meant little. It did mean that a lot of work, work beyond the capacity of her department's budget, would be necessary to disprove Forbes's denial. Her offer to have her bank records checked could either mean Forbes was telling the truth, or just that she had done something else with the money other than putting it in her bank. Karen Forbes's name stayed on the two-suspect list—at the bottom. Frank Knowles's name now rose to the top.

The office of Silvio Rossi Enterprises occupied the second-floor of a converted warehouse a block and a half from Restaurante Lucretius. Waiting for the elevator, Donna remembered the question she had intended to ask Patrizia Nuvolari: Did anyone use the door to the spiral staircase while she and John Seabold were sitting in that side room? She fervently wished now that she had asked it. Frank Knowles would have found it so easy, drifting around looking at Rossi's art collection, to slip onto the stairs and be out on the side terrace with Rossi in a matter of seconds.

The elevator door opened and interrupted her thoughts. She walked in and pressed the button that read, "Silvio Rossi Enterprises". When the door reopened, Donna found herself directly looking into a large office-space. A high ceiling supported by ornamental iron columns drew her gaze upward. Her attention was abruptly redirected to life back at floor level, when she heard her name spoken.

"Deputy Roper?"

An attractive dark-haired woman wearing a sari sat looking at her.

"Yes. Yes, I'm Deputy Roper. I have an appointment with Frank Knowles," she replied, while immediately realizing she was stating the obvious.

The woman smiled, guessing Donna's thoughts. "Yes, he is expecting you. Please come with me."

The room the receptionist led Donna across was light and airy due to the many floor-to-ceiling windows. Several people were working at computers and copiers. Donna now noticed that three corners of the space had been separated into cubes, creating offices which were insulated and private. The receptionist knocked on the door of the cube in the northwest corner. At a response, she opened the door for Donna and announced her name.

"Deputy Roper," exclaimed Frank Knowles, striding forward to meet her. "What a pleasure to see you again so soon."

Donna doubted very much that he was happy to see her.

"Thank you for seeing me today, Mr. Knowles."

"Frank. Please call me Frank."

"Right," thought Donna. "As part of our investigation," she said, "We are interviewing some of the party guests again."

"Ah, I see. And why am I one of those you have selected?"

"Because you are one of the few people who have no one to

verify where you were while someone killed Mr. Rossi."

"But I was with the others doing the party thing."

"So you've claimed."

Knowles was among those who had met the first sally of colder weather into the city by coming to the office in a black turtleneck sweater of an exotic blend. The construction and drape of the material caused it to hang in those indefinable lines that declared to the world that the wearer is a member of a superior class—at least a class able to afford that garment. The sweater once again proved a fact that Donna, with the small sum she could afford for the purpose, hated to admit; expensive clothing made you look better. Frank Knowles looked comfortable: comfortably well off, comfortably secure in his opinion of himself and no doubt living an enviably comfortable life style. Donna intended now to destroy the comfort he may be enjoying, thinking he'd gotten away with murder.

"Mr. Knowles, when we last spoke, you told me the television show was dead. I believe your words were, 'It was the Silvio Rossi show, without him, nothing.' When I asked you what plans you had for the future, you told me the answer to the question ranked with the question about life's meaning." Donna paused as Knowles recalled the conversation with a satisfied appreciation of the nonchalance of his answer that day and the fact that this gorgeous young woman had remembered it. Donna waited two beats and added, "To see you now, one would neither think your prospects were dead, nor that you had less than a confident notion of where you were heading."

"Really? Seriously, is it that obvious? Things can change in such unexpected ways. Sometimes life really does behave like a Dickens novel; just when it appears there is no hope, an event occurs that causes the black clouds to vanish and the sun to shine.

"I'll stop being obscure: a dandy job came along that I never expected."

Puzzlement showed on Donna's face.

"Let me explain. The show is dead as I said, but I never gave any thought to what would happen with the other aspects of Silvio Rossi Enterprises. I never thought of it, because I'd never been involved. I produced the show, nothing more. Rossi Enterprises involved a vast commercial exploitation of the Rossi name. A managing and marketing firm created it and managed it. I'm only—and with awe—just learning the imaginative inclusion of products whose marketing seems enhanced by adding Silvio's name. One is not surprised that a chef would have his name on cookware, or a commercial grade stove that every home kitchen must have—but on a line of house paints? And, how about ski wear, sports wear, aftershave and a laughably expensive brand of boutique rum, Rum Rossi?

"I'm told that for a time an actual spike in sales can be expected. Partly this is because of the publicity connected with the murder, and then there are the collector types, who believe the termination of the manufacture of Rossi cookware will mean an increase in its value.

"This means there are a lot of assets and continuing income still to be generated by Rossi Enterprises that must be dealt with. This, to my surprise, is where I come in. You see Gina Rossi is not interested in having to think of these details. She has set up a trust to receive all the assets and income and the money will afterward be distributed according to the stipulations of the trust."

Donna followed all this with an ear cocked toward anything bearing on her investigation.

"Stipulations of the trust?" she repeated.

"See how quickly I'm adapting myself to legal lingo? It means charity usually—good works of some kind."

"And, in this case?"

"To my knowledge, Gina hasn't spelled this out yet. Maybe she and the lawyers have drafted something recently."

"I'm a little confused. How is your future affected by all this?"

"Gina has asked me to be a Trustee. Beyond that, as I said before, since she doesn't want to think about and deal with management firms and such, she is paying me a more than decent stipend to act as liaison between her and all those other guys."

Well, well thought Donna, another way he profits from Rossi's death. Did he indeed have no notion that such a job would be in his future?

Frank Knowles continued on, reminiscing now about how chance enters one's life.

"I had made up my mind, as Karen Forbes and I were driving home from Michigan, that I would move to western North Carolina where my two children live with their families. They have been urging me to do this." He smiled impishly. "The coast is clear for me now, since my ex-wife and her husband have moved to Arizona.

"I would buy a small condo and create a web-site on which I would gradually sell off much of my porcelain collection, while communicating with my fellow collectors."

He paused, but Donna said nothing.

"I shall do that eventually," he continued, "But this new opportunity will allow me to build up a bit more reserve, so I need never become the burden that we parents always fear we may become. Besides, I want to help Gina out. She is a very nice person and has always been very friendly towards me. She is not at all the type of person who could cope with business. Having to do so would change who she is—an artist really—and I wouldn't like to see that happen. My job here will be limited: sooner or later Silvio Rossi Enterprises will be terminated and liquidated. After all, I

182

doubt if Sears still sells Mickey Mantle bats.""

It occurred to Knowles that the course of the conversation so far could hardly have coincided with the deputy's purpose in seeking an interview.

"As the saying goes, 'I've talked enough about myself, now what do you think of me?'"

Donna laughed. She remembered that he had made her laugh the day of the murder. "What do I think of you, Mr. Knowles? I think you faced the necessity of contemplating a forced retirement before Silvio Rossi died."

Frank appeared surprised. "I don't understand."

"Oh, I think you do. You see, we have had access to Mr. Rossi's e-mail. We have his computer."

It began to make sense to Frank Knowles. "Ah, yes. I see. Of course you would have read his e-mail. Yes, the messages about an exchange Silvio and I had at the elevator."

"It looks to us as if you were about to be replaced as the producer of Cucina da Silvio by a man named Logan Burgess."

"Yes, that's the way it looked to me too. And, I am belatedly understanding that you are not here today because you find me irresistible—a common wish that men who meet you must have." Frank Knowles laughed, "I mean that, by the way, I'm not trying to divert your attention. Yes, I can see clearly how you'd consider that I'd had a good motive for murder. I confess my thoughts and feelings with the prospect of Burgess succeeding me were murderous —not to the point of any real thought of action, but I was damned angry and afraid, afraid of the embarrassment of it all. But, after I got over the first rush of feeling, I began to weigh what Silvio had said in his e-mail. I had been neglectful of keeping the show on the cutting edge. Hell, he was right. I was bored and I really did desire to retire and pursue my hobby. I went to Michigan with the intention of telling Silvio this at the first opportunity I had to speak to him alone. Talking with Karen Forbes, I learned he was alone at the barbecue kettles and I was actually making a move in that direction when the waitress screamed."

Donna had carefully followed his every word. He had spun a convincing story to wash away his motive for murder. Many possess the facility to build convincing arguments if they can get you to accept but one premise, a false premise that is at the very center of their argument, and the good tale they spin lulls you into missing the falsity—just as one tends to overlook the fact that there is a stick at the core of cotton candy. Donna saw the weakness in his story.

"Mr. Knowles, I have to point out that it is easy for you to make that claim now."

"Yes, I see what you're getting at. What proof have I got?"

He got to his feet and went to a filing cabinet where he opened a drawer and withdrew a letter. He walked over to Donna and handed it to her.

"It's a copy of my letter of resignation. To make sure I wouldn't change my mind if Silvio were to ask me to reconsider my decision, I wrote a letter of resignation and carried it to the network vice-president responsible for the show. I asked him to not contact Silvio until I'd had a chance to tell him myself at his party. I'll make you a copy and you can take it to the network office and compare the letter and the date to the one I gave the vice-president."

Knowles went back to his chair and faced Donna, his smile friendly. "I hate to disappoint you and your sheriff, but I had no reason to kill Silvio Rossi."

When she returned to her friends' apartment, Teresa, Sheridan, and the nanny were there. The nanny and kids spoke only French in the afternoon. Donna made an effort, but the remnants of her high school French were not up to the task and the others gave no quarter. She had two phone calls she wanted to make, so she left the three French speakers and went to the guest bedroom.

She called John Seabold first. She got a machine and left a message thanking him for finding time to talk with her, but the meeting was no longer necessary.

Next she called Patrizia Nuvolari at her unlisted number and she answered.

"I'm sorry to bother you again, but I do have another question I had intended to ask you, but forgot. I hope you have a moment to answer it now."

"Yes, all right, if I can."

"When you and Mr. Seabold were sitting alone in that side room before the waitress screamed, did any one go in or out of the door located on the inner wall of the room?"

Patrizia Nuvolari cast her mind back to the time and place Donna referred to. "You mean the closet? Did anyone go into or out of the closet?"

It was Donna's turn to be momentarily confused. "No, it's not a door to a closet, but to a stairway."

"Really? Maybe that's what I heard."

"Heard?"

"Yes, while we were talking there we did hear a rumbling, tumbling sound like something falling off a shelf. I suppose I had that association, because I thought it was a closet. I went over to the door to look inside, but found it locked."

"What was the noise like?"

"Like, bump, bump, bump, bump. Perhaps it was something falling down the stairs."

"Could it have been someone running down the stairs?" Donna asked.

"Why yes, I think that could account for what I heard."

"Exactly when sis you hear the sound?"

"I'm not sure. Before the waitress screamed, certainly, because John and I left the room then to go to the deck as others were doing."

"Can you time it more precisely?"

"Well, John and I were talking perhaps half an hour—toward the end of that time rather than at the beginning. I'm sorry, that's the best I can do."

"Thanks anyway, that helps me."

Donna hung up telling herself: Yes, I would have thought that door belonged to a closet also. The author's ingenuous answer made Donna even surer that she and Seabold had not killed Silvio Rossi. At the same time, it started her thinking seriously along another line.

23

Dan Pollock and Art Brock sat up late. Fatigue, dashed dreams and too many beers all contributed to their pale, sagging faces. They didn't talk much; they were just reluctant to end the day that would close such a—on the whole—successful epoch in both their lives. Neither had any doubt about the fate of the show, but it wasn't until early the next morning that they knew for sure that their fears were fact. Dan knew it the moment the network president's secretary didn't say, "Hi Mr. Pollock, how are you this morning? Mr. Bondi wants to speak with you." Instead, the secretary began to deliver the message herself. She stated that the program's major sponsor had cancelled its contract and was busy disassociating itself from the show. She also told Dan to instruct all the network personnel there in Michigan to return to New York ASAP. So there it was, no reprieve. Dan put down the phone chuckling grimly. He would be famous—more famous than if they'd managed to pull-off this last act gracefully. His would be a fame to last for generations throughout the industry, the fame that goes with the really bad screw-up.

On top of this, Dan genuinely felt sad and guilty about the Thomas woman's death. He had seriously thought he had identified the killer, but he'd jumped the gun and the results were bad, very bad. He consoled himself some by thinking that since the woman was depressed, she may have killed herself anyway.

As the morning wore on he tried to have positive thoughts about the future. He had enough money to live out his life in a modest way. There was no point in trying to make more. The path to the easy buck had closed for him. He would go to a warm place, sit in the sun and read all the Elmore Leonard novels. Maybe he'd study them, see how Leonard did it and write one himself.

Art Brock undertook the miserable job of tying up the loose ends, paying off the staff, responding to inquiries from the press and so on. Dan got his personal things together and asked his secretary to get him a reservation back to New York. A first-class seat was available that afternoon.

Pollock started the drive to the airport early, because he'd thought of one final thing he wanted to do. On the way into the city, he asked the young local driver they'd hired if he knew of an auto parts store located in a part of Traverse City close to houses or apartments that rented reasonably.

"I've never inquired about the rents in the area, you understand, but there is an established business near Union Street that might fit the bill."

"Take me there."

When the young man pulled up at the door of the business, Dan jumped out saying he'd only be a minute.

Inside at the counter, Dan asked to speak to the owner. The clerk opened an office door and Dan heard him say, "That television reporter, Dan Pollock, is asking to speak to you."

A moment later a gray-haired man came to the doorway and peered out with a hesitant look, as if his boys were playing a joke on him. The expression changed to one of pleased curiosity.

"Welcome, com'on in," he said stepping back to make way for Dan. He held out his hand and Dan shook it. "Have a seat, Mr. Pollock. What can I do for you?"

"First let me say what I'm sure you hear all the time: You've got a very nice city here. I'm glad I got a chance to come here and see it. I wish I could stay longer, but that's not possible in my business. I'm on the way to the airport now, but I had an idea—spur of the moment—that might be useful to you, so I asked the driver to stop at your place. This might be a waste of your time, in which case I apologize."

The owner listened with wide-eyed interest. Seated across from him was one of the most famous people in the country talking about an idea that involved him.

Pollock looked at his watch. "To get to the point, I had occasion while here to meet a most interesting individual. He helped us a lot. He is a young man who possesses a rare aptitude. He is able to memorize vast amounts of data. I think he's better than a computer in selected and focused subjects."

Pollock saw he had managed to completely confuse the other man. "What I'm saying, in a not very clear way, is that he would be able to memorize all the part numbers in your entire inventory and be able to put his hand on any item faster than you could bring up the screen on your computer—and he'd make no mistakes. Do you think you could use a man like that?"

"You're talking about me hiring this guy, right?"

"I know it's none of my business. Like I said it was spur of the moment."

The owner considered the idea. "Has he worked in a parts store?"

"No, but he's worked in the inventory department of an auto company supplier in the Detroit area. He has a good work history, but the business he worked for had to close its doors as so many have."

"He lives here now?"

"Yes. He moved here recently. I think he now lives not far from your place." Pollock looked at his watch again. "I've got to get on my way, but I thought if I could put you and him together, I'd be doing you both a favor."

"Actually, I do need for someone in the stock room. I . . ."

Pollock stood. "I'm sorry to interrupt, but I have to leave. If you do decide to contact him," Pollock laid a piece of notepaper on the man's desk. "Here is a number. His name is Gregory Abbott. Keep in mind he is someone who would mind your stock like no one before, but he is not a person who meets the public well—not like these guys out front." He waved his hand toward the service desk, and ended the motion by extending his hand once again to the overwhelmed owner of the parts store.

Back in the car, Dan Pollock took out his notebook and looked up the same number he'd given the man only moments before and dialed it.

"I'd like to speak to Margaret Dennos please . . . Ms. Dennos, I'm Dan Pollock. I believe my secretary talked to you about Gregory Abbott. She told me you found him a halfway-house here in town. Right. Well, I just talked to a guy who might call you about employing him at an auto parts store. I want you to be prepared, so you can respond in a way that presents Mr. Abbott as a, shall we say, reasonable choice. Yeah, right. I see we're on the same page. So long and . . . good luck."

Dan Pollock sat back in the car's seat. He felt much better.

• • •

"You realize, of course, I sent you off to New York with four very good suspects and you've come back with half a suspect." Hoss said this over the phone after Donna had related the results of her New York meetings. The half suspect, of course, was Hoss's current estimate of Karen Forbes.

"Sorry about that." She then added, "Seriously, I'm very disappointed. I had high hopes that one of them would make a mistake when I confronted him or her with what we knew of motives. "

"You haven't yet experienced handling a case that must be accepted as unsolved. It's not easy, but it's a fact of life in law enforcement. In large cities, a third of murders go unsolved."

Right, Donna thought, but most of those are related to the drug trade, not famous chefs killed at their own parties.

Donna, talking on her cell phone, had just paid the parking fee at Traverse City's Cherry Capital Airport and began the drive back to her apartment.

"By the way," Hoss said, "Pollock and his pals have packed up and left town."

Donna gave a short snort of a laugh. "I'll miss them."

"The other person about to leave is Rossi's wife. This morning, I stopped for coffee at The 45th Parallel Café and ran into Gil Wolf. He told me Rossi's wife put the house on the market. Gil was a very happy guy; she gave him the listing. She's asking two and a half mil, while according to Gil, it's easily worth a million more. Gil told me it was a steal and I shouldn't pass it up."

Donna laughed. "Did you give him a deposit?"

"How about if everyone in the department chips in?"

"Pretty quick, don't you think?"

"What?"

"Putting her house on the market," Donna replied.

"Maybe. "

"And, why the low price?"

"Gil said she wanted a quick sale."

"Just let me get out of here," Donna said.

"What's that?"

"Just imagining what Gina Rossi must be thinking. I learned of an interesting observation made by one of the New Yorkers that bears on this, but I need to think about it a bit to be sure of what it might mean."

"OK, I like a mystery. I always waited until Christmas morning to open my presents . . . but not a second longer."

"I've got to work at wrapping this one first."

"Nothing fancy."

"I hear you."

What did the quick sale of the Rossi house tell her? The house here had been all Silvio's idea? A grieving wife couldn't come back to a place where her beloved husband had been brutally murdered? Or, could there be another reason why she wanted to wash her hands of her association with Leelanau County? And what about Patrizia Nuvolari's description of the sound coming from the door to the spiral stairway? At any rate, here was a bird in hand, who needed to be interviewed one more time before she too became a bird an airline ticket away.

"I'd like to run up to Cathead Bay and talk to the lady."

"Better make it quick. I got the impression from Gil Wolf she's packing her bags."

Donna had just passed the Blue Goat wine shop on Front Street. She continued on to the Culinary Institute, where she pulled into the parking lot in order to get out her notebook and look up and call the unlisted Rossi number.

She told the woman who answered that she'd like to speak to Mrs. Rossi.

"I'll see if she can come to the phone," the woman said. "Who shall I say is calling?"

Donna needed to get Gina on the line. Her experience as a sales rep told her she'd experience an easy brush-off otherwise.

"I just need some information before she leaves town."

This was certainly no identification, but it got by the woman.

"Just a minute," the woman said.

"Hello, this is Gina Rossi. How can I help you?"

"Mrs. Rossi, this is Deputy Roper of the Leelanau County Sheriff's Patrol. I understand you are planning to leave the area soon. I would like to meet with you before you do."

"Tomorrow. I'm leaving tomorrow. I'm very busy. I must do so much before I can go. It would be very inconvenient to meet with you. Is there something I can tell you right now?"

"It won't take long, but I prefer to talk to you in person," Donna persisted.

There followed a silence pregnant with reluctance. "I see. Very well. I will stop what I'm doing for a few minutes. At what time?"

Donna had to go to her apartment and change into her uniform—twenty minutes. Drive to headquarters to get her patrol car—twenty-five. On up to Cathead Bay—another twenty-five.

"I'll be there at one o'clock, Mrs. Rossi."

After hanging up, Donna felt irritated with herself for arranging such a tight schedule. She could have told Gina Rossi two o'clock just as well. Was she that afraid this bird would fly away?

Donna parked in front of the Rossi home at one minute past one. Gina answered the door. Donna could discern displeasure that Gina tried to cover with chatter about the many things she still needed to do. Another thing Donna noticed were intrusions of stereotypical Italian speech mannerisms into her English. She didn't know what to make of this.

Gina led the way to the alcove off the living room, the room where Nuvolari and Seabold had sat together talking. The space was bright with the early September afternoon sunshine. Two cardboard boxes, one filled with newspaper wrapped objects, the other partially filled, rested on the hardwood floor. Donna had obviously interrupted the task of taking down and packing-up those small but valued objects from the shelves of this room.

Donna had no agenda for this interview; she only intuitively felt its importance.

"I heard you are selling this house."

"That'sa true."

Donna smiled and said jokingly, "I hope your leaving so quickly doesn't mean you didn't like our little peninsula."

"No that'sa not true, but New York is'a my home and the business and everything."

"I understand, of course, and I wasn't serious," Donna assured her. "Mrs. Rossi, I talked to you the first time just after your husband's death. At that time you said you had no idea who might have wanted to kill him. You've had more time now to think about it."

"No, I can think of no one. Everyone liked Silvio," came the instant reply.

Donna felt a need to break into these safe responses. The suicide of Sandra Thomas had no direct bearing on the murder investigation and she would normally not have brought it up with this woman, who knew now, for certain, about her husband's affair.

"I'm sure you've heard about the suicide of Sandra Thomas."

Clearly, Gina had not expected this but said, "It's so sad. Poor woman and her poor family. It was the fault of that television program, don't you agree?"

Donna had not anticipated the sincerity of her empathic response and it deflected any thought she had of pursuing the subject.

" Mrs. Rossi . . ."

"Please call me Gina. I believe your name is Donna."

"Yes, that's right. I was going to ask . . . Gina, if you normally lock this door leading onto your spiral stairway?"

"No. No, it's always open."

194

"I'm puzzled by a fact that I've only just learned. The door was open, as you say, when the other deputies and I were searching through the house right after your husband's death, yet a person sitting in this room at the time of his death tried the door and found it locked. Why would that be?"

The Italian shrug. "I have no idea. Perhaps the person was mistaken, or perhaps that little button in the handle," She pointed to the locking button in the door knob, "got pushed in by accident. Who can tell?"

Gina sat very calmly, smiling at Donna.

Gina's last sentence resonated in Donna's mind, "Who can tell?"

"Yes, well—Gina—would you actively keep my question, about who might have had a motive, open in your mind and call me with anything that occurs to you." While saying this she had taken a card from her notebook and handed it to Gina.

Gina took the card saying, "I have thought hard about your question since you first asked me. I am not able to help you any-more than I could at that time. I, of course, understand it's your job to continue to look for the guilty person."

The words Gina had just spoken were appropriate. Donna remembered, however, her days as a sales rep, when a really disinterested customer would take her card with the promise to call whenever he or she needed anything. Right!

24

Donna didn't need to look at the menu. A green salad, the spinach ravioli and a glass of pinot grigio made up her favorite early evening meal at Stella. She and Derek had just sat down in one of the shallow nooks off the long hallway the waitresses called "The Arches". The small alcove lent an intimate tone to a candle-lit meal.

The restaurant occupied the basement of what had been one of the gothic pavilions of the long-abandoned state mental hospital, now rescued from the demolition ball and restored into up-market office suites, shops and restaurant space.

"This must have been the hospital morgue, don't you figure?" Derek commented, his gaze running along the exposed brick walls.

"You did that on purpose to get a reaction from me. Confess."

"I don't know what you mean," he pleaded with mock innocence.

"You're teasing. You know how I like this place and that was a typical doctor's attempt at black humor. I'll bet you delighted in taking your dates to the anatomy lab when you were in medical school."

Still acting the innocent, Derek threw up his hands in surrender. "I promise I'll never comment . . . on the obvious again."

"You can't stop, can you?"

"OK, OK. I'm sorry. But can't you picture a body laid out in each of these alcoves . . . where do you think the morgue would have been located if not r-i-g-h-t HERE!"

She picked up one of the rolls the waitress, in passing, had placed on the table, and was making as if to throw it at him, just as the waitress turned toward their table and saw her.

Derek said quickly, "When I asked you to pass me a roll, I didn't mean the forward pass."

The waitress went on her way and Donna threatened, " 'Just you wait, 'Enry 'Iggins. Just you wait'."

She broke the roll and dipped it in olive oil. "Can I now assume you've gotten over this breakthrough of adolescent behavior?"

"Now wait a minute: Who was about to throw food at the table? I never give way to childish behavior, but if I did, let's assume it's over."

"Good, because I want to get serious about a talk I had today with Gina Rossi."

"They give you no rest. Your feet are barely back on the ground, when they send you off for interviews."

"Not quite the serious demeanor yet that I require," she admonished.

"OK, I've got my serious hat on."

"I got some impressions, vague impressions, when I talked to her today that bother me."

Derek listened now.

"Hoss told me she had put the house on the market—and at a very low, quick sale price. She wants out of our little bit of paradise. So, I thought I should talk to her before she leaves. I called to make an appointment to see her and she clearly made an attempt to duck out of it, claiming she was busy packing. I felt strongly she didn't at all want to talk to me and she only used the packing as an excuse.

"I had no real idea of what to ask her when I drove out to her house. There was no specific information I thought she could—or rather would, be willing to give me, but . . . Well, let me tell you about our little talk."

Derek sat, quietly curious.

"I'll just run through what she said and I hope you can help me understand what's troubling me."

These last words, presented as they were, automatically shifted Derek's set from listening to a conversation in a restaurant to the kind of attentiveness he employed in his office.

"OK, first I met her at the door and she took me back to an alcove off the living room. No, the first thing that struck me was her accent. I had been impressed when I met her the day of the murder that she spoke English with very little accent. When I first arrived at her house today her accent seemed heavier, and the cadence was different—a stereotypical Italian cadence. Later on, at the end of our talk, this had changed. Looking back to the day of the murder—I'm not sure of this—I seem to remember the same change in her speech when she explained why she had used the spiral stairs that day."

Derek frowned. "I'm not sure I know what significance you're giving this."

"It's only an impression, but I wonder if she reverts to an Italian's natural tendency to speak with that cadence—rhythm— when she's anxious. Later in the interview today, when she saw I had nothing threatening with which to confront her, she relaxed and her English became perfect."

"OK, so you're saying your calling and wanting to talk to her caused her to fear you might be a threat to her," Derek summarized.

"Right. The next thing I noticed—that is I noticed on a subconscious level, because I didn't consider its meaning at the time—was that she didn't ask me right off about our investigation. If your spouse had been murdered, wouldn't you ask the police right away about the investigation?"

"Hmm, sure, I believe I would."

"Nothing. Nothing until I asked her if she'd had any further thoughts about who might have had a motive, and even then she didn't inquire about any progress we might have made. And finally, I couldn't see that she was feeling any grief over her loss. I saw only a woman who was interrupted in the urgent task of packing up some of her more valuable things before the moving men arrived. Looking back, I think the same was true right after the murder when I first talked to her. There was so much demanding my attention then that I wasn't sensitive to her behavior, but now I believe I noticed the same absence of real grief. Wait! There was one other thing. This complacency of hers was getting to me, so I brought up Sandra Thomas's suicide."

"You did?"

"Yes. It would normally be an insensitive thing to do, to confront a woman with the name of 'the other woman.' I know that, but I felt pushed to do it to see if I could make something happen— disturb her self-control. The important thing now is the way she handled it. She said, 'that poor woman and her poor family'. I swear it was unsettling. No anger with Sandra Thomas. No anger with her husband. No anger with me for bringing it up."

"What we have so far is she wants to get out of town fast before you could ask too many questions. And, she suffers no grief for the departed chef, but is saddened by the death of his lover."

"Not quite right. I didn't sense she had to 'get out of town fast'. I sensed she had simply and coolly finished with this phase of her life. Like a person who'd waited impatiently for retirement and when the day arrived was eager to clear out his or her desk and leave, while at the same time trying to still appear to be the loyal employee—if at all possible—for a few minutes more."

"You sensed all that."

"Maybe."

Derek made an attempt once again to pull together what she had been hinting at. "So, you think she could give a damn about the affair with the woman. She could give a damn about Silvio Rossi. This phase of her life is over and good riddance. She is impatient to move on."

Donna sipped from the glass of wine that had been placed before her. She thought about Derek's summary.

"You didn't include her anxiety."

"OK. She is nervous and it affected her speech until she discerned that you were harmless."

"I think that covers it."

"It has just gotten through to me that you're seriously considering her to be a suspect." Surprise was in his voice.

"The wife who is cheated on has a strong motive."

Derek let a moment pass to consider this point, and then pressed her. "But she has an alibi."

"Maybe, maybe not."

"Now you're being mysterious. I thought we were to be serious," Derek countered.

"I'm afraid to tell you what I began thinking, because you'll think I'm desperately clutching at straws. But since the interview this afternoon I've been obsessed with a teeny, tiny loophole in her alibi. She was with the other women on her supposedly spontaneous little tour, until one of the women became suddenly ill and vomited. She began tending to the sick woman, but then she gave that task over to an older woman. There is a suggestion that she was absent from the bathroom for a time. She was back, cleaning up the stricken woman shortly after this, but there just may be a period that isn't accounted for."

"Yes?"

"Well— and I haven't told anyone this before—I learned from a woman I talked to in New York that at a point in that critical time when the murder was committed, she heard a noise like someone running down the spiral stairs."

Derek frowned and drummed his fingers on the table. "Now wait a minute. This sickness thing happened on the second floor— third floor really, since the barbecue, as I understand the layout, is on the basement level. You think she could run down two flights of stairs, stab her hubby and run back up quickly enough so her absence wouldn't seem overly long?" He squinted his eyes, sending the message that what she suggested was indeed unbelievable.

"OK, but would the women in the bathroom notice? Remember one was busy being sick and the other was holding her forehead over the washbasin while she puked. How many minutes, in a situation like that, would she have to be absent before it seemed overly long?"

Derek could discern the depth of Donna's investment in this wild idea and he knew better than to scoff in the way his rational judgment dictated.

"All right, let's consider your solution soberly: How much time would actually be needed?"

"We could check it out roughly right here in this building. You could run up two flights and back and I could time you."

"That's a great idea, only you've got our roles reversed. This becomes official police business and you've told me before that participation by citizens is not permitted. Consider also that I might stumble and break my leg and be forced to sue your department. A more serious fact is that our ravioli might come and get cold while you are chasing about and I'm timing you, but for the sake of argument let's say it could be accomplished."

"Of course, I know what I should do; I should ask the two women involved what they remember of Gina's absence."

"Right, but, for the moment, we're assuming Gina had time. Why would she want to kill him?"

"Silvio was having an affair with Sandra Thomas."

"Just a minute ago you said her attitude indicated she didn't give a damn. According to your information he'd been fooling around for years. Why become murderously angry over this particular fling of his? She would have him safely home in New York soon where he'd be sure to forget Sandra Thomas, and why do it in this flamboyant, almost operatic way? If she must kill him, why not wait until she could feign dizziness at home and drop the hair dryer in his bathtub?"

"Because."

"Because? What kind of a serious answer is that?"

"I haven't thought through this notion that she could be the killer very well yet. I really only had the beginning of suspicion yesterday in New York, when Patrizia Nuvolari told me about hearing the sound of someone running down the stairs."

"So you base your theory on that reported sound and your hunch about her reaction to your paying her a visit this afternoon?"

"Pretty slim, eh?"

Derek thought it was time for a little more placating. "I don't disregard your intuition. I really do believe you have a finely tuned antenna for those subtle signs that tell us about the emotions of others. Your recognizing the possibility that her accent comes and goes with tension deserves a merit badge."

She smiled, partly as an acknowledgement that she had been pushing her idea too forcefully and partly pleased by the compliment.

"Now that I have you softened up to accepting my brilliant

deduction," she said, "I'll tell you there is a huge flaw in my theory. Let's say there was something about the affair with Sandra Thomas that sent her over the edge, and say she figured the party to be an excellent time and place to do the deed. After all, there were plenty of other suspects there to seize our attention. And let's say she flew down the spiral stairs and out onto the patio. Silvio would not be surprised to see her. But, if to her disappointment she found him talking to some party guest, or a cook or a waitress, all she would have to do is say, 'How's the food coming along, darling?' and go right back up to the women upstairs, no harm done. She had the option to skewer or not to skewer depending on whether she judged the moment to be perfect for her purpose. If not perfect, she could put off the offing until he was in his bath."

Derek tried to follow her. "OK, but what has that to do with this flaw in your theory?"

"The flaw? Don't you see it? Don't you see the whole caper depends on her being able to predict that a member of her tour would start vomiting and provide her with the excuse for her absence—provide her with the time to pull it off."

"Oh, is that all? A little syrup of ipecac would take care of that problem."

"Syrup of ipecac? What's that?"

Derek was alarmed that she was taking him seriously. He had made a joke. "I was only kidding."

She was too serious to let anything pass that, even in joking, offered a solution to the problem with her theory.

"What is syrup of ipecac?"

"Donna, really, I . . . "

"What is syrup of ipecac?"

"OK, OK. It's a medicine, an emetic, something that induces vomiting. I really don't know its composition. It's an old-time remedy that mothers kept in their medicine cabinets in the event one of the kids swallowed some noxious substance."

"How is it given?"

He was sorry now he had mentioned the stuff. Donna had jumped headlong into the hope that this would solve her problem.

"By mouth. You get the person to drink some and voila."

"Does it take long to act?"

"I only saw it used once and it worked pretty quickly, maybe three or four minutes."

"So, Gina could have given it to this woman, Marla."

Derek laughed. "Hi, Marla, would you mind drinking this for me? You'll only be sick for a very short time, but it will give me time to run downstairs and stab Silvio. That's a good friend."

Donna ignored his attempt to be funny. "What does it taste like—look like?"

"I never tasted it for an obvious reason. It looked like cough syrup."

Derek reached across the table and took Donna's hand. "This is really very unlikely don't you think. Maybe you were right when you said your theory was flawed." He felt her hand stiffen. "At least sleep on it, here comes our ravioli."

25

Donna didn't sleep on her theory, at least not well. She felt an unusual degree of excitement and agitation. She had come to strongly believe Gina to be a murderess. Accompanying this she felt an equal quantity of inner warning. She recognized she had an unreasonably great need to find the killer and show-up Dan Pollock and through his further humiliation, make him pay for Sandra Thomas. She remembered a recent occasion when she had wanted to make another suspect pay for a crime and how badly she'd been wrong. She tried to temper her zeal. She suspected the odds were heavily on the side of Derek's reasonable view that she was distorting the facts in order to make her theory valid. OK, she needed to ease up, not push her idea too hard. But even so, there were a few reasonable steps she could take to test it.

Driving to headquarters the next morning, Donna stopped off at the pharmacy in the village of Suttons Bay where she usually got her few prescriptions filled. The pharmacist, a friendly, fatherly man in his sixties, she trusted to be honest with her. It pleased her to see he was on duty this morning and alone, because she feared the question she wanted to ask would seem a little strange.

He recognized her and left what he was doing to come to the counter and greet her. "Good morning, officer. Can't you feel autumn in the air this morning?"

"Yes, I certainly can. It seems like a discovery every year. Maybe the year is twelve months long to give us time to forget what each season feels like."

He laughed. "You may have something there. How can I help

you today?"

"I need some information—a case I'm working on. Do you carry syrup of ipecac?" Her tone carried the expectation that he'd react as if she'd asked whether he stocked powdered rhino horn.

"Now there's something I haven't heard of in a long time. Syrup of ipecac. I'll bet it's been ten years since I've sold it. A while ago, it could be found in the medicine cabinets of many households—those with children anyway. It induced vomiting in case Junior swallowed something like silver polish or ant poison." He remembered that Donna had asked if he had the substance. "But no, we don't stock it anymore."

"Is it still made do you think?" she asked.

"I really don't know, but I have a vague recollection of hearing there were problems—liability perhaps."

"Liability?"

"There are cases where inducing vomiting can be harmful, for instance if the person has swallowed a caustic substance like lye. Induced vomiting could cause a rupture of the esophagus."

"Really."

He recognized that Donna still wanted to know if the product was available. "I don't have the catalogs used to order drugs here at this store and there is no one in the main office this early. If you like, I could find out what I can and call you."

"That would be great." She took one of her cards out of her notebook and handed it to him. "Thanks."

He was happy to be able to do this beautiful young woman a favor. Her smile could jump-start a guy's day.

"Any luck?" Hoss asked Donna as she walked past him after the usual morning briefing.

206

Donna hesitated. "What do you mean?"

"You were going to try to talk to the Rossi woman. Did you have any luck?"

"Maybe yes, maybe no."

"That's the way I like to have my deputies report, clear, to the point, without ambiguity."

"It's great to have a boss who can pronounce ambiguity this early in the day."

"I can also pronounce insubordination."

"Well almost. You only get a 'c', but I'll save you the trouble of trying again and explain what I meant."

"OK, but let's grab a cup; Kate bought us a new brewing machine."

The new coffee maker was in the conference room, so they settled there and Donna went through her interview with Gina and the suspicions it had aroused in her. She recited the exact steps in her reasoning as she had the night before to Derek Marsh. She left out the subject of syrup of ipecac. She thought it would be too much to expect Hoss to accept her complete theory at the first sitting. And, she'd have been right, because without including it, Hoss still looked stunned. He had the appearance of someone who had just bitten into a green apple.

"There are more 'ifs' in that idea of yours than in Kipling's poem," he commented finally.

"It's still possible."

"There is one glaring problem; it all hinges on the lady being a sorceress who can cause people to vomit on command."

"I'm working on that."

Donna's cell phone buzzed and she excused herself and answered it.

"This is Deputy Roper."

"Hi, Fred Gamble, the pharmacist. The person who does our ordering looked up ipecac and found out it is still available, but there is so little demand we've stopped carrying it. I made a couple of calls, however, and located a pharmacy that has it."

He then named a national drug chain that had two stores in Traverse City and gave her a phone number.

"Thanks very much for the trouble you've taken."

"No trouble."

She hung up and said to Hoss, "As I said, I'm working on that problem and if you'll excuse me, my work calls." She yelled back as she went through the door, "I'll talk to you soon."

So, Gina could have bought the drug. "So what," Hoss would say. He'd be right. Being able to buy it wasn't proof she had bought it or used it. Donna had an idea.

Those retailers that ring up all the merchandise by bar code are, at the same time, registering the sale in the inventory log. It is from that information that supplies are sent out to the individual stores. Wouldn't the sale of this one bottle of ipecac be recorded, and probably also be recorded by date. She was on her way to her car before she finished the thought.

She was on patrol for the morning as was Becky. She called Becky as soon as she was in her car and told her where she was going and asked her to cover for her. She needed to talk to one of the pharmacists in person.

One branch of the pharmacy chain was located near the mall on highway 31, and here she sought out the head pharmacist and presented her request. He, like most other people who live in the area, was readily willing to help. He said it would take some time to get the information she sought, since the request would have to go to the Midwest regional office where the records of inventory were kept and shipments to the individual stores were assembled.

He assured her he would make sure they understood it was a request from the Sheriff's Department. Implied in this was his doubt about willing helpfulness at that location.

Whatever had motivated the promptness, Donna had her answer before her shift ended. A single bottle of ipecac had been sold last month from the city's other branch store. She was given the date of the sale—one week before Silvio Rossi's death. Still dressed in her uniform, but driving her own car now, she hurried to the store. She explained to the man who came to the prescription drop-off window who she was and how she had learned of the sale of the single bottle of ipecac and she asked if one of the pharmacists remembered selling it. He turned to two women pharmacists and relayed the question. One of them came over to the window.

She studied the uniformed woman who was asking this odd question. "Yes, officer, I sold a bottle of ipecac a while back—maybe two, maybe three weeks ago. What is this about?"

"It's related to an investigation in progress. I can't say more than that, but it would help us if you'd be willing to tell me what you remember about that sale." Donna tried to represent authority, while at the same time making the appeal a friendly one.

"I remember the sale very well, because of what the woman said. She asked if we carried 'ipecaca'. At that moment it sounded funny, ipe - caca." She added, with an embarrassed smile, "Maybe I was tired. Anyway, I asked if she meant ipecac. The woman nodded and said, 'yes', with a strong Italian accent."

Donna's heart pounded. "What did the woman look like?"

By this time the third pharmacist had joined the group.

"Interesting," the pharmacist went on, "that she should be the person you're interested in, because she struck me as being different. First of all I had this strong feeling she wasn't . . . local, not from around here. There was something about her that said large city.

It wasn't the clothes—I couldn't see much of what she was wearing. She wore a raincoat and a kerchief over her head as if to protect her hair from the rain, only it was a sunny day. And, she had on dark glasses.

"I remember her," the third pharmacist put in. "I remember your joking that you had just waited on Sophia Loren incognito."

"Yes, that's right."

"Did you notice anything else about her? Did you notice her hands?"

"Her hands?"

"Was she wearing a ring, for instance?"

The woman thought about it but shook her head.

"Not that I remember."

Donna was disappointed with this answer, but it figured that Gina wouldn't wear anything so readily identifiable. It made no difference: Donna was sure the pharmacist had identified Gina Rossi. There was no question in Donna's mind. Gina had purchased what she needed to stage the tour charade—the charade that gave her time to race to the patio and kill Silvio.

Donna bought all three bottles of ipecac the store had in stock.

26

Hardly aware of her automatic moves while making spaghetti with oil and garlic, her default meal when in a hurry, Donna's absorption in the Gina Rossi problem was total. What had been a theory anchored in mid-air by her feelings concerning Gina's mood and responses, had just taken on factual underpinnings. What possible reason could Gina have wanted with a bottle of emetic other than to cause someone to throw up? Gina had no children who were likely to swallow daddy's charcoal lighting fluid or mamma's nail polish remover. Damn it, she had solved the case! She had not let Hoss and her friends down. What must she do to shut the door?

She felt herself to be in the position of a deep-sea angler, who, turning from the joy of just having hooked a prize marlin, now faces the problem of getting the sucker into the boat.

As with scientific discoveries, the establishment of one fact makes possible the consideration of other questions. If Gina had made such a grand plan for murder, wouldn't she carefully plan each element in its execution? Did she leave the composition of her "spontaneous" house tour to chance, or did she choose the participants ahead of time for the parts she wanted them to play. What was there about the three women, which perfectly served her purpose? Would any one of these three be more likely to succumb to the effects of the emetic? Why three women, instead of two—or, why not one instead of two? OK, Donna thought, I'm Gina, what if I only took one woman on a tour and arranged for her to take the ipecac and get sick. I take her to the bathroom, where she continues to throw-up. Can I leave her for the time to run down to the patio and kill Silvio? Not easily. Wouldn't the sick person become very aware of the time I'd been gone, since she'd want my assistance? OK, then I have two on my tour, one to get sick and one to take care of her. Who would I choose to be the kind of person to give the care? She reminded herself that Rosa DeSica ended up with that assignment. Was she chosen for the role? Donna pictured Mrs. DeSica. Motherly was the first descriptor that leaped to mind. And, she's someone capable of becoming engrossed in the task of helper and losing track of the time.

"Yes," Donna said aloud, as she captured a strand of spaghetti for testing between her teeth. Rosa DeSica, what a perfect choice.

Then, why take three women on the tour? Wouldn't a third person standing around be a witness to my absence? But, Donna reminded herself, Judy Bombard, the third woman didn't stand around; she took off. Interesting.

Donna tossed the cooked pasta with the oil and garlic, sprinkled the whole with grated Romano cheese, poured a glass of cabernet from a liter bottle, lit the candle stub in the holder on her kitchen table and sat down.

Her next step became clear to her. She needed to call each of the women on the tour in order to learn more about them and their relationship to Gina. She was as sure as she was that the pasta would be delicious that Gina had left nothing to chance. She had acquired an appreciative fascination for Gina Rossi.

It was not until the next evening that Donna managed to complete her project of talking to all three of the women. She had put in a busy day of her usual duties as a deputy plus the multiple calls necessary to connect with the three New Yorkers. In addition she heard of Gina's departure from the peninsula and of a pending purchase of the Rossi home.

212

Donna told each of the women that a routine review of statements made by all the guests was being done. She asked what each remembered of the tour and then probed for anything which would have given each of them a special qualification to be chosen by Gina for a role in her plan.

Right away a significant fact emerged. Rosa DeSica had already seen the upstairs of the house. She and her son had been staying in the Rossi home since coming from New York. Rosa remembered Gina saying to her, "Rosa, please come with me. I want to show two women the rest of the house." Rosa didn't really know why Gina wanted her to come along, but she went without question.

Gina had told them she wanted to keep the group small and planned to take others on the same tour as the party progressed. Gina had proposed the tour to the women when they first arrived at the house and when the time came, she quickly went around and in a whisper told each of them to come with her to the kitchen. Each of the women, when asked for her reaction to this whispered approached, said she put it down to Gina's wish to keep the group small. In the kitchen, on a small counter, Gina had four champagne flutes waiting. Each woman confirmed that the glasses already contained an inch or more of red liquid. Each woman also thought the liquid was probably the currant liquor, cassis, when Gina began adding champagne to the glasses. Gina then led them to the balcony where she proposed a toast. OK, Donna thought, so Gina would probably have already added the ipecac to one of the glasses. She then had to be sure the right person ended up with that glass. Here, Donna did some careful questioning, since she believed Marla Phelps must have been the one Gina intended to drink the emetic. Gina would also need to see to it that Marla Phelps drank most, if not all, of it in order to achieve the intended effect. All of the women agreed that Gina had not urged them to drink up. Marla remembered her impression, however, that Gina took many sips, interrupting her comments about the little balcony study and the use Silvio made of it, to take a swallow of her champagne. This, she believed in retrospect, caused her to do the same. She remembered having finished most of her drink there on the balcony.

Marla Phelps also supplied the information that she had a "delicate stomach". She had been at a party with Gina where a dip, left too long in the sun, seemed to be the responsible agent for several guests feeling unwell. Marla had, however, become very nauseous and vomited.

Judy Bombard supplied the fact that among her friends, she—Bombard—was known to be phobic about illness, and especially vomiting. Her husband had been the one who had had to attend to their kids' childhood GI problems—a topic he brought up repeatedly as a family joke, much to her irritation.

It was from Rosa DeSica that Donna learned the most vital fact. Donna told Rosa that when she had questioned Marla on the day of the murder, Marla had mentioned that Gina had taken her to the bathroom and supported her head while she vomited, but then, she remembered Rosa taking over this task.

"Why was that? Why did Gina have you change places with her?" Donna asked.

"Because'a Gina had'a to go to get'a the towel. There was'a none in'a the bathroom."

"Really?" No towels in the bathroom? How very convenient!

To Donna's mind now, a Broadway casting director couldn't have assembled a more perfect cast for Gina's script. One element didn't make complete sense to her. Why include Judy Bombard? Why have a person who could be relied upon to run from the scene? Maybe . . . sure: She saw it now. Who would suspect Gina

214

of planning this scenario when she had included a witness who could have been there to see her run down the spiral stairs? No one! But knowing of Bombard's phobia, Gina knew there would be no witness.

She had to tell Derek. She wanted him to share her excitement. She knew he was still seeing patients in his office, but she called and left a message on his machine to come to her apartment as soon as he finished.

Derek came an hour later, and went straight to the refrigerator and got himself a beer. Donna had already begun to relate the conversations she'd had and declared, with mounting certainty, just how the murder had been committed.

Derek listened. What she'd described made some kind of sense, but only if one were willing to suspend disbelief. Her certainty reminded him of the kind of conviction one sees in paranoia. A person holding a paranoid theory, say of a conspiracy, can present an argument that superficially seems convincing. It may, in fact, convince a large group of people. But, it breaks down if examined in the light of what one knows to be true about common human behavior. A conspiracy, for instance, posits a number of people keeping the object of their conspiracy a secret—not a common human trait.

Donna, realizing she'd ignored the fact Derek might be hungry at the end of a full day of seeing patients, gave some thought to what her larder could provide.

"I'd be happy to make spaghetti, or I can do turkey sandwich and leftover orzo salad, or . . ."

"A sandwich would be great."

"You're sure?"

"I've dreamt all day of a turkey sandwich."

She began the preparation and Derek settled back sipping the beer and thinking how lucky he was to be there with her. He wanted this scene to play permanently in his own, comfortable home, but he knew she wasn't yet ready to alter her present life. He counted on her not feeling this way much longer and so he was content—for a few more months anyway.

Donna served the food, poured herself a glass of wine and sat down opposite him.

"So, what do you think?"

"All the pieces seem to fit together nicely."

"That's all, 'seem to fit nicely'?"

He certainly wasn't going to mention his earlier thoughts about paranoia, nor was he about to speculate on what it might be that she must be ignoring to make her formula work. He also didn't want to change the subject and cause her to think he was disinterested.

"I say, lady, you're not giving the chap a chance to shed the mantle of a long day's work, and have his supper."

She relaxed. "Sorry, chap."

Derek thought about his options and decided on a question.

"What's your next step?"

"I'd like to go over the Rossi house again."

"What do you hope to find?"

She shifted uneasily before admitting, "I'd like to find the ipecac bottle." She saw Derek framing an objection and beat him to it. "It's unlikely, I know, but you never can tell. I mean a person plans to dispose of an incriminating article, but he or she delays, waiting for the right moment when no one will notice and then forgets to do it."

Again Derek felt an impulse to argue and again he reminded himself that Donna was in no mood for an objection.

"Finding the bottle would be hard evidence, all right. You have none now."

"I have the earring. Gina said she used the stairs to check on there being charcoal but now, in the light of this new information of Nuvolari hearing the sound of someone running down the stairs, the earring there on the stairs takes on new significance."

"You still have the earring? You told me you were going to give it back to her."

Her look said she'd been caught committing a social misdemeanor, like not having returned a borrowed book you'd had for a year.

"I just didn't have a good opportunity the next day and then we got caught up in the interrogation of Bruce Thomas and Sandra's suicide." She stopped trying to find excuses. Her reason for holding on to the earring had already been acknowledged. Until the pharmacist described the woman who bought the ipecac, the earring remained all she had of substance in the whole case.

"May I see the earring?" he asked.

"Sure. Just a minute."

She left the table and went to her closet and returned with the small purse she used when she traveled. Opening it and a zippered inside pocket she withdrew the earring and laid it in front of Derek.

"Wow. That certainly didn't come out of a Cracker Jack box. Shouldn't you put it in a safe-deposit box or, better still, isn't there this place you mentioned at headquarters where you keep evidence?"

He was right, she admitted to herself, but that could be awkward; Hoss thought she had given it back to Gina already.

"It's perfectly safe here. I keep it in an inner pocket of this purse that I only use when traveling. It hangs in the back of my closet behind a garment bag," she answered.

Derek ran his fingers over the buttery leather of the purse. "Am I right in thinking this 'H' stands for Hermes?"

"Yes, a case of irresistible impulse."

A note of worry came into Derek's voice, all of which wasn't put-on.

"Are you given to these impulses often?"

"Not often. But I love this purse and want to keep it and use it forever. That's why I only use it when I travel. Besides it's really very practical; see how secure the fastener is."

"You're absolutely right; no bag less than two thousand dollars would do the job."

Behind the playful banter lay his concern about her whole idea about the murder. He experienced the feeling one has when one hears a friend tell you of a step he or she passionately plans to take that you're afraid is very wrong. At a time like that, you're happy if there is another person in the picture, one with some authority—a variation on, "Ask your father before you do that."

"You are presenting your, ah, conclusions to Hoss, of course."

"Of course, but first I want to have another go at that house."

"You said that she'd gone back to New York."

"I could, of course, re-enter the house as part of our investigation, but I'd rather not be that direct. Gina has left, but all of her things aren't moved out, which almost certainly means the maid is still there to continue packing and supervising the movers."

"I see." He also decided the time had come to make a strategic withdrawal. He had managed to have dinner with a zealot and raise some questions while avoiding the role of naysayer.

27

"Can I talk to you a minute, boss?"

Hoss, who had been reading the morning's Traverse City Record-Eagle, swiveled his chair a bit to answer.

He held up the newspaper. "They say the widow has left for New York and she leaves without the murder being any closer to being solved. I hope you have come to tell me this isn't so."

She was tempted to use this opening for a full account of her thinking about the ipecac, but she forced herself to stay with her schedule.

"No, but it bears on the problem. I want to go through the Rossi house again—now that she's gone, and see if I can come up with something like hard evidence."

"You don't say. I understood the four of you searched the house the day of the murder."

"True. But, it's always more fruitful if you know what you're looking for."

"And you know now?" Hoss challenged.

"I don't want to say more just yet, but I do have an object in mind."

"Is this the beginning of twenty questions?"

She stood in silence; her reticence said she was serious.

"OK. Am I right in thinking that you want to make this search without Mrs. Rossi's knowledge?"

"You're right, and I know it's a problem with the maid there. She might feel it her duty to inform her employer."

Hoss saw the problem. "Hmm, maybe," he muttered to himself. "I've heard the maid is a member of the Band. Just maybe."

The Band he referred to was the Grand Traverse Band of Chippewa and Ottawa Indians, whose reservation in Peshawbestown lay several miles to the north of Sheriff's Headquarters.

"If I'm to handle this in the best way, I've got to drive up to Northport and have a little chat with an old acquaintance. Can your plan accept a little delay?"

"Sure. Thanks, Hoss."

Hoss stopped and looked in first one display-window and then the other on each side of the gallery's front door. He had known that Harry Swifthawk and his bride Mary had opened the business in Northport several months earlier, and he had been telling himself he should really stop by and congratulate Harry. But in spite of positive changes in their relationship since last year, theirs wasn't an easy friendship. Harry had taunted Hoss for years, before their mutual participation in a murder investigation cleared the way for peace. If Mary was inside the gallery, Hoss could more smoothly satisfy the social obligation with a breezy visit, but in order to ask for the kind of help he now needed from Harry, finding him alone in the store would serve him better. Hoss opened the door and Harry, who sat unpacking tissue-wrapped, Hopi kachina dolls, looked up. His look contained a composite of attitudes from his history with Hoss: wariness of authority, rebellion and the fear of retaliation, anger over discrimination, finally segueing into the tentative friendship and mutual respect they'd established.

"Hoss! Glad you stopped by."

"Hi, Harry," scanning the interior, he added, "Impressive place you've got here."

"Marti and Mary get the credit for the decoration. The fine work that the artists did on these pieces is what is truly impressive. I'd like to take you on a tour." The two women Harry had mentioned were his half-sister and his wife.

Hoss relaxed. Harry seemed to have truly put aside old grievances. "Great, but I have to tell you right off I also came here to ask for a favor."

What kind of favor would Hoss ask of him? Harry waited to hear.

Hoss cleared his throat. "As, of course, you're aware, we are in the midst of investigating the murder of Silvio Rossi."

And, not making diddly progress, Harry would have said tauntingly in the past.

"Donna Roper wants some information concerning the inside of the Rossi house, but doesn't want to stir up the attention that getting the widow's OK would cause. We know one of the women from the reservation has been working there this summer and might have the info Donna wants, or if not, could help us get it."

Harry thought he understood the request. Hoss had come to ask him to approach Doris Pinesong about doing some snooping. Hoss was afraid to ask her himself, because he was afraid Doris would turn him down. Harry didn't know if Hoss knew Doris, but he'd be right. Doris wasn't a fan of white people, but she'd been treated very well by the Rossi woman and would be reluctant to do anything behind her back. Harry doubted very much that Mrs. Rossi would approve of a sheriff's deputy nosing around the house without her knowledge.

"You really think this secret shit is necessary, Hoss?"

"To tell you the truth, Harry, I don't know. Donna Roper is technically leading the investigation and she's got something on her mind she's reluctant to tell me about until it . . . ripens more. I trust her; that's what's important. I know you better than she does, so I came to open the door, so to speak. If you're willing to hear

Donna out, I'll let her take it from here."

"You've put me in a spot, Hoss. I don't know Donna all that well, but if she asks a favor of me, Mary would kill me if I didn't do it. Ever since Mary met that deputy, she thinks she's a super-hero on a level with Wonder Woman."

"Wonder Woman?" Hoss faked a serious tone. "I know a compliment doesn't get much better than that, but I don't think I'll pass it along to Donna."

Harry laughed, "Have Donna come and see me. Now, Hoss, I'd like to show you these things we've got in the gallery."

• • •

Harry couldn't help from looking over every few seconds to where Mary and Donna sat behind the gallery's front counter, and signaling to them, with a subtle smile, that the couple he was attending at one of the displays in the next room seemed about to open wide the family wallet to Indigenous Design.

Mary chuckled, "Harry believes he's made a sale. That couple is looking at some big-ticket items. I think you've brought luck with you."

"I try never to leave home without it."

Donna, dressed casually for this meeting in jeans and a sweater, guided the conversation back to the reason for her coming to the gallery. "The situation is this, Mary, I need several pieces of information and I want to perform an experiment in the Rossi house. I can go about this in the direct way, and I and other deputies can conduct a search of the house. I can go to Doris Pinesong and ask my question, but I . . . ah . . ."

"You're not sure you'll get the honest answer you want."

"No, it's not that I think Doris would be dishonest, it's that I

222

need more than an honest answer. I need her cooperation, her extra effort to think about my questions and want to help."

Mary nodded. "I understand. And, you are quite right to come to us. I know for a fact that Doris has strong feelings of loyalty to Mrs. Rossi. The woman has treated her very well—has been a friend, in fact. I believe you would get from Doris just what you imagine, short answers and a determined attitude to protect Mrs. Rossi's privacy. You would get nowhere. The question is; can I do any better?"

Harry approached the counter, his pleasure obvious. In each hand he carried a large multi-colored ceramic bowl. Just the way he handled them as he placed them on the long table used for packaging stated their value.

Donna recognized that an event with a higher priority had inserted itself into their discussion and understandingly looked to Mary, who said in a low voice, "I'll meet you on the back deck as soon as I help pack the bowls."

Donna walked through the gallery to a back door that opened onto a small deck overlooking the rapid and crystalline creek running through downtown Northport. The village was very quiet this morning. Donna could see past the corner of the gallery to the parking lot at Tom's Market. Vacant spaces there had been as sought after as on a Chicago street a mere three weeks ago. Now only two cars were parked. She could even hear the creek several yards away churn its way among rocks and clumps of watercress. She heard the happy note in Harry Swifthawk's laughter coming through the gallery. She also heard the answering laughter of people who had just taken possession of objects upon which they had set their hearts. Mary came through the back door.

"Why don't we sit here," she said. When they were both settled in the folding lawn chairs, she continued, "As I was saying, it will be hard for Doris to let herself adopt your point of view. And, even though I know her very well—I went to school with her older sister and went to their house a lot—it may not move her. Can you tell me more about this?"

Sitting beside Mary now, Donna felt the absence of any barrier between them. None of the normal, continuous layers of restraint that exist between people—all the way from the unyielding façade of officialdom to one's polite laughter at a friend's unfunny joke—was felt by either of them. She should tell Hoss about the ipecac idea first, but she needed Mary's help right now.

"Mary, I've got a crazy idea. I think Gina Rossi killed her husband."

"Oh."

"In itself—wife kills husband who has been cheating—is not a stretch to believe, but it's asking a lot to expect someone to believe she killed him the way I think she did."

Donna hesitated. It was as if she were about to tell this woman, whom she respected, that she, too, was one of those who had seen a UFO, or one of the suspect local group who swear they have seen a cougar in Leelanau County.

"What I strongly believe is this: Gina led a group of women on a tour of her house and arranged to have one of them begin to vomit. This created a few moments when the attention of these women was drawn to the stricken person and allowed Gina time to run downstairs to the patio, stab her husband, then return without being missed."

Mary immediately picked out the absurd element that made Donna's theory "crazy". "You say she 'arranged' to have one of the women get sick?"

Donna took a deep breath and let it out slowly like a parent about to launch uncomfortably into what must sound like an absurd

224

explanation of how babies are made. She withdrew the small ipecac bottle from her pocket.

"This is a substance, which at one time would have been found in many household medicine cabinets. It's called syrup of ipecac. Mothers used it to make their children throw-up any possibly poisonous substance they had swallowed. It . . .

"Yeah, I know. We had some in our house and I saw it work on one of my friends who ate a crayon. Mom ran and got it and made her swallow the whole bottle and in a minute or so . . ." She laughed. "We had a full set of crayons once more."

Donna relaxed. She could, at least, sell one part of her theory.

"Mary, I have a witness, a pharmacist, who sold a bottle just like this one to a woman who exactly fits Gina Rossi's description. This happened only a short time before Silvio's murder."

"Really?"

"Yes, only Gina was so covered up with kerchief and sunglasses that the witness would never be able to absolutely swear to it in court. It would help my case greatly if I could prove a bottle like this one had been in the house. Especially since Gina had no children to explain the need for it."

"You want to ask Doris to look for it?"

"Yes, that and a couple of questions about Gina."

"You want Doris to help you prove the woman who befriended her is a murderess? You're asking me to talk her into doing this?"

Mary had said this as if Donna had just asked her to donate their new gallery to a fund to save the beach sweet pea from extinction.

Donna nodded.

"You believe she killed her husband because of the affair the TV guy, Pollock, talked about."

"Yes, but there had been other affairs also."

Once again Donna heard someone go to the heart of the problem of motive. "Why now if there had been other affairs?"

Mary continued. "And why in this difficult way? Why hadn't she done it before by—let's say demanding he go out into Manhattan after dark to buy her some aspirin."

Donna's head hung a bit as she answered, "I honestly don't know the answers to those questions." She hurried to add, "But Mary, I'm sure she did it."

Mary studied this woman whom she had envied and respected since they'd first met. If this woman had said to her, "Jump into the fire," she'd be inclined to do it and ask questions later.

"You said there were other questions?"

"Yes. I'd like to know if Gina Rossi asked Doris if she had found a ruby earring. Did she, for example, ask Doris to check the vacuum cleaner bag for an earring?"

Finally, Donna said she wanted to conduct an experiment to see how long it would take Gina to run from the upstairs bathroom down the spiral stairs and back.

Mary nodded. "OK, I'll see what I can do." Her tone did not inspire optimism. "You'd better loan me that bottle of medicine."

Three days had passed without a word from Mary Swifthawk. Donna, who had until then only been thinking of the information she needed to back up her theory, now began to realize she probably had caused trouble for Mary with her friend and maybe even more broadly in her community. She began to feel like a loose cannon. She had just gotten back into her patrol car after having stopped Jacob Schaub to tell him that one of his brake-lights was burned out, when her mobile radio came on with her number, directing her to call the dispatcher.

"This is Donna, Kate."

"You got a call from a Mary Swifthawk. She gave me a number

for you to call. I didn't think you wanted me to broadcast it."

"Right, Kate. Thanks."

"I'm sorry it took this long," Mary said when Donna called. "Doris did hesitate about taking part in anything behind Mrs. Rossi's back, but our friendship is strong enough so she'd at least listen to me. Also, to get the information you wanted, I didn't think it necessary to tell Doris that you thought of Mrs. Rossi as a suspect. Incidentally, Doris didn't think the idea of using the medicine to cause the woman to vomit was strange. There had been a bottle in the medicine cabinet in her home, also. I showed her the bottle but she had not seen one like it in the Rossi house.

"In the end, she agreed to our searching through the house and I drove out there this morning. We found nothing. Also, Mrs. Rossi did not ask Doris if she had found an earring and didn't inquire if Mary had emptied the vacuum bag. My question about the bag, however, caused Doris to remember an odd occurrence. She said that when she finished vacuuming after the party, she remembered noticing the indicator on the machine showed that the bag was full and Doris made a mental note to change it before using it again. She was surprised and puzzled yesterday when, before beginning to use it, she opened the machine and discovered the bag had already been changed.

"Gina must have opened the bag herself to see if the earring was there!" Donna said with certainty. She also noted that Gina had done this surreptitiously. If she hadn't been trying to hide the fact that she was looking for the earring, wouldn't it be more normal for her to have asked Doris to check the vacuum bag?

"Oh yes, one other thing," Mary said. "I ran the time experiment running down and back up the spiral stairs. It took me exactly one minute and ten seconds. That is, if Silvio Rossi had his back turned and I could stab him and start the return trip immediately. While I did this, I had Doris imagine that she was attending to a person who was retching. She concluded she would not, in that circumstance, have experienced my absence as excessive."

"Great, Mary. It would have helped if you'd found the bottle, but this has helped a lot. I'm very grateful."

"De nada. Oh, there is an idea that Doris had. She said she really had little to do with the kitchen, except clean the counters and the floor. The person who she thought would be able to tell you more about the contents of the cupboards and pantry would be Paul Treviso, one of the chefs at the party."

"That's a good idea. I'll look up his New York number and call him."

"You won't have to look that far; he and his wife have bought the Beech Tree property here in Northport. They're going to open an Italian restaurant. I saw cars parked there this morning."

"Really! He did mention to me he'd like to stay here instead of returning to New York. Thanks, Mary, I'll go there right now."

28

Northport's copper beech was the largest specimen of its kind most people had ever seen. The venerable tree anchored the south border of the village the way the Washington Monument secured and defined one end of the National Mall. Its strong, twisting branches and healthy, shining foliage reassured the village that hardship is a temporary and man-made concept. "Stick with me," it said, "and we'll see it through together."

The well-proportioned building, which had taken on many identities over the years—residence, restaurant, gallery and museum—was about to be born again as an Italian restaurant. Whatever name the new owners gave it would be secondary to its main identity—the restaurant under the beech tree.

Donna entered through the front door and headed toward the voices she heard. Paul and Laura Treviso were at each end of a measuring tape they had stretched across the back wall of a small kitchen. Donna waited until she saw that Paul had written down the measurement before she spoke.

"Tight quarters," she said sympathetically.

Both Trevisos wheeled around.

"Ah, Deputy Roper," Paul said, surprised as anyone would be to see a uniformed officer-of-the-law standing in one's kitchen. He recovered and introduced his wife with an explanation of where he had met Donna and then joked, "We're not breaking and entering; we and our giant mortgage are about to become local citizens and tax payers."

"So I've heard. I can't tell you how much I hope you're very successful. This whole village, I assure you, feels the same."

"Thanks. As you've pointed out," his gesture took in the entire kitchen, "there are challenges here."

Donna pointed toward a door that opened on a lawn at the rear of the building. "At least, there's room for expansion."

"If there hadn't been, we would not have taken the risk," Laura said. "It will have to wait until we see that the mortgage payments are being met."

"Hence, the challenge," Donna added.

Paul knew Donna had come there on business other than wishing them well on their venture.

"We're pleased by your interest in the restaurant—Il Albero is the name—Italian for tree. But I know there must be another matter that brings you here and I suspect it has to do with Silvio Rossi's murder."

"You're right. I like the restaurant's name, by the way. But yes, I have a question or two concerning the Rossi house—something you may have seen."

Paul handed the tape measure to Laura.

"I suppose you want to talk to me alone."

"It would be better." She stepped back into the empty room, originally the front parlor of the house and walked over to a window. Paul followed her.

Donna took one of her other bottles of ipecac from her pocket and handed it to him. "When you were working in the Rossi house, did you see a bottle like this anywhere?"

Paul turned the bottle over examining it. "Ipecac Syrup. Is it some kind of flavoring I haven't heard of?"

"No, it's what they call an emetic. It induces vomiting, but your question brings up a point. By the way, Paul, I'd like what I'm about to tell you to remain between us—well, it's all right to tell your wife, but no one else. OK?"

"Sure."

Donna went over her suspicion about Gina's house tour and the description of it given by the three women. As she did, the look of surprise she'd expected appeared on Paul's face.

"I've never seen a bottle like this, but I did notice the champagne flutes on the small kitchen counter as you described. Each glass contained maybe two inches or so of a red liquid. I thought to myself that someone was preparing to make kir royales—you know, champagne and cassis. Out of curiosity, I picked up one glass and took a sniff. Smelled to me like cassis all right."

Possibilities and questions flooded Donna's mind.

"Paul, do think that adding this ipecac to the cassis would alter the taste enough to make it noticeable?"

Paul unscrewed the top from the bottle he held and smelled the contents and then poured a drop onto his finger and cautiously tasted it. He considered the impression he'd just formed.

"It would depend on the ratio of the two liquids. This stuff doesn't smell like cassis, but it's mild and not unpleasant. The same goes for the taste."

"Something, then, a mother could get a kid to swallow," Donna said.

"Yes, and in equal parts with cassis, I'd doubt that you'd notice it."

Paul handed the bottle back.

"What about the champagne glasses; did you see them later on, after the murder was discovered?"

"No, I didn't."

"Thanks Paul. You've helped me a lot. When you open Il Albero, I'll be here to direct traffic."

29

"Wake, for morning in the bowl of night
 Has flung the stone that puts the stars to flight.
 And lo the hunter of the east has caught
 The Sultan's turret in a shaft of light."
Donna nestled deeper into the covers.

Derek shook her shoulder gently. "Tis your big day, beautiful. Even now the arbiters of justice are showering, dressing and polishing their shoes in anticipation of your presentation. Awake and receive the encomiums you deserve."

Donna had requested a meeting with Hoss later that morning, where she would report her evidence and conclusion about Gina Rossi. Hoss had suggested they ask Pete Dreisbach, the D.A., to sit in.

She pulled the covers more tightly around her ears.

Derek shook her shoulder harder.

Suddenly, she rolled over and looked at him. "I had a dream in which I had a huge blue ribbon around my neck. Immediately, I remembered the time I won a blue ribbon for running the one hundred yard dash at my grade school field day. I wore it home, of course, and could hardly wait until my father came home to show it to him."

Derek smiled down at her. "You mean, to show you with a blue ribbon to him."

"Right."

"Why do you suppose you had that dream last night?"

"I don't know. What do you think, Dr. Freud?"

"I like to analyze your dreams; they are so pure and simple."

"Childlike."

"I'd never say that."

"Go on, you were saying."

"Do you think it could have anything to do with today's 'field day', the one you're having with Hoss and the DA?"

"What do . . . Oh, my God!" Donna blushed deeply. "Oh, Lord. You're right, of course. The case I've put together against Gina is the blue ribbon and I want Hoss and Pete to make a big fuss over how smart I am."

Donna began pummeling Derek and he defended himself with a pillow.

"Hey, I didn't do anything."

She punched the pillow. "You think you're so smart."

Derek grabbed her wrists and forced them down on the bed and then he kissed her. "Now get dressed like a proper deputy and go make your report. Your solution is correct, of course, and they'll have to agree. Hoss is even capable of picking you up over his head, as your father must have done."

She made a big child-like smile. "You really think so?"

He let go of her hands and she immediately grabbed the pillow and threw it at him as he dodged off the bed.

An hour later, when she walked into Hoss's office and saw him and Pete Dreisbach talking, she couldn't suppress a smile.

"What's so funny?" Hoss asked.

"Oh, nothing. Something someone said earlier."

Pete spoke. "Haven't seen you for a while, Donna."

"That's so. Seems no one has fought my speeding tickets."

"My hunch is you don't hand them out unless the person has been truly flying and he or she knows damn well they can't fight it."

Donna laughed. "Could be."

"OK," Hoss said, intending to shift to the subject for which Donna had requested the meeting. "I've told Pete you've been in charge of the Rossi investigation from the first and you've been pursuing a line on your own, which you tell me has proven to be the correct one. We're both eager to hear what you've come up with."

She had prepared notes so she wouldn't forget a single element in her case. She began by describing the murder scene and the result of their interrogation of those at the party. She then dealt with each of the guests who had no corroborative alibi and their apparently strong motives that dissolved upon closer examination. Finally, she came to the conversation she'd had with Gina Rossi just before Gina left the county.

"Her behavior just didn't ring true for me—not a grieving widow. That caused me to look closer at her story."

Consulting her notes frequently, she gave a detailed account of the way Gina had gone about planning and carrying out the murder. She told of the sound the two authors had heard coming from the spiral stairs. She ended by describing the results of an experiment of her own where she made two glasses of kir, one with and one without added ipecac.

"The cassis took over. That's all I tasted. And, the drinks, after adding the champagne, looked the same."

Donna closed her notebook and studied the reactions of the two men. They weren't exactly tossing her in the air the way her father had.

Hoss spoke first. "Pete, that's our case. If we were to arrest this woman, how easy would it be to prosecute her?"

Dreisbach looked sharply at Hoss. He couldn't believe Hoss had seriously asked about the ease of prosecution. Pete sensed that Hoss had just tossed a hot potato to him rather than confront his deputy himself. The look he gave Hoss also said Hoss owed him one.

Dreisbach awarded Donna with a smile and an affirmative nod. "Nice work. It's a very convincing argument." In spite of what he said, he really believed her idea was totally bizarre. "The problem for me is there isn't one single thing you've given me I'd dare take to the courtroom. Any good criminal lawyer would convincingly discredit every one of your points. And, you've got to believe this woman would have the best lawyers in the country."

This wasn't what Donna had expected to hear and she was speechless.

"OK, from the top." Dreisbach began. "Everything, of course, that you discerned about her lack of appropriate widow-like behavior or disinterest in the investigation is of no consequence. 'Ladies and gentlemen of the jury, my client had been through so much in those few days; who can say how she should react? Those of you who have lost loved ones know what I mean; so many well wishing friends have to be listened to until one's feelings are worn away, worn flat. You are just waiting for people to leave you alone so you can grieve in private.' Can't you just hear the defense lawyer?

"The whole idea of someone planning a murder that hinges upon assembling the right cast—an old woman who will only concentrate on the sick person and pay no attention to how long the murderess is absent and a woman who is phobic about vomiting and is sure to run away— borders on fiction. Can't you just see our lawyer presenting it to the jury, while not being able to suppress his laughter?

"Of course, Mrs. Rossi will be dressed in high fashion with her hair styled to make it stand out and her expressive dark eyes accented to the fullest. I will ask the pharmacist, 'Look around the room, can you point out the woman who bought the bottle of ipecac?' What do you think the pharmacist will answer? At best it will be, 'I can't be sure.'

"And then we come to the chef, Paul Treviso. The defense will ask, 'Can you say that the liquid in one of the glasses looked different to you?' You know what he will have to answer—you just told us about your own experiment.

"By the way, did the Nuvolari woman volunteer that the sound she heard was of someone running down the stairs, or did you ask her if that's what it sounded like?"

"I believe I asked her."

"You can see that her lawyer will object that you planted the idea in her mind. Right?

"Finally, I have a question. Let's say Gina Rossi did kill her husband—why then? The only motive you've suggested is Silvio's infidelity, yet you've also said he had a reputation for affairs. So why then? And, why there? I've got to say it's not where I'd attempt to do such a thing."

When Dreisbach had finished, Donna felt foolish. She was happy she had not mentioned the earring. On her own now, even without Dreisbach's parody, she could imagine the defense attorney. "Is it unusual for a woman to loose an earring?" And, "Would a woman whose husband had just been murdered—a woman for whom money meant little—be concerned about her earrings? Would she bother herself to rush to make a report of its disappearance to the police?"

Things hadn't gone as Hoss had anticipated. Hoss realized acutely he should have gone over Donna's "case" with her beforehand. He felt guilty for the hosing Dreisbach gave her.

"Thanks, Pete, for stopping by and cluing us in on the legal point of view. We'll have to review our options and get back to you."

Dreisbach understood the cue to make an exit. "As I said, Donna, your argument is plausible, but you've got to give me something I can use in court."

"Thanks, Pete," Donna managed.

When they were alone, Hoss said, "As I said before, there are a lot of cases relegated to the unsolved tray, in which the police know very well who the perp is, but they haven't got the kind of evidence Pete needs—evidence a smart lawyer can't discredit."

Donna couldn't help the tear that rolled down her cheek. She wiped it away quickly. "I'm sorry Hoss. I'm afraid I fucked this case up."

"Not at all. Believe me, if I had had one good idea about another line of investigation, I would have told you. My sole hope depended on those New York interviews. I went over the facts daily and never thought of anything I would have done differently. You, at least, came up with a reasonable theory."

"I don't have any 'good' evidence and I can't see that changing. What do you think I should do?"

"Many cases become 'cold cases' until the perp makes a mistake, usually talks too much. Perhaps we'll have to wait for something like that to happen. This is a murder, so it is never closed. The file will remain open and in your case load."

Donna got up. She shook her head as if to free herself from this case and her disappointment. "I've got to help Becky. We're part of a program at Glen Lake High School—a civics class. We represent law enforcement on the county level."

"Right. Have a good talk."

Donna walked outside into the warm September day. She thought of the embarrassing session she'd just experienced. Lighten up, she told herself. All right, she didn't have the proof the law demanded; she knew she had caught her man—or, rather, woman.

What Hoss said was probably true; many murders go unsolved until the murderer screws up. We'll have to wait, he'd said. Her problem: She didn't believe Gina Rossi would ever screw up. But if she did, Donna resolved, she'd be waiting—she and the ruby earring.

She reached her patrol car and had her hand on the door handle when she had the unwelcome and chilling thought: maybe there had been no ipecac in the drinks. Maybe, after all, that and Gina's guilt were totally creations of her own imagination.

Part Two

30

Her name was now Mrs. Donna Marsh. It had been so for two years. Her valued independence had finally become an encumbrance and she had succumbed happily to Derek's pressure. She was very happy. She was also a little bored with the present circumstances. Derek had accepted the chairmanship of the Program Committee for an international psychiatric conference being held in Zurich. His best friend during their training years now served as President of the American Psychiatric Association, one of the meeting's sponsors. A combination of pressure from Jim and his own curiosity and a need for an adventure had led Derek to agree to take on the position. The program chairman's job had lived up to his expectations, or rather his fears; dealing with unforeseen cancellations or delayed arrivals of speakers due to illness or spite, hurt feelings over lecture room assignments and so on. He, as he had also feared, found no opportunity to attend the presentations he would really liked to have heard. His duties required his presence for eight days. Four had passed already, during which Donna had seen him only at breakfast and dinner time.

The sun shone brightly on the snow-topped mountains of the Lepontine Alps to the south of the Swiss city. The air here at the shore of the Zuricher See was balmy in late September. At home, the leaves had begun to change color, but Donna noted little evidence here of summer's end. She stood on a promenade above the water and tossed bits of a roll she had saved from breakfast to a group of grateful ducks.

When Derek had first asked if she'd be interested in taking

some vacation time from the Sheriff's Department to go with him to Switzerland, she had agreed with excited anticipation. Later, when Derek expressed second thoughts about having accepted the job, she had worked right along with his friend, Jim, to reverse his hesitation. They were making their first trip together outside the country, several factors having combined to limit their honeymoon to a long weekend in Chicago. However, the realities of Derek's function at the convention here in Zurich had proved deflating. Busy from breakfast until dinner, he had also been called upon to attend two, late post-dinner meetings on two of the four nights they had been here. She was restless; Zurich had only proven good for three days, at least if you're alone.

Maybe she could take a side trip during the day: Lucerne or Basil. Then, standing looking to the south and the snow-capped peaks of the Alps, the perfect idea sprang to her mind; just over those mountains lay the Italian Riviera. Donna had been to Rome, Florence and Venice, but never to northern Italy. To go there now would mean being away for two, even three days. She, of course, really wanted Derek to be with her, but that was impossible. At that moment one of those wonderful, problem-solving maneuvers occurred that the mind is so good at. She could go and scout out the area for a return trip with Derek. Yes, that's what she'd do!

She threw the last morsel to the waiting ducks and hurried back to the hotel to call Derek.

Luckily Derek was still in the Program Committee's office when she called the Congress Hall. He was very surprised to hear her voice so soon after they had parted at the breakfast table.

"I think I'd like to take a quick trip to the Italian Riviera. I'll be back the night before our plane departs. That is, if it's all right with you," she added.

Her announcement made Derek blink. He also noticed the lilt

of anticipation in her voice, a lilt that hadn't been there at breakfast. He knew the demands of his duties had created a less than ideal holiday experience for her. Although he would miss her company at the end of each day, he recognized her need for diversion.

"Sounds good. When are you leaving?"

"Right now. I'll throw a few things into the small bag I carry on the plane for books and my iPod, and I'll catch a cab to the train station."

Derek had memories of such spontaneity in his college years. He envied her and wished he were going along.

"Where will you go, do you think?"

"I thought I'd go to the nearest point on the Mediterranean and play it by ear."

"What point would that be?"

"I'll have to look at the map, but I think Genoa is directly south of here. I've never been to the Italian Riviera."

"Same here."

"I wish you were going with me."

He said the perfect thing. "Play the part of a scout and find the perfect place for us to stay at some future time."

"I'll call you tonight and tell you where I've lighted."

"Have fun. I love you."

"Love you, too."

From Zurich the train first climbed to the St. Gotthard Pass surrounded by awesome white peaks and then began its descent through the Italian Piedmont toward Milan and the Mediterranean coast. Donna experienced a Disney World ride from the temperate Europe of the north into the sunny Europe of Italy. At twelve thirty, she stepped onto the platform in Genoa. She wondered if she should get a hotel and explore the city or, it being early, go further along the coast. The sign identifying the train standing on the neighboring track read "NICE", and under this, listed in smaller letters, the cities of "Monte Carlo, Savona." She asked a man wearing a conductor's uniform when the train departed and he held up six fingers.

"Can I buy a ticket on the train?"

He shook his head and pointed to the ticket booths. "Run," he advised in English.

At Savona she descended from the train into a contemporary, utilitarian and uninviting terminal. Discouragement of loitering had been built into the design. Coming out of this sterile interior into the sunlight, Donna saw a prosaic, commercial city—not the romantic sunny Riviera she'd expected. It looked like she'd made a mistake—should have stayed in Genoa—but she felt too tired from the journey to return immediately. She would stay here one night.

The rule she'd adopted when traveling as a Kellogg sales rep was to get settled first, get oriented with the help of the hotel staff and then immediately eat something. Here in Liguria that would have to be *pesto Genovese*.

She thought she could do better than the vicinity around the station for a hotel. "The old city" had to be more interesting and she knew every European city had one if it hadn't been destroyed in a war. She asked a woman just entering the station for the direction to the *citta vecchia*. The woman's answer went over her head, but the gesture told her that what she sought existed, and it lay to the east of the railway terminal. Donna started to walk away, but the woman called to her and pointed to a taxi. Donna understood this advice.

The taxi she took let her off at the harbor, a cozy enclosure filled with yachts and watched over by a great, grey, brooding fortress. She decided she'd find an outdoor café where she could get a drink and ask the waiter to recommend a hotel. The only café' in sight was very busy. She wanted something quieter. She turned and began to walk down a street away from the harbor. On the train from Genoa she had recalled that early in the investigation of Silvio Rossi's murder she had learned that Gina Rossi had originally come from Savona. She began, now, to imagine Gina as a young girl walking along this very street. She stopped abruptly and stood, bag in hand, oblivious to her surroundings. Disbelief and embarrassment seized her. Did the idea for the entire trip into Italy originate in an unconscious curiosity about Gina Rossi? It was true that she had always wanted to see this part of the Riviera, but why now and why Savona? Her motive had become too transparent for her to deny it any longer. Had Derek understood this? If he'd remembered that Gina had come from the Riviera, of course he had. Before allowing self-criticism to advance too far, she rallied, telling herself she'd think about it no more until she'd found a cafe and had that drink. Facing her at the end of the street stood a long, three-story building with a row of classic columns running along the second story supporting a lintel. As she got nearer to it she realized the whole three-dimensional effect of the façade was a trompe l'oeil. The façade was flat, the columns painted. The discovery of having been fooled knocked her further off-balance. Where was that pleasant little café when she needed it? A couple of blocks more brought her to the perfect place nestled into an angle of a small renaissance palace, the Palazzo Gavotti, now the city art museum. She took a seat at a sunny table.

Donna had lost track of Gina Rossi. Gil Wolf, the realtor, mentioned that he had been told to send some papers relating to the sale of the house to an attorney in Turin, and she had wondered if this meant Gina had returned to Italy. For a while she had checked out the website of Silvio Rossi Enterprises, but about a year ago she got back the computer message that the site couldn't be located. She'd figured the time had come when, like Mickey Mantle bats, Silvio Rossi merchandise was no longer in demand and Frank Knowles had gone to a happy retirement in North Carolina.

Here is where chance entered in the way it does constantly in our lives, usually unrecognized and unacknowledged. You sleep late and miss your usual train into the city and are forced to take the next one and you take a seat next to a person who will become your future spouse.

In the present instance, the waiter who saw Donna sit down and who started toward her table was called away to take a phone call. The waiter who had brought him the message then came to Donna's table instead. Had the first waiter been the one she talked to, almost certainly her experience here would have unfolded much differently.

The young man who stood smiling at her in his starched white jacket possessed an easy, casual manner and spoke very good English.

Instead of doing as she normally would and asking for coffee or a glass of white wine, she, because of rising pleasure at finding this pleasant little café, playfully outlined her situation to the waiter.

"This is my first time here. I love this square and I'd like your recommendation of the perfect drink to go with it."

The waiter matched her mood. "Yes, yes, I know what you mean. A stein of Augustinerkeller beer in Munich, eh?" He didn't have to think long before saying, "I think Cinque Terre," and without waiting for her to agree, hurried into the café.

She became aware of just how happy she felt sitting there in the sun and wished again Derek were with her to make the moment complete. She thought of him cooped up in some dreary conference hall and gave a mental shudder.

The waiter reappeared with a glass of white wine, set it down, obviously waiting for her to taste it and approve of his choice.

Donna complied and while savoring it let her gaze pass around the piazza. "*Perfecto*," she pronounced with mock solemnity.

"And what is the perfect drink if I visit your home?"

"Let me think. I live on a small peninsula surrounded by the waters of Lake Michigan." She studied him to see if he knew of the lake.

"Yes, I was in Chicago several years ago."

"Much farther north, on the opposite side of the lake is my home. The drink—although we make very good grape wine—would have to be cherry wine. Cherries are what we are known for. Cherryland."

The waiter laughed, "Like fairyland."

"Yes, only I don't think it snows as much in fairyland. Did you acquire your excellent English in Chicago?"

"I only visited Chicago for a few days. I worked in New York City for two years. I knew a little English before that, but I really learned to speak there."

"What were you doing in New York?"

"My cousin got me a job in a restaurant. I liked New York, but it was too big for me. This is where my family is, so I came back."

"I don't blame you." Donna could see that he may have misunderstood the idiom and added, "I mean, I can understand you'd want to live—work right here." Her gesture took in the whole of the square. "I passed an interesting building walking here—large with painted columns across the front. Another palace, I assume."

"Yes, yes. The Palazzo della Rovere."

"What's its history?"

"A local boy made good."

She decided his idiom repertoire wasn't so bad.

"He became a pope, Sixtus the fourth" the waiter went on. "Back then, the job paid very well. He is best remembered today for building a chapel in the Vatican. His cousin, another boy from Savona, who also became a pope—Julius the second—had the good sense to have Michelangelo decorate the ceiling."

"Really. So, it all started here."

It pleased the waiter to find Donna curious about his city, so he ventured into becoming her guide.

"It's nice here, but the best I think are the small villages in the hills. I was born and grew up in Carreto."

He accompanied this information by pointing inland to the rising land behind the narrow coast.

"It's a beautiful place," he added. "You can look out over the sea."

This was getting ahead of her agenda. Before she could think of side trips from the city, she first had to find a hotel.

"You can help me if you would recommend a hotel."

He considered this for a moment. "Hotel Fortuna is in the next block. It's nice."

"Good. And, what in your opinion is the best restaurant in the city?"

"The best restaurant in the area, of course, is in Carreto, the Pera Dorada."

"Really?"

"Yes, everyone will tell you that. If you don't need to stay here in the city, it is also a very nice hotel. Very pretty and not expensive. The owner's English is also very good."

His enthusiasm resonated with Donna's growing openness to adventure, awakened by her discovery of the piazza and this new acquaintance.

"Does a bus go there?" she asked.

"To Carreto? Oh, sure, every hour. The bus leaves from in front of the train station."

"If I took the bus there now, do you think I would need a reservation?"

"At this time of year, I'm sure you wouldn't. But, if you seriously want to go there, I'll call right now and make a reservation for you. And your lunch, have you had lunch yet?"

"No, I haven't."

"I'll ask them to keep the kitchen open until you get there."

The feeling of the moment swept her along. "That would be great."

• • •

"Marcello said I must give you our best room." The woman's attitude was pleasantly easy going and friendly. It is instantly possible to identify the owners of small hotels from the hired staff and Donna had no doubt from the moment she'd walked through the door that this diminutive, energetic woman owned the Hotel Pera Dorada. She had just opened the door to a large, white-walled bedroom with colorful accents. She walked ahead of Donna to a bay widow with a view to the south and the coastline. Over the woman's shoulder Donna glimpsed the scintillation of the afternoon sun off the Mediterranean.

"Marcello said you will have lunch with us," she said after opening the window to a fresh breeze.

"Yes, if I'm not too late. Marcello told me yours was the best food in the region."

"That Marcello. I guess I owe him a drink. But, what can I say, he's right."

They both laughed and the woman said, "My name is Anna, Anna Lohngi. If I can help you in any way, please let me know. Marcello didn't say how long you might stay."

Donna had liked what she'd seen of the village from the bus and the hotel was charming. Maybe she had stumbled upon the special place she and Derek would return to together. She'd stay until she had to return to Zurich.

"Two nights, then I have to meet my husband in Zurich for our flight home."

"Ah, too bad you can't stay longer . . . maybe another time."

The day being clear and warm, Anna Lohngi had asked Donna if she would like her lunch served on the terrace, which offered the same view of the sea as her room. That's where she now sat. The young waitress confirmed that *pesto Genovese* was, indeed, on the dinner menu, so Donna decided to save that for dinner and ordered a light calamari salad for her lunch. She continued to sit on the terrace and sip her wine after the dishes were removed. She'd ordered a bottle of sauvignon blanc from Friuli after the waitress assured her that the unfinished portion could be saved for her dinner. The afternoon sun cast shadows of the moving leaves of a nearby tree across her table, creating a mesmerizing effect.

Anna Lohngi, bringing fresh flowers for the vase on her table, broke the spell.

"I saw from your passport that you are from Michigan," Anna said as she arranged the flowers.

"Yes, a small town in the north."

"I have a friend who had a house in Michigan. Her husband died there," Anna said in the way one will, when gathering together every association to a fact a stranger has just revealed about him or herself.

Donna was caught between an impulse to say an automatic, I'm sorry, and the thought that sympathy may be inappropriate; this may only be an acquaintance the woman spoke of. Still, she felt she had to say something.

"How did he die?" Donna asked

"He was murdered."

"Murdered?" This was the very last thing she expected the woman to say. "When was this?"

Anna thought for a while, each slight nod of her head counting off a year. "Maybe four years ago."

"What is your friend's name?" asked Donna, totally alert for the answer.

"Gina del Carreto."

Donna had been listening for Gina Rossi, not del Carreto.

"del Carreto?"

"Yes, but when Silvio was killed, her name was Rossi. Silvio, her husband, was a famous chef. Maybe you heard about his murder?"

"Yes, of course," Donna replied. An inner warning told her to go slowly about how much she knew. This woman's willingness to talk freely to a complete stranger about a friend might become restrained if she were to know of Donna's closeness to the case and Donna eagerly wanted to hear more.

She added quickly, "Everyone in the whole country knew about the murder because of his fame as a television celebrity. What a terrible thing, to have your husband murdered."

"Yes, and almost before her eyes."

What was this? "Before her eyes?" Donna repeated.

"No, Gina didn't see it happen. She would have known who killed him in that case and they never discovered who did it. I mean she saw him, Silvio, right after it happened. He was stabbed in the chest—right through the heart."

In her mind, Donna began to object that it had been through the back, but caught herself. Afraid that direct questions about Gina might cause Anna to question her motives, Donna decided to focus on Anna's relationship with Gina—Gina del Carreto.

"She is your friend?" Donna prodded.

"My best friend—since childhood. We went to school every day together." Anna Longhi had motioned with her head as she said this toward the hill above the town.

"She lived here?"

"Yes. The del Carreto family has lived here for hundreds of years. The town, of course, takes its name from the family."

"Now? She lives here now?" Donna worked to make the question sound of only casual interest to her.

Anna stopped to consider how to answer. "Yes and no. That is, her family lives here, her brother—although he is in Turin much of the time—and his wife and the children live here, but Gina is in Genoa at school."

School? Donna had just heard more than she could ever have expected about the woman who had apparently drawn her, through a powerful curiosity, to Savona.

"This seems such a wonderful place to spend ones childhood," Donna said and then added, "Won't you sit down with me, join me in a glass of this very good wine?"

Anna Longhi smiled and pulled out a chair next to Donna. "Thank you. Yes, *Le Due Terre*, it is very good." She called through the door to the waitress to bring her a glass. When it was brought, Donna half-filled it with the crystal clear wine.

Anna, recalling Donna's remark about the town and with nostalgia entering her voice, agreed with her. "It was wonderful . . . back then. Life was very simple. Oh, we tried to make it complicated, Gina and I, with our secrets, but what innocent secrets they were. Gina took a lipstick from her mother's dresser and we hid in the orchard—just down there—and put it on. Then we had to sneak into the restaurant toilet to scrub it off. How innocent we were."

The waitress came to see if they wanted anything more and then left. Anna said, motioning in the young woman's direction, "Not like today, tattoos, piercing. My father would have cut my head right off if I had put a ring through my eyebrow like she has. And, we went to the convent school. The nuns were very strict."

"There is a convent in Caretto?"

"No, we went to Savona, to the convent of Santa Clara. Old Sesto, who worked on the del Carreto estate, drove us down in the car every morning and came back to pick us up in the afternoon."

"You say estate."

"Yes, Castello Carreto. Gina's family have been the—how you say—ah, I can't think of the English word, but the important people of this area since the middle ages."

"Gentry?" Donna offered.

"Yes, but more."

"Nobility?"

"Yes, like that. *Condetorre*, cardinals and rich. They owned all the land. Not so much now, but still much."

"And the brother runs the estate now?"

"In a sense, but Senor Tocco does the day-to-day managing. Roberto, Gina's brother is a lawyer. His office is in Turin."

Donna put together a new image of Gina Rossi as each new fragment of information came from Anna. She had assembled the picture of a rich girl from a locally very important family, who was raised in a conservative, probably strict, catholic ethic. Did this fit with the Gina she'd known in Leelanau? This wasn't how she had thought of her before. Initially she'd viewed her as a passive, long-suffering woman who had been content to live in the shadow of an active, outgoing and domineering husband. A woman who, probably out of financial insecurity, had tolerated her husband's infidelity while presenting the persona of the loving, loyal wife to the world. Donna had had difficulty back then reconciling that image with the person she had finally thought Gina to be, one, who could brutally and dramatically murder her husband. How could the new facts she'd learned help reconcile the apparent incongruity? Totally, her thoughts were captured by the challenge, but she reminded herself that she had to go easy. She needed to change the subject.

"This hotel, apparently it's been in your family for some time."

"My grandfather's father—grand grandfather?"

"Great grandfather," supplied Donna.

"Yes, great grandfather. He built it in 1858. My grandfather added to it."

"It is so very . . . comfortable."

"Yes, old things. We say the edges wear off."

"But, there is also the restaurant and its reputation."

"My husband, Umberto, that is his passion," said Anna laughing and raising her glass as if toasting.

"So, you and your best friend ended up marrying chefs. That's quite a coincidence."

"Ah, well." Anna's mood abruptly clouded. She caught herself and smiled ruefully saying, "But that's another story."

Donna ached to ask about this other story, but waited, hoping Anna would take the lead.

Anna finished her wine and got up. "Thank you for the wine, and the conversation, but I must go to Savona to do some shopping. You'll be dining with us tonight?"

"Yes, certainly. How could I not, after Marcello's praise?"

31

Donna continued to sit at the table and stare out toward the sea, but she didn't see a thing; she thought only about what she'd just heard. She was amazed at what a rich mine of information about Gina she'd happened upon. Foremost in her thoughts was the tantalizing phrase Anna had used, "But that's another story."

Donna left the terrace and walked through the hotel lobby and out into the town's main piazza that the hotel faced. At the square's center stood a fountain. A central obelisk supported four dolphins. Each probably faced a cardinal point of the compass and each let a steady stream fall from its mouth into a basin circling the shaft. A man busied himself skimming leaves from the surface of the pool with a net. "1780" was inscribed just above the level of the water. In her experience, fountains of such a vintage in small towns had long since ceased to function. The people of this place must care. She wondered if the man performed his task as his civic contribution.

She wandered out of the piazza along a street leading eastward. She passed venerable buildings housing brightly furnished shops with enticing goods: a butcher shop, a fruit market that also had a showcase of dozens of cheeses. All the while, a direction was subconsciously beckoning—the direction of the hill behind the town where Anna's gesture had pointed. At the next corner she turned into a street leading upward and her pace advanced from a leisurely stroll to a determined march. On this side street she passed a cabinetmakers shop, an electric appliance store and what came close to what she'd call a hardware store. After this there came a long two-story building of apartments and then several individual homes with small gardens. Where would this "estate" be? Right, left, farther up the hill? The paved street she'd been walking on came to an end and a narrow, cobbled lane led back toward the west, the direction she'd come from. Her pace slowed along this lane, because breaks in the foliage afforded tantalizing glimpses of gardens and the sea beyond. Ahead of her she saw a paved road lead farther up the hill. The possibility that this road might lead to Gina's house re-ignited her curiosity. At the junction of the lane and the paved road, Donna could see that the road descended to enter one corner of the main piazza; looking upward, the road disappeared over the crest of a hill. Upward she climbed until she reached the hill's top. Before her now stood a perfect gem of a small castle. Perched on a low outcropping of rock, the building, even to the unschooled eye, harmoniously combined architectural elements representing styles reaching back many centuries. The part that appeared to be the oldest stood nearest her. A crenellated twenty-foot wall and a small turret presented a bold challenge to anyone approaching and to the world below. This was apparently the only remnant of a wall that originally must have encircled the entire promontory. At the side of the turret the paved road ran on between sturdy, stone gateposts on which hung heavy, wrought iron gates of elaborate scrollwork. The gates stood open. Beyond them Donna could see a graveled forecourt and the baroque façade of the main building—not a royal palace, but a very significant edifice nonetheless. Donna had no doubt she had found Castello Carreto.

She certainly hadn't been prepared for this. It was like observing a fellow worker being picked up at quitting time by a chauffeured Bentley limousine. She stood for several minutes, taking in the details of the architecture, until a man pushing a wheelbarrow came out of the entrance gate and noticed her. She turned slowly and made her way back down the hill to Carreto's main piazza and her hotel.

The gnocchi with pesto and the red mullet were both deserving of her full attention, but on Donna's mind was Derek's absence. She almost resented the soft ambience of the dining room, its burnished old wood and simple but solid appointments, because they created a perfect romantic setting that she was barred from fully enjoying without him. Neither Derek's nor her cell phone worked in Europe. She could call only the Program Committee office or the hotel. She'd been fortunate to reach him at the Committee office in the late afternoon and to report all she had unexpectedly learned about Gina Rossi. She went only as far as saying that she'd found Carreto to be interesting, not that she'd discovered a treasure. She could sense that his wish to be there with her was already placing a strain on his patience with his duties.

In spite of her lonely feelings, she made herself display the appropriate appreciation and ask intelligent questions about the meal when Umberto, Anna's husband, came to her table in his full chef's garb minus toque. He answered her questions then he intuitively addressed her loneliness.

"Anna tell me you husband in Svizzera. You see him soon, yes?"

Donna smiled as she realized his purpose. "Yes, very soon. I only wish he were able to enjoy your town and this hotel."

"That easy," he shrugged. "You two come again. When I know you come, I make my special, *capon magro*."

Donna laughed, "Then we must . . . as soon as we can."

Later Anna who, along with the young waitress from lunchtime, served the guests, came to the table with the cheese trolley.

Donna told her of her brief conversation with Umberto and of his promise to make his specialty.

"Ah, capon magro. A sign he likes you, my dear. It takes much preparation—too much to be on the menu. And, now that you have promised to come back, you must do it."

"Anna, I walked up the hill and found what must be your friend, Gina's, house. I was surprised at its size."

"Like I said, the del Carretos are a very important family. The garden is my favorite part. Of course the reason it is special for me is because Gina and I spent so much time in it when we were children. If you would like, I could take you through the garden tomorrow."

You can do that? Donna wondered, and then remembered that Anna had said she and Gina were best friends.

"Yes, I'd like that very much."

"I can be free to do it right after breakfast."

Donna went to bed contented. Derek wouldn't miss out on Carreto. Her pact with Umberto assured this.

As soon as Donna finished her coffee the next morning, Anna came to the table and said she was free to set out on their expedition. She said she had called the house, hoping she would be able to introduce Donna to Gina's sister-in-law and the children, but they were in Turin today.

Just as well, Donna thought. Learning more about Gina was one thing, getting involved with her family was another.

When they passed through Castello Carreto's entrance gate, they came upon the same man Donna had seen the day before. He worked at reattaching an errant wire that supported an espaliered pear tree, heavy with fruit. He clearly had his hands full and could only smile and nod to the two women.

Anna waved back. "Guido. Guido's father used to drive Gina and me to school. They maintained the garden better back then. To Gina's father, Massimo, the garden was very important. He employed two full-time gardeners."

They passed through another gate and into a walled space of perhaps three acres. To Donna's eyes it looked very well tended. A small area of formal design with trimmed hedges and a gravel walk stretched across the rear of the house. The remainder of the garden was given over to fruit trees, flowering shrubs and informal, free-formed flower beds. An ideal playground for two little girls.

Anna's thoughts paralleled Donna's. "We spent many hours here. Paula—she was the cook and a second mother to Gina after her mother died—she, Paula, would lay out some ingredients on the kitchen table and let us think we were inventing original dishes. Then we'd take what we had made and hike out among these trees and pretend we were lost in a jungle and only had the food we'd brought." She laughed. "Otherwise, we may not have been able to stomach what we'd made."

"How old was your friend when her mother died?"

"Only twelve. Fortunately, Gina and her father were very close."

Anna pointed up ahead. "At other times we'd take our lunches to the raised terrace called the Belvedere. You can't see it from here; the trees are in the way. You can see across the whole countryside from there. We'd sit and draw. I'd draw horses and Gina always drew buildings: cathedrals, palaces things like that."

"Natural for her I'd guess, growing up in a house like hers."

"Yes, but she had a real talent. She wanted to study to be an architect. That's why she went to Bologna; it was the best school."

Another unexpected side of Gina. "That's quite a shift of direction—from architectural student to chef's wife," Donna observed.

258

The focus on Gina had developed in natural sequence. Anna had supplied the leads and Donna responded. She had the feeling that the topic of Gina had now become something the two women could discuss as a phenomenon of life, rather than as an intrusion into the privacy of a friend. Donna waited, hoping her appraisal was true.

Anna continued, "It was more than just a change of direction; it meant a tragic destruction of her life." Anger had entered her voice.

"How do you mean?" Donna said, surprised by the emotion Anna displayed.

Anna did not answer immediately. Donna sensed that this was not a subject Anna talked of readily—maybe not even to her husband.

Then it all burst forth. "She was raped! That egotist raped her!"

Donna, unsure how to respond, remained silent.

"I blame myself. We talked on the telephone almost every day. I encouraged her to go out with him. It was like this; I went earlier to visit her in Bologna, and we went out to a nice restaurant. He was a chef and he came out of the kitchen and talked to us—Gina really. He was young and handsome and a good talker. He had us laughing. He also sent glasses of expensive dessert wine to the table. About a week later, after I'd returned home, he called her. He had found out her name and telephone number. He asked her to go to a party with him. Gina hesitated. She told him she was unsure if she would be free and asked him to call back. She called me that same night to talk with me about it. Neither of us had had much experience with men. Around here we had always moved in groups of boys and girls. There was little pairing off. She said Silvio seemed too fast for her. Besides, although she had only spoken to him in one of her classes, Gina had become interested in one of her young instructors and she thought the feeling was returned."

Donna worked to both follow what she was being told, and at the same time, to place this into the context of her professional interest in Gina Rossi. Anna sensed the intensity of Donna's interest and went on with her story.

"Anyway, and that is what I blame myself for, I encouraged her to accept the date with Silvio. I said he seemed to be lively and she would probably enjoy the kind of flamboyant attention he'd give her. When she still hesitated, I said, 'What harm can it do?' This convinced her she was making too much of a simple invitation to a party."

Anna had brought them to the belvedere. "See what a view," she said motioning to the panorama before them.

Donna feared this interruption had put Anna off her passionate tale. But, there had been too much emotion awakened for it to settle so quickly.

"At the party, one of Silvio's friends came up to him and asked Silvio if he had remembered to bring along the new camera he'd forgotten at Silvio's apartment. I'm now sure the two men had made this up between them. Silvio made as if he was very sorry to have forgotten to bring it and said he would go to his apartment right then and get it. He asked Gina to go with him and keep him company. "

Anna lapsed into silence, empathically reconstructing Gina's experience.

"Did he do what I'm afraid he did?" Donna asked.

"Yes, yes. She was barely in the room when he grabbed her. She tried to fight him off, but he acted as if by coming to his apartment she had given him a sign of her willingness. Everyone would agree with him he claimed, and since she had agreed, she owed him what he wanted. She struggled, but he got what he wanted anyway. As I came to know more about him, it became clear Silvio always got what he wanted. He couldn't stand the word 'no'.

"Gina was devastated for a while, then she told me one day, 'Things can happen to a person; they should make you wiser, but they shouldn't spoil your life.' She, of course, stayed away from Silvio and he could see in her eyes that he should stay away from her. She became immersed in her studies and the relationship with her instructor advanced. She seemed to have forgotten the incident with Silvio. Then she missed her period."

"Don't tell me."

"Yes. And only a short time later, one of the girls at school guessed it and told Silvio. This was about twenty years ago, and even back then most men in his situation would have just ignored the news or would have given the girl the money to make a trip to Switzerland. Silvio could see other possibilities for himself. He had learned about the wealth and importance of Gina's family. A marriage would give him opportunities he may never be able to arrange on his own. Gina had her own needs and fears. She worshiped her father, for whom the family's honor was as important as life itself. She would give anything to avoid that look of deep disappointment she knew she'd see on his face if she had to tell him she was pregnant. Silvio wouldn't agree to an abortion and threatened to go to her father if she dared to act without his agreement."

"So, she decided to marry him," Donna concluded.

"She could see no other way. And, if it was to be done it should be done right away to protect her father and the honor of the family. She told her father she had met the man of her dreams and wanted to marry right away."

"What did her father think of Silvio?"

"The news surprised him, of course—the suddenness. But he tried to make the best of it. I suppose there were tales of how the family had, over the centuries, taken unlikely candidates to the family's bosom and made proper del Carretos of them. Anyway, a big wedding was quickly arranged. In spite of the short notice, three cardinals, the Secretary of the Holy Office, four Senators and Gianni Agnelli himself attended."

Without Donna being very aware of walking, they had left the high terrace and were now moving along a path next to a bed of roses.

"And Gina . . . "

"I was about to say she did that mental trick women seem destined to do; she did her best to love Silvio."

"And, did she accomplish it?"

"She didn't tell me she didn't . . . at that time."

Donna waited, giving Anna an inquiring look.

"In her third month she miscarried."

"Oh!"

"It hit her very hard. The following weekend she came home. I went to the station to pick her up and when I saw her, I became very worried. It was as if a plug had been pulled on her mental and physical strength. Silvio had not given her the support she needed. Her father didn't know of the miscarriage but he saw that she was ill and in no condition to return to school and persuaded her to remain with him until she felt better.

"I saw her every day. I got her to talk. I could see she had placed great hope that the birth of the child would give meaning to her marriage. Toward the end of the week, she had begun to think about getting pregnant again. Little by little she began to regain her vitality. When I saw her off at the station, I thought things would be all right."

This puzzled Donna; she had understood during the investigation that Gina had no children. "Did she have another child?"

"No. I don't know the full story about the reason, but I have a good idea. She had built up this idea in her mind of investing herself once again in the relationship. Full of this optimism, she returned to Bologna. She wanted to surprise him, so she didn't let him know she was coming. I guess in her fantasy she pictured him surprised and pleased to see her. "

Anna looked over at Donna to see if she had guessed the next part of the story. That look plus what she already knew about Silvio Rossi's extramarital sex life tipped Donna off.

"I think I know what you are about to tell me."

Anna nodded. "Gina walked in on them, right in their own bedroom—a waitress from the restaurant where he worked."

Donna shook her head as if in disbelief. She wanted to hear more. Would Anna suddenly realize how much she had told a stranger and stop.

"Anna, you said you had a good idea why your friend didn't become pregnant again."

Donna didn't need to worry that the flow would cease. Anna wanted to talk.

"I think when she discovered her husband and the other woman, she was finished with the marriage. I think she didn't want a child with Silvio."

"Yes. I see what you mean. But, she didn't divorce him?"

"That would be hard for an American to understand. You would have to understand a man like Gina's father. He didn't go tilting at windmills, but in essence he was a Don Quixote. In his mind, he still lived in a feudal—no, more of a renaissance world. A world in which a man of noble family strives to lead the perfectly balanced life, what we Italians term, *La bella figura*. Gina loved her father above all else. She could not let herself disappoint him. A divorce would have done that. It seems to me the main thing that gave her life purpose from then on was to protect her father's last years from any pain of disappointment. She never let him know there was a problem. She let her father believe she and Silvio were happy together. Massimo gladly put up the money for Silvio's restaurants. I don't know if Silvio ever repaid him. He, Gina's father, died only a month before Silvio was killed. Gina came home for the funeral, of course. Silvio chose not to make the trip."

Instead of continuing in the role of the passive listener, Donna dared to follow an impression she had just formed. "Am I right to think a change took place in your relationship with your friend at the time she discovered her husband and the other woman?"

Sadness fell over Anna. Donna could sense a new closeness with her as Anna accepted this understanding on Donna's part.

"Yes, you're right. We remained best friends, but Gina did not confide in me all her thoughts and feelings as she'd done before. She became . . . what you say, 'sadder, but wiser' and kept her deeper thoughts to herself."

Donna, thinking back to her own experiences, murmured, "Yes, that can happen with best friends from childhood." A gap in the story occurred to her and she asked, "What about school? Did she continue at the university?"

"Yes, she did, but she gave up her plan to study architecture—for then. She knew that Silvio would be moving wherever he thought he could find advancement, including an eventual move to your country. She took courses on child development and filled her time later with volunteering in school programs. In New York she worked in an orphanage."

Anna's tone changed to a lighter, more up-beat one. "But, that has changed. She seems to have brought that phase of her life to a close and started anew after she returned here from America. She took all the money from the sale of the restaurant and the rights to the cookbooks and such and gave it to orphanages—but mostly to the one run by our old school in Savona. Then, she enrolled in the architecture program at the University of Genoa. That's where she is now. And, she changed her name back to Gina del Carreto."

They had just passed through the entrance gates and back out onto the public road. Donna stole a look over her shoulder at the magnificent house. Her head spun with all the information she'd received. She couldn't wait to talk to Derek.

• • •

Looking back on the week's highs and lows, Derek Marsh decided he was glad he had agreed to be on the convention's program committee. He also decided he would never do it again—not his thing. For him, it was like cleaning up the pots and pans, someone had to do it and the completed job gave satisfaction, but the task itself held little joy. He was free for the evening and wished Donna was with him. She'd be back tomorrow and they'd have the final evening in Zurich all to themselves. Last night on the phone, she'd talked of her good fortune to have Gina Rossi's best friend as her hostess. She had been excited to have managed to form the beginning of a relationship with the woman and hoped this day would provide answers to satisfy more of her quandary about Gina. Donna had been patient with his professional obligations; he supposed he should be as patient with what, after all, did amount to an unfinished professional task.

He planned to shower and change into something comfortable and then walk a long way along the Zuricher See until he came to some small, cozy *Gasthaus* and order a sinful platter of cheese *raclette* and a bottle of wine. The blinking light on the phone got his attention as he entered his room. The message waiting for him was from Donna. She wanted to be called.

Derek took off his tie and threw it on the bed, where he sat and dialed the number of her hotel. Her voice filled with the excitement of discovery poured into his ear. She began telling him about the magnificent house and garden and was prepared to go on with the full story of Gina and Silvio, when she remembered to ask him about the final day of the conference.

"Everything wound down nicely. We've been invited to visit about a dozen cities spread across Europe. Stay as long as we like."

"Did you accept them all?"

"Of course. And, of course I invited them all to come to Leelanau."

"And stay as long as they like?"

"It was only fair."

Nothing else was said for a moment as they let the playful banter come to rest. Derek knew Donna had serious thoughts to discuss.

"Did you learn anything more about Gina Rossi today?"

"Yes. I learned she hated Silvio and why."

"Really. You always said she wasn't the grieving wife."

"Exactly. First of all he raped her—."

"Raped her?"

"Yes, and she became pregnant. He refused to permit an abortion and forced her to marry him and when she miscarried and she needed his support, he cheated on her instead."

This lump of information would have been difficult to digest, except that it resonated with similar stories he'd heard in his office.

"'How much do I hate thee? Let me count the ways,'" he said.

"Exactly. Do you agree she had an adequate motive for murder?"

"It's been done with less motive. But remember, she'd had

266

those motives for a long time. According to your information from that publicist, the extramarital affairs in New York had been a regular diet for Rossi."

"I hear where you're going," Donna responded. "It's the same argument the district attorney hammered me with. Why then?"

"Do you think there was something particularly nettling about his affair with . . . what was her name?"

"Sandra Thomas. I don't know."

"I take it that everything you've learned about Gina has made you more sure than ever that she killed Silvio."

"Yes. Still, a piece is missing. Like you just said, 'Why then?'"

"You said it," Derek corrected, laughing.

Donna laughed too. "That's right, I did." She sighed. "And, of course, I haven't a shred more evidence."

"But, do you feel your trip down there has been worth it?"

"Yes, on two counts: First, I think I've put this problem to rest—a bit more, anyway, and second, the discovery of this town and Anna Longhi."

"Good. I miss you. When will you be getting here tomorrow?"

"There's a train from Savona at eight in the morning. I change at Genoa and Milan. I'll have to sprint in Genoa, there's only ten minutes between trains. Then, it's on to Zurich to meet my lover at six eighteen."

"I wish you were here now. I love you."

"I wish *you* were *here*. Love you too."

32

With hugs and a promise to return soon, Donna left Anna at the Savona railway terminal, where Anna had insisted on driving her. The one-hour ride to Genoa followed the coast and the changing scene out her window held Donna's gaze. Her thoughts, freed now from the immediate demands of dressing, breakfast and the farewell to the Longhis, were now drawn to last night's conversation with Derek. Before coming here to Savona, Donna had truly managed to let her experience with her unsuccessful investigation settle in her mind like residue in a bottle. Daily life, her marriage, her new home and her work served the task of suppressing the displeasing memory of what she regarded as her failure. Vividly detailed memories of that time were now awakened, the residue stirred-up. She had many new facts about Gina, much was explained—strong motives for murder—yet that one objection remained a puzzle. Why had Gina chosen that particular time to act?

The loud grinding of brakes filled the car and the train slowed and lurched forward again causing standing, rush-hour passengers to grasp seat backs to keep from falling. Then the train came to a dead stop, accompanied by the hissing of the brakes. Those sitting next to the windows reflexively strained to look ahead for an answer, but nothing could be seen. Five minutes later, a conductor passing through Donna's car said they had to wait for another train to leave the station. A young man sitting next to her, recognizing her to be an American, made the translation for her. "Right away", as promised by the conductor, turned out to be fifteen minutes. Unless her connecting train was late starting, she would miss it. Descending from her car onto the platform of Genoa's central station, Donna ran up to the same conductor she had spoken to only days before and asked about the Milan train.

He responded with the now familiar shoulder shrug and the depressing answer, "It'sa go."

She knew from having consulted the timetable at the hotel last night that there was another train to Milan that would get her to Zurich about two hours later. She went to the departure board and saw that it left Genoa an hour and ten minutes from then. First she would call Derek and tell him she'd be late. Then she'd sit down and wait. He wasn't at the convention hall, so she left a message for him there and at the hotel and hoped he'd receive it. She started toward the waiting room when once again the interior of the station contrasted with the sunshine coming through the station's entrance, suggested she should find a place outside to wait. An espresso—that would be just the thing, if she could find an outdoor table. She left the station and began walking along the Via Andrea Doria looking for a place to have her coffee.

She hadn't walked far before she realized she'd been looking closely at the faces of the women she passed. She was looking for Gina. Gina went to school here in the city. Donna wondered where she'd be at this time of day. Probably in class. Donna pictured Gina leaning over a drafting table laying down the lines of a . . . what? What would Gina del Carreto be interested in designing? She had walked three blocks and was afraid of going much farther since she certainly didn't want to miss the next train. She'd walk a block to her left and, if she didn't find the spot for her espresso, she'd turn and head back to the station. Half a block farther, she spotted Campari umbrellas ahead in what turned out to be a small piazza.

A large and commanding baroque church dominated the

square. Donna's eyes followed the boastful, confident curves of the cornices. What had happened to all that ebullience, she wondered? What had tamed it? In addition to her family's home, was it this very building that had stimulated the young Gina del Carreto's interest in architecture? She glanced at her watch. Her train left in forty-five minutes. She sat down at one of the café's tables. About half of the tables were occupied with handsome Italians, either talking rapidly to friends at the table or talking just as rapidly into their cell phones—gesturing equally in either case. A waiter made a quick detour from his path to come to the beautiful woman's table. When he returned with the coffee, Donna asked to pay so she wouldn't be delayed when she needed to leave to return to the station. The waiter made a semi-flirtatious comment that she shouldn't rush away. Left alone she took a sip of the strong, delicious coffee and exhaled deeply. She felt very happy she had impulsively left Zurich and made the trip south. Now that she knew Gina's story, it made it easier to accept her own failure as a police officer, her failure to prove Gina's guilt. Donna brought the cup to her lips and looked over the brim into the piazza. The combination of having just pictured in her mind the del Carreto palace and the baroque church must have conjured up the idea of noble stature and pride.

"Gina's father," she said aloud.

Anna had suggested the special meaning he'd held for Gina, but Donna had heard and compared it to the kind of love she'd had for her own father. No! This was an almost entirely different thing Anna had been talking about. Like the congealing of gelatin, the bits of information that had been separately suspended in her awareness came together in a solid form. She now understood Gina del Carreto. She knew it in her bones. She had become Gina. She understood how Gina's concern for her father's honor had prevented her from getting a divorce. Now she understood why

Silvio had to be killed and when it had to happen. Gina no doubt lived all those years for that very moment. And, this is why she no longer confided her thoughts and feelings to her best friend, Anna. She had committed herself to a plan she could tell to no one.

All that Silvio had done and continued to do to Gina until his death constituted an insult to her father. Silvio had treated the daughter of Massimo del Carreto as if she were worthless. He dishonored her, and by doing so, he dishonored her father. Silvio's payment had to match the debt. He had to die by Gina's hand, but it could not happen until her father died. She could take no chances that she'd be charged with or convicted of murder while her father was still alive. That would be the greatest harm she could do him. Her father had died a month before the murder. She'd returned to Italy for the funeral—all reinforcing her identity with her father's code of values.

"My God," she said aloud. "It's true!"

It was the stuff of Italian opera, a drama form that had remained passionately alive because it portrayed true, but harsh human emotions. Honor or death. An eye for an eye. Silvio Rossi had even died by the sword! And the question others had raised of why after years of his infidelity she had chosen that particular time to react was answered. With her father dead and beyond any pain that her action might inflict, it was Silvio's time to die.

Donna sat back in her chair, emotionally spent from this flight of insight. The missing piece of the puzzle now fit in place. It wasn't the kind of proof that would convince Hoss to close the case. The file would remain among the Department's open files but she had now mentally closed the cover forever knowing she did not have and never would have the evidence for an arrest.

She looked at her watch. She would have to get moving. She finished the last sip of coffee and started to rise when she saw a woman walk up to an unoccupied table two tables away from hers. It was Gina. Gina laid a briefcase on the table and sat down. She faced in Donna's direction, but had not seen her. Gina was four years older, but she looked younger than the last time Donna had seen her. Gina took a paper from the briefcase and made a note. Donna noticed she wore no rings. It was when Gina looked up, obviously still thinking about what she had written, that she noticed Donna. Perhaps what Donna saw was brief alarm in Gina's expression, but that passed quickly. Her gaze became steady now, even bold.

Donna's absolute certainty of Gina's guilt continued to dominate her thoughts and it showed. In Donna's face Gina read, "I know you did it."

It wasn't a smile that Donna saw in return, but something like a relaxed acceptance of Donna's message. Gina's look said, "Yes, I can see that." Donna would tell Derek that next she discerned a change in Gina's expression to one of understanding sympathy. "You know it, but there's nothing you can do about it."

The two women held their eye contact for a few more seconds and then Donna glanced at her watch and got up. Opening her purse, she walked over to Gina's table. She reached into the inside pocket of the purse and took out the ruby earring and laid it on the table.

Gina looked at it for a long moment and then she looked up into Donna's eyes.

"*Grazie.*"

Printed in the United States
117696LV00001B/24/A